THE JOURNEY PRIZE

STORIES

WINNERS OF THE $10,000 JOURNEY PRIZE

1989: Holley Rubinsky for "Rapid Transits"

1990: Cynthia Flood for "My Father Took a Cake to France"

1991: Yann Martel for "The Facts Behind the Helsinki Roccamatios"

1992: Rozena Maart for "No Rosa, No District Six"

1993: Gayla Reid for "Sister Doyle's Men"

1994: Melissa Hardy for "Long Man the River"

1995: Kathryn Woodward for "Of Marranos and Gilded Angels"

1996: Elyse Gasco for "Can You Wave Bye Bye, Baby?"

1997 (shared): Gabriella Goliger for "Maladies of the Inner Ear"
 Anne Simpson for "Dreaming Snow"

1998: John Brooke for "The Finer Points of Apples"

1999: Alissa York for "The Back of the Bear's Mouth"

2000: Timothy Taylor for "Doves of Townsend"

2001: Kevin Armstrong for "The Cane Field"

2002: Jocelyn Brown for "Miss Canada"

2003: Jessica Grant for "My Husband's Jump"

2004: Devin Krukoff for "The Last Spark"

2005: Matt Shaw for "Matchbook for a Mother's Hair"

2006: Heather Birrell for "BriannaSusannaAlana"

2007: Craig Boyko for "OZY"

2008: Saleema Nawaz for "My Three Girls"

2009: Yasuko Thanh for "Floating Like the Dead"

2010: Devon Code for "Uncle Oscar"

2011: Miranda Hill for "Petitions to Saint Chronic"

2012: Alex Pugsley for "Crisis on Earth-X"

THE BEST OF CANADA'S NEW WRITERS
THE JOURNEY PRIZE

STORIES

SELECTED BY
MIRANDA HILL
MARK MEDLEY
RUSSELL WANGERSKY

EMBLEM
McClelland & Stewart

A cataloguing record for this publication is available from Library and
Archives Canada.

Published simultaneously in the United States of America by McClelland
& Stewart, a division of Random House of Canada Limited, P.O. Box 1030,
Plattsburgh, New York 12901

Library of Congress Control Number: 2013938799

Typeset in Janson by Random House of Canada, Toronto
Printed and bound in Canada

McClelland & Stewart,
a division of Random House of Canada Limited
One Toronto Street
Suite 300
Toronto, Ontario
M5C 2V6
www.mcclelland.com

1   2   3   4   5   17   16   15   14   13

ABOUT THE JOURNEY PRIZE STORIES

The $10,000 Journey Prize is awarded annually to an emerging writer of distinction. This award, now in its twenty-fifth year, and given for the thirteenth time in association with the Writers' Trust of Canada as the Writers' Trust of Canada/ McClelland & Stewart Journey Prize, is made possible by James A. Michener's generous donation of his Canadian royalty earnings from his novel *Journey*, published by McClelland & Stewart in 1988. The Journey Prize itself is the most significant monetary award given in Canada to a developing writer for a short story or excerpt from a fiction work in progress. The winner of this year's Journey Prize will be selected from among the twelve stories in this book.

The Journey Prize Stories has established itself as the most prestigious annual fiction anthology in the country, introducing readers to the finest new literary writers from coast to coast for more than two decades. It has become a who's who of up-and-coming writers, and many of the authors who have appeared in the anthology's pages have gone on to distinguish themselves with short story collections, novels, and literary awards. The anthology comprises a selection from submissions made by the editors of literary journals from across the country, who have chosen what, in their view, is the most exciting writing in English that they have published in the previous year. In recognition of the vital role journals play in fostering literary voices, McClelland & Stewart makes its own award of

$2,000 to the journal that originally published and submitted the winning entry.

This year the selection jury comprised three acclaimed writers:

Miranda Hill won the 2011 Writers' Trust of Canada / McClelland & Stewart Journey Prize for her story "Petitions to Saint Chronic." Her debut collection of short fiction, *Sleeping Funny*, was published by Doubleday Canada. She is currently at work on a novel that weaves a story of Pittsburgh's fine houses and steel mills with Muskoka's cottage country. Hill received her BA in drama from Queen's University, and her MFA in Creative Writing from the University of British Columbia. She is also the founder and executive director of Project Bookmark Canada, an initiative that installs text from stories and poems in the exact physical locations where literary scenes are set. She lives in Hamilton, Ontario. Please visit www.mirandahill.com.

Mark Medley is the *National Post*'s Books Editor and oversees the paper's books blog, *The Afterword*. His work has appeared in magazines and newspapers across Canada, including the *Globe and Mail*, *The Walrus*, *Toronto Life*, *This Magazine*, *Spacing*, and *Taddle Creek*. He currently sits on PEN Canada's board of directors and serves on the advisory committee of the Humber School for Writers. He lives in Toronto.

Russell Wangersky's most recent fiction collection, *Whirl Away*, was a finalist for the Scotiabank Giller Prize, the BMO Winterset Award, and the Thomas Head Raddall Atlantic Fiction Award. He is also the author of *The Glass Harmonica*, winner of the BMO Winterset Award; *The Hour of Bad Decisions*, a finalist for the regional Commonwealth

Writers' Prize for Best First Book; and the memoir *Burning Down the House: Fighting Fires and Losing Myself*, winner of the British Columbia National Award for Canadian Non-Fiction, the Rogers Communications Newfoundland and Labrador Non-Fiction Book Award, and the Edna Staebler Award for Creative Non-Fiction. It was also a finalist for the Writers' Trust Non-Fiction Prize. Wangersky lives and works in St. John's, where he is an editor and columnist with the *St. John's Telegram*. Please visit www.russellwangersky.com.

The jury read a total of eighty-one submissions without knowing the names of the authors or those of the journals in which the stories originally appeared. McClelland & Stewart would like to thank the jury for their efforts in selecting this year's anthology and, ultimately, the winner of this year's Journey Prize.

McClelland & Stewart would also like to acknowledge the continuing enthusiastic support of writers, literary journal editors, and the public in the common celebration of new voices in Canadian fiction.

For more information about *The Journey Prize Stories*, please visit www.facebook.com/TheJourneyPrize.

CONTENTS

CONGRATULATIONS TO THE JOURNEY PRIZE
– FROM THE AUTHORS

"I was naturally thrilled to have a story included in the *Journey Prize* anthology. Particularly when you're just starting out, being accepted in an anthology – an actual book instead of a magazine, something with a spine, something that people might buy in a bookstore – feels like donning a tiara. But it wasn't until I sat on the Journey Prize jury myself, fourteen years later, that I realized how tough the competition is, how many stories are submitted, and how many good ones aren't included for lack of space or jury consensus. If I'd known this back then, I probably wouldn't have settled for that tiara feeling. I'd have gone around with the darned book strapped to my head."
                                      – Caroline Adderson

"The *Journey Prize* anthology does many things: it gives affirmation to a work, it piques the interest of agents and publishers, but most importantly, it creates an opportunity for emerging writers to be recognized and it supports our Canadian literary magazines. It searches out fresh and daring voices trying to gain ground and gives them a boost. We need *The Journey Prize Stories* now more than ever."
                                      – Théodora Armstrong

"Way back in 1989, I got lucky with my first published story when it was selected for the *Journey Prize* anthology. Then I got lucky three more times. It is astounding to see how many writers published in the anthology have gone on to publish great story collections and novels. The anthology is a windfall for both writer and reader."   – David Bergen

"Reading *The Journey Prize Stories* helped me grow as a writer, gave me a sense of permission, threw down a stylistic gauntlet, and then, when I found my own stories in its pages – oh, glorious day! – gave me a fantastic sense of accomplishment and confidence.

It's true that developing writers need *The Journey Prize Stories*, but really, we all need the *JPS* – to show Canada and the world that our short story writers just keep quietly, keenly, creating; to show discerning readers that the whole world can haunt and glow in a few pages, that a small shift in a character's consciousness can be as thrilling as any sprawling saga, and that size really *does* matter, but never quite in the way that you might think."   – Heather Birrell

"A great jolt of electricity startles the heart and jump-starts the writing career when you get the nod from the Journey people. It's a thrill to find your name included amongst some of the leading new voices in short fiction."   – Dennis Bock

"Some writers are blessed with an innate, bulletproof confidence, coupled with the sturdy conviction that what they write matters. But for the rest of us, doubt and insecurity are the acid bath in which our literary ambitions are born. And there is nothing like a Journey Prize nomination to prop up a nascent writer's fragile hopes. Like the little boy's love for the Velveteen Rabbit, the affections of the Journey Prize eased my transition from 'Who are you kidding with this writing stuff?' to 'Maybe you should write more of these things.' And the truly wonderful thing is, I know I'm not alone."

– Michael Christie

"Being a part of the anthology was something of a landmark in my own progression as a writer. I'd read previous editions, and to be a part of it myself was a great surprise. It provided me with some confidence, a commodity highly prized by writers, especially when you're just starting out." – Craig Davidson

"Many years ago, a kind relative who knew I had literary aspirations gave me a copy of the *Journey Prize* anthology. It was bright red and contained stories by new Canadian writers. Would I ever be one of those? So far I was just Canadian. A decade later I got a phone call that changed my life. Are you sitting down? I was living in a tiny apartment in Calgary and I had one chair. I was so excited I couldn't find my one chair. Wait, wait! I sat down on the floor. I had won the Journey Prize! How did I feel? Like a superhero. Very proud. Very grateful. And completely cured of my worst fear – that I wouldn't be a writer." – Jessica Grant

"What a thrill! A 'yes' instead of a 'no.' I had done something right, and now I would have to figure out what it was."

– Elizabeth Hay

"I remember feeling ratified, authenticated, which of course was an illusion; no journal or anthology or prize ever proves you are a real writer (whatever that is). But being chosen for

an anthology as important as *The Journey Prize Stories* gave
me a lift when I especially needed one, and I still think of that
with gratitude."   – Steven Heighton

"Winning the Journey Prize was the largest, and most public
acknowledgement my work had received. But more than the
money, or remembering the moment my name was called, I
treasure the fact that my name and the title of my story will sit
forever in the back pages of subsequent *Journey Prize* anthologies, side by side with the names of writers I admire – those
I know about already, and those whose work is still to come.
It's a great privilege to be part of that tradition. How lucky I
am – how lucky all we writers and readers are."
                                              – Miranda Hill

"The writing apprenticeship is a long one, perhaps neverend-
ing, and an appearance in the *Journey Prize* anthology is a
boost of encouragement along the way. I am especially pleased
that several of my former students have been included. Bravo
for continuing to celebrate this challenging and exact genre –
the story in its short form."   – Frances Itani

"I feel like I've been travelling alongside the Journey Prize for
a substantial chunk of my life. My dad (Alistair MacLeod) was
the judge for the first award, and I very clearly remember the
winning story, Holley Rubinsky's 'Rapid Transits,' and the way
that inaugural prize transformed her career. Later on, like lots
of young writers, I was a loyal annual reader of the anthology.
Sometimes I loved what I found in there, sometimes I hated
it, but I was always thrilled when editors at journals would

nominate my stories and then devastated when my pieces didn't fit into the final puzzle. When 'Miracle Mile' got the call in 2009 – selected by editors I really respected – I felt like this was the beginning of a real writing life, and when I was asked to be an editor in 2011, that was like being invited behind the curtain by the great and powerful Oz. Last year, I celebrated like a fool when one of my students, Kris Bertin, made the cut. I was proud of him and proud of the editors and proud of the whole series. It felt like a completed circuit, a journey all the way around and back again. A quarter century of great work has gone onto the pages of *Journey Prize* anthologies and into the production of these twenty-five books. Canadian Literature is flat-out lucky to have such an institution."

– Alexander MacLeod

"David Bergen is a loser. André Alexis: also a loser. Anne Carson, Lee Henderson, Heather O'Neill – all losers. And I can claim to losing the Journey Prize not once, but *twice* myself. Being in the company of some of Canada's best, brightest, and most beautiful losers is fine and good, but ten grand for twenty pages of typing? It would have been *awesome* to win."

– Pasha Malla

"The *Journey Prize* anthology has become the proving ground for new, young Canadian writers, a who's who of the coming generation. . . . I, for one, owe everything to the Journey Prize." – Yann Martel

"I'd been collecting the *Journey Prize* anthologies and dreaming of one day appearing within those pages, so every step of

the process left me almost beside myself with happiness. To work harder than you've ever worked before – and to have your work acknowledged in that very public way – is hugely encouraging for a writer. It's special, too, because it almost never happens. I felt I was forever becoming part of this tradition that I had revered and which stood for something important to me, connecting me to writers whose work and careers I admired."
                                        – Saleema Nawaz

"Like a secret handshake or the password to a speakeasy, inclusion in *The Journey Prize Stories* feels like the first, magical entry to the tribe of Canadian writers. It's an honour to be part of this heady heritage, alongside writers I grew up reading and whose work I adore. The Journey Prize is one of Canada's most important literary institutions, because it ensures the continuation of great Canadian literature through its encouragement, support, and celebration of the next generation."
                                        – Grace O'Connell

"There is no guarantee, ever, that a writer's work will be read and recognized, and as a beginning writer there are many moments of self-doubt in this regard. Inclusion in the *Journey Prize* anthology was invaluable to me in terms of the encouragement and boost in morale that it offered me."
                                        – Nancy Richler

"I remember buying twenty copies of the fourth *Journey Prize* anthology, and giving them out to family for Christmas with my story helpfully Post-it marked. I finally got up the courage to ask a cousin what he thought of it, and he said, 'Yeah. It was long. Didn't finish it.' Which seemed to be the reaction of most of my family, except for my mom and dad, who kept their copy on the coffee table. The press and the attention I received from being in the anthology were important to my career, but not as crucial as my family finally referring to me as 'The Writer' instead of 'The Most Educated Bum in Kitamaat Village.'"   – Eden Robinson

"The Journey Prize provides something valuable, sincere, and joyful: a celebration of short stories, a way for them to be appreciated in public, right out loud. Every writer has to write for him- or herself – there's no way to work that hard if you don't love it – but it really does help to know that there's a community out there, waiting to cheer if you get it really, really right. The Journey Prize is a huge cheer, and a huge support to short story writers."   – Rebecca Rosenblum

"The day I received the letter that told me my story would be included in the *Journey Prize* anthology was one of the most memorable days of my writing career. I felt that it meant my writing had been truly seen, and that my story had been included in a large literary conversation, with authors I admire and respect. It was like I'd been given a ticket to fly to another hemisphere! It gave me the confidence I needed to finish my first book. Being a part of the Journey Prize – both as a writer and as a juror – has been a privilege."   – Sarah Selecky

"I owe a huge debt to the Journey Prize. Before my nominations, I didn't even know I wanted to be a writer. I saw my writing as arts and crafts, nothing more serious than macaroni that's spray-painted gold and glued to a tissue box. When my first story got nominated, I thought, 'Fluke.' When a second story got the nod, I thought, 'Another fluke.' When a third story was picked, I thought, 'Career change!'

If there were no Journey Prize, I wouldn't have kept writing. I wouldn't be sitting in a room all alone, making up stuff in my head. Obsessing over my fiction. Looking at somebody and thinking what a great character he'd make in my novel.

When people ask how I've changed since publishing my first book, I reply that I'm now more neurotic but also more content. So a big thanks to the Journey Prize and McClelland & Stewart for feeding my neurosis and making me a happier person."
                                                          – Neil Smith

"Quite a few years before I would have dared call myself a writer in public, while I was still working at a bank, I began to buy the *Journey Prize* anthology yearly. I did so because I understood it to collect the best new short fiction of the year, and I hoped quietly that I would be inspired. One afternoon, a colleague caught me reading the anthology at my desk. Knowing a little about my literary interests, he asked bluntly: 'Are you in it this year?' I wasn't, and I said so. But after he left my office, I remember my astonishment, my disbelief at his suggestion. These are 'real' writers (I wanted to shout), and while I aspire in the same direction, I have yet to publish a single story! About eight years later, I was included in the anthology and I remembered my colleague. It occurred to me that – despite the years I'd been at it and the stories that had since been published – nothing up to that point had convinced me that I could be a real writer. And while I remained astonished to see my name in those pages, the *Journey Prize* anthology now marked a beginning in which I could really believe. I've continued to read the anthology, and count it as an honour to have adjudicated during its fifteenth year. To me, its ongoing contribution is found on every page: new writers, new voices, new confidence."   – Timothy Taylor

"'Simple Recipes' was my first published story, and the one that, to my utter amazement, made it into the *Journey Prize* anthology. I remember getting the phone call, and remember sitting on the couch for a long time staring at the wall. I had a strange sense of vertigo, to think that it might actually be possible to one day write a book, and for that book one day to find readers. I had always quietly hoped for that possibility, but hadn't really thought it was within the boundaries of reality until that day."   – Madeleine Thien

"Looking back over two decades of writing fiction, I find to my amazement that the greatest imaginative feat required of me thus far has been the conception of myself as a writer. The early years were the toughest. Every published story helped, but the day I learned that my work was to be included in the eleventh volume of *The Journey Prize Stories* – and thereby in a national tradition of literary discovery – was the day when the writing life I had long imagined finally began to seem real."   – Alissa York

INTRODUCTION

Sitting on the Journey Prize jury is nothing if not daunting. After agreeing to serve as jurors, we each received a rather sizeable package in the mail. It contained a great bundle of short stories, which stretched across an impressive spectrum of genres. Fantasy and science fiction, works that travelled back in time or sprang forward into the future, works that could be categorized as traditional literary fiction alongside experimental stories that pushed the boundaries of what a story can be. The package contained work by many of the most promising of this country's emerging writers, a bounty we were ordered to whittle down into the anthology you now hold in your hands – or that you're reading on your iPad. In these pages, you'll discover, we're confident to say, twelve of the best short stories written by Canada's emerging writers over the past year.

On the one hand, the task was like comparing apples to oranges to, well, dragon fruit; every story had its own flavour. On the other hand, it was a rather straightforward job: judge the story's excellence, nothing else.

This is as pure a prize as you'll find in Canada. As judges, we read and ranked the stories without knowing who the authors were. This is not a prize that rewards friends, nor does it favour reputation. It is a collection – twelve stories, three finalists, and one winner – that is based solely on the strength of the individual stories themselves.

This year, eighty-one different stories battled for our affections, ranging in content from a post-apocalyptic suburb coping with rumours of cannibalism, to a movie theatre in Mauritius where dreams of a better future flicker on-screen, to a mattress store where a long-lasting friendship threatens to come undone.

For each of us, it was a chance to partake in a process that now stretches back twenty-five years, a sneak peek at authors who – in the future – will likely become favourites. Like an appearance in a volume of *Granta*'s "Best Young Novelists" or the *New Yorker*'s "20 under 40" or the *O. Henry Prize Stories*, being in this anthology often marks the start of a long, and celebrated, career.

It's trite to say that it's an honour just to be nominated, but check out the list of previous contributors at the back of this book: simply being in the anthology can be a mark of things to come. Included in past anthologies have been non-winners like M.G. Vassanji, Frances Itani, David Bergen, Steven Heighton, Marina Endicott, Anne Carson, Elizabeth Hay, Dennis Bock, Michael Crummey, Madeleine Thien, Lee Henderson, Karen Solie, Annabel Lyon, Emma Donoghue, Charlotte Gill, Sarah Selecky, Craig Davidson, and Pasha Malla.

It's also fitting that the Journey Prize should mark the beginning of a journey for the writers included in its pages: the impact of James A. Michener's donation of the Canadian royalties for his novel *Journey* has clearly set many careers in motion.

And how was it behind the closed doors?

Like any jury, ours was one with argument, humour, complaint, and the occasional attempt at horse-trading, coupled with the knowledge that this is an anthology with real heft and value. The decisions mattered. We were three individual jurors making difficult, careful choices – but in the end, our choices were only the opinion of three people, three readers. This is not a yes or no judgment on new careers as a whole – for all of us, what mattered was that the talent in the individual stories was humbling.

And where do they all come from? That's critical, too. It's worth noting that the eighty-one submissions were initially selected by this country's literary magazines, a segment of the literary world that is among the most financially precarious. They are out there, picking and publishing new and emerging writers; they are the farm teams, the incubators, the discoverers of Canada's writing future.

Remember that when you get a chance to subscribe to any one of them – to these magazines that are carving out the new frontiers – you will see things there that you will see nowhere else in this country.

And the greatest wonder for all three of us? Seeing the names, finally, of the people behind this crop of stories, and welcoming them to a great fraternity.

Here's to twenty-five years, and then twenty-five more. The literary industry is changing in many ways: it might not even be fair to call it solely the "book publishing" business much longer. But there will always be new voices, new talent, and in whatever form, this anthology will continue to shine a bright light out into the darkness and reflect back new and hungry eyes.

Miranda Hill
Mark Medley
Russell Wangersky
June 2013

LAURA LEGGE

IT'S RAINING IN PARIS

There is so much work to be done.

Rain has been pounding Paris for weeks. Whole swathes of pavement have come untied, sidewalks once ribboned into four-way intersections, ravelled now with seams exposed, ragged hems no longer travelled by bicycles, sedans, wandering feet.

They say my blueprints will pull us headfirst from this emergency.

In my office, an eight-by-eight cork cubicle on the eighth floor of the Institut de la Ville, I hunch over an early draft I've called "Centre City Contingency," using a line gauge to lay out a series of stormwater drains. Until I sense my boss hovering.

Digging my heels into the linoleum, I turn slowly to face him.

—We are in shit, Serge, he says.

—

Two days ago, I saw a girl lose her life in a lemon sundress. She was crossing avenue de Choisy, past dusk on a Thursday, parting smoky sheets of rain. I was the only one near her when she was hit. Strangers crowded against the smoggy glass of dim sum restaurants, Hong Kong bakeries, stared hollow-eyed from the whale's belly of the 183 bus.

Her skin barely held her bones together.

Time passed, who knows how much of it, before those same strangers poured onto the wet pavement. A man with pock-marked cheeks folded his nylon windbreaker in half, angled the makeshift pillow under the crown of her head. A woman in a silk turban knelt beside the body – marking with fluttering eyelashes the moment when *her* body became *the* body – and let a storm fall down her cheeks.

At some point, an ambulance arrived. Two young medics pressed their ears to the girl's chapped lips and waited for breath that never came. Every evening for the past two years, I have followed the same ritual: rolling my blueprints into a drawing tube, buttoning my vinyl raincoat, and fording avenue Kléber to my suite at Hotel Raphaël.

The greatest joy of living in a hotel is that hardly anything you use belongs to you. The bed you sleep in, the tub you bathe in, these are tools you do not have to maintain.

With my forearms, I iron my plans flat across the suite's Victorian dining table. Bicycle boulevards, civic squares, aquatic reserves, the barbed wire of railroad tracks – a miniature city balances on the Carrara marble.

My boss has fixed a slew of pink sticky notes like chicken pox on the plans. *Remember, downtown is our town; the Seine is the yolk that flavours the egg of Paris.* I tear them off one by one.

Tonight my hands migrate south on the blueprint, to Chinatown, the shaded elevations of trauma centres, pediatric hospitals. And, as there must be, the depressions.

—You're unbearably vague, Colette is saying to me. I've been with her once, maybe twice. She has deep-set eyes that are at once inviting and distant, like a memory just beyond reach.

She picks up a vanity jar of ground cardamom from the bedside table and rubs the fine powder in the flexures of her palms. I flash to lamb tagine, my Formica mother in a Formica kitchen, shag-rugged and minimal, her slack lips forming unreadable words, *proud* or *pound*, *love* or *loaf*.

—You're not handsome enough to get away with being vague. If you were better looking, you'd be mysterious.

I'm lost in a long-gone Christmas, cardamom braids rising in a redbrick oven, an autumn-haired woman riveting her arms around my neck, ornamenting me with eggnog kisses, while Harry Belafonte croons "Glory Manger" on our worn-down record player. I say nothing. Colette turns her back on me.

—You're afraid, she sends over her shoulder. You're a hunter with no heart.

And how beautiful her bare spine looks, straightened as if to underline her unkindness. I think I'm beginning to love her.

It seems that my boss has been crying.

—Avenue de Choisy? he asks from the doorway to my office. His hair is rumpled with stress and humidity; he is a stray dog, river-eyed and wild, his matted coat licked against the grain.

—I know what I'm doing.

His cheeks burn red. —If there are sinkholes in rue de Rivoli because you want to pump all of our efforts into Chinatown, you'll be out of a job. I won't think twice.

Through my office window, I make out the north face of Hotel Raphaël – the lace balustrade, the limestone carvings of pomegranates and lions' heads – and I want, badly, to go home.

My boss lowers his gaze to his polished Valentino loafers. On his left toe, he notices a pigeon dropping and looks as if he might cry again. He is a tweed suit with no man in it; his body has slipped out, vanished into tedium, rain poised to wash away any trace that he may have existed.

In any flood, there are abandoned vehicles. I have flown to Chongqing, Queensland, and Cologne to plan for rebuilding after natural disasters, and seen miles of sedans deserted, dead headlights wired to dead batteries.

Down de Choisy, the water is low enough to walk through – or, we walk through it because we can't be still – but nothing smaller than a bus can clear the overflow. I follow the road like a salmon going downriver, netted by the quiet pull of magnetic fields, to Chinatown. At some point, the wind picks up, and I huddle under the domed awning of a magazine stand.

I settle beside the gossip glossies while the proprietor, a man with a puddle for a chin, clears his throat over and over. From there I look out into the street, to an imagined chalk outline overwhelmed by the flood but not washed away, the nipped waist and tulip hem of a sundress.

Here, it takes work to filter beauty from the ugliness, the vibrant trains of mounted paper lanterns from the ones that have fallen, detritus scattered in the ocean, taking on the shapes of pried-open clams, sunfish bones, red coral caked in salt. How to find anything beautiful while sadness folds itself around us, a beach blanket of steel wool?

Before stepping out from under the awning, I raise a newspaper over my head. Two steps into the road, the newspaper is already soggy. Still I cling to it; not for shelter, but for its semblance of structure, as something I can hold in my hands.

Colette paces the Alcove Suite, an architect surveying her building site, industrious but aware of its limitations. I perch on a red-velvet bergère, watching her luminous face as she decides what, together, we have room to construct.

—I can't believe it, she murmurs. Hotel Raphaël.

While she slips off her slingbacks, I unseal my rainboots from my calves and peel away my socks. We line up side by side on the king bed, each half-starfished on the silk duvet, nowhere touching.

—I went on a vacation once, Colette says, after so much time has passed that I thought she was asleep. When I was twelve, my father and I took a charter flight to Dakar.

Across my mind runs a panorama of a clammy city, the opening montage of a New Wave movie: high-rises sweating like leather, women ripe on hot-waxed mopeds, men with rickety carts hawking dried plums and chevron beads. In this world I expect Colette's words to be silver floss, to glisten.

—He grew up there, but he was ashamed of growing up without money. When we visited, he rented a hotel room for me to stay in, alone, while he stayed in his childhood home.

—Bet your hotel wasn't like this one, I answer, unsure of the shades in my voice.

—It was a Radisson. No shred of personality in that place. Not a single honest smell or mismatched piece of linen. Who can stand beige throw pillows?

The sun, which had, for a spell of fifteen minutes, poked out from behind the cirrus clouds, disappears from view. Colette fits her palm to mine, and the darkness we are left in doubles for the low light of intimacy.

Hell or high water, the suggestions have trickled in. Alternative routes for public transit, wider boulevards, new fountains. The people want to revive Old Paris.

I refuse to reshape this city into its own shortcomings. Wider boulevards will only increase traffic; pigeons will drown in new fountains. I will not suffer for someone else's nostalgia.

The public doesn't understand. Simply because the city is broken, and we are forced to rebuild, doesn't make this an opportunity to carve out a dream world.

I uncap a 0.18 millimetre pen – with it, I could perform surgery – and steady the nib in the heart of Chinatown.

In the next room, my boss is singing Josephine Baker in a vaudevillian boom, filling each wordless bar with the mimicked lilt of an accordion. *Paris! Paris! Paris!* For people like him, this city is a Vincente Minelli movie – Leslie Caron sipping from a champagne flute, lovers picnicking on the Seine, Gene Kelly serenading a baguette.

As I'm plotting pedestrian crosswalks at the south end of de Choisy, I can almost hear his voice. *For the love of God, focus on the downtown core.*

A feeling steals into the bones at the base of my skull, not a pain but an awareness, blood pulsing over and over against my temple, like a madman throwing himself endlessly at the same idea. It must be a shift in the weather.

Before Colette, I loved someone as hard as anyone can be loved. Claire called herself Ourson, the masculine of little bear, because she said she felt like a little boy hibernating. She was twenty-six when I met her, and by that time had already lived ten years on the street.

Cities work in a different way for people with no home to return to – subways, gravel alleys serve a distinct utility; sycamore-treed parks far outgrow aesthetics – and I knew that. In my head, I knew that.

We dated for months. We went to second-run movies, and she kissed me in the dark. I often tried to get her to stay overnight, without sounding lonely or expectant. And when I finally bought a place for us to live together – lofty popcorn ceilings, a claw-foot tub that looked like it might run away – I still felt the weight of that trying.

She would wear jackets inside the apartment, two or some- times three, double her jeans, pile on extra socks and sweaters, no matter how many times I would say, *Make yourself comfort- able*. On her body, she carried everything she owned.

She fled after midnight on New Year's Eve, while I slept, champagne-tongued. I wish I had been surprised when I woke up alone.

—You really don't have to stay, Colette says, passing a tur- quoise ring from one finger to another as she waits for her tailor to finish hemming one of her pantheon of yellow dresses.

I unbutton the front of my overcoat to indicate my intention of remaining with her.

—When the rain stops, I will wear nothing but sundresses, she says. I will be a little sun myself.

She tilts her face down and looks up at me, the coy angles of a child. I can tell she is looking for a response, so I search the hurricane of my brain for a way to please her.

—Lovely as Saturn, but close as the sun.

These the tailor's words, spilling out as he rises to his full six feet. He hands the dress to Colette, who studies the seams, makes sure no golden threads have been left loose. The little sun needs secure hems.

—Oh, Ray, she tells him, you are a dream.

She leads me outside. Or maybe just walks ahead of me.

—I need to buy persimmons, she says, again twirling her turquoise ring. Will you walk me to the Peking Market?

My nod is a mechanism no more thoughtful than a sneeze. Satisfied, she squeezes my hand.

She begins to walk south, her feet fragile as glass under all the flood water, and suddenly I draw her to my chest, moor the ferry of her body so it does not float – it must not float away from me – but catch her palm in the swing of my arm, knocking her delicate ring to the ground.

My boss sits with legs crossed behind his seagrass-teak desk, imported from Copenhagen on the city's tab, and flutters visibly between comedy and pain, as if a shadow puppet show is playing on the crystal stage of his cornea.

—I looked at your plans, he begins, amusement deepening

his laugh lines. And then, darkly, —Do you think nothing of our city's golden past?

I imagine he is watching two paper cut-outs scale the lattice of the Eiffel Tower, propelled by the power of love, belting out a duet that, at some point, rhymes "bébé" with "mais oui."

—You mean my work around the 13e arrondissement? It's vital.

—You're saving Chinatown and letting the heart of Paris stop beating.

I flex my wrists. —Blood can't circulate without arteries.

His sweaty, overgrown eyebrows form a road map of mixed emotions, hills of wonderment at the centre bottoming out into vales of anger near the pink pulp of his tear ducts.

—I have to submit the plans to city council tonight, he tells me.

The choice for him is simple: submit my plans and seem illogical, or ask for an extension and seem weak. A wet sound passes between his lips, the last bubble rising to the lake's surface above a drowning man.

With his back turned, he carries the blueprints past the recycling bin and folds them safely under his arm. —If you have nothing more to say, he manages, then show yourself the door.

Colette is a lover of cubism. She tells me on our walk to Montmartre that, at one time, she had a tattoo of Georges Braque's *Le Portugais*, but had it removed because too many people asked her what it was supposed to be.

I have come to this neighbourhood only once, to step inside the Sacré-Coeur after Claire slipped away. I was afraid, racing against a riptide of darkness, and had little left to believe in but the spirit of the ancient basilica.

—Look at that townhouse, Colette says, pointing to a grey box with a For Sale sign. Just look at the stone siding.

All I can think of is the gutters to be swept of cypress leaves, the faucets to be sponged and polished, the furnace air filters to be replaced.

—Do you want to live in a hotel forever? she asks, scratching down the realtor's number on a folded receipt.

—The room service is nice.

—Well, then, she says, slapping the receipt into my palm, it's me or the lobster canapés.

What I remember of childhood autumns is Bordeaux, hunting wild boar with a recurve crossbow, rifling the life from ring-neck pheasants. I would swat horseflies into the oil slicks of my forearms, pressing hard when I caught one between my thumb and forefinger, until I heard a crunch and saw what was inside.

On a boar, tusks gleaming through the gooseberry bushes, you would aim straight for the meaty bell of the mid-shoulder. But the only way to hunt a pheasant is to gun into the air a foot ahead of them, in the direction of flight.

—Boys are mean by nature, my mother would say, and then fold me, star-eyed, into sleep.

In the pond beside our cottage, I sometimes caught flashes of a Rouen duck – black banding on the crown, royal-blue speculum feathers – when it flickered between the bulrushes. Though it moved like this from place to place, it always went alone.

I was in bed, laid up in eiderdown, when through my window I saw the duck catch his webbed feet on a jag of basalt and snap his legs like sticks of cinnamon. I watched him tumble through the thistled border of the pond, plunge deep below its canopy of lily pads. For hours, I heard the awful scraping of his wings against the water, and then nothing.

I know now, as I knew then: I could have saved that bird.

A cold front has sliced through the humidity, Paris slipping off its mantle of rain. For the first time in weeks, I can sit comfortably in my office.

My boss enters the room wig first. —I'm letting you go, he says, so nonchalant that he might as well conclude the sentence with "for an early lunch."

Any possible reaction of mine would satisfy him. So I look straight ahead and ask, without ceremony, —What's the city decided for you?

He looks down at the carpet, which is argyled in an unsettling shade of papaya whip, so that his wig stares me square in the eye.

—How I envy you, Serge. You don't have a family to disappoint.

In the street, a battleship fleet of half-smoked cigarettes floats past my ankles. Though the storm sewers are still overwhelmed, brimmed too full to function, at least, for the moment, things are not getting worse.

Colette runs to meet me in a tunic dress the colour of otter bone; from a distance, she looks airy, figmental, a forward-floating ghost from some unforgotten past.

—Hope you haven't been waiting long, she says, when she is close enough that I can smell cardamom on her breath. —The traffic is hell right now.

She must see the clouds forming on my forehead because she pauses. Fashions her hands into small canoes and glides the watery channels of my cheeks.

—Did something happen? she asks.

—Something happened, I say.

She takes me by the bulb of the elbow, where my jacket sleeve is patched with grey suede, and steers me across the flooded street. I feel I could float with the tide, lay back and let it move me, like a sprig of sea kelp, like a caravel skimming some long corridor of blue, easily, with the sun as its sentinel.

ANDREW FORBES

IN THE FOOTHILLS

Marty came down out of the mountains in early March, trailing a string of bad decisions. He started high up in the Rockies and swept into Calgary, coasting at great speed, almost like his brake lines had been cut.

I was working in a big sporting goods store, selling skis and running shoes and golf clubs. I had been thinking about heading back to Ontario, but that would've required putting my tail between my legs, and I wasn't ready for that just yet.

He'd been married to my sister for a short time, before she cracked up. My mother still says Eileen's "taken ill." Most recently Marty had been in Hundred Mile House, doing I don't know what, exactly. The details were vague. Before that he'd been in Vancouver. Trouble trailed him like a wake; bad ideas poured off him like a stench. Every time I saw him he was driving a different car. Not new cars, but different ones. This time it was a blue Cavalier with lightning bolts down the sides.

Since he and Eileen split and she walked herself into an emergency room wearing a nightgown, Marty has drifted like pollen from place to place, his welding papers in his back pocket. He'd stay for a time, use up his luck, then move on to the next town. He'd done like that after he got out of the Air Force at Cold Lake, but then he met Eileen and they had a couple of years where they imitated normal people, settled in one place, rented a nice house east of the city. They stayed in nights. Then real colours began to show through and things went haywire, like I'd felt they would.

Since then he and I have kept in touch, in a fashion, and all the while I've battled feelings of guilt for some sort of disloyalty to my sister. But then again I have since childhood suspected my sister to be the cause of all bad things.

Marty is big. Not obese, just large, built on a different scale than most human beings. He stands about six-foot-four, and his limbs are like telephone poles. His torso is like the front of a transport truck, and on his feet he wears a size thirteen or fourteen pair of boots. When he drinks, which he often does, it's usually from something big, a jar or a big plastic travel coffee mug. He drinks vodka mostly, Russians or Screwdrivers. Drinks them like water. Sometimes the only way you can tell he's on his way down is that his face and neck get beet red. Eventually he just collapses. Finds a bed or a sofa and you can forget about Marty for twelve hours or so.

The thing with Marty is, when he comes to stay with you, there's no way of knowing how long he'll be there. He arrived on a Saturday afternoon and immediately went to sleep on the futon in the other room, the room that had been empty since my roommate skipped out on me. Marty stayed there until midday Sunday. I could hear him snoring. Once or twice in the night I heard him get up to use the washroom, a bear of a man, a lumberjack, shaking the whole apartment as he moved, then planting his feet before the toilet and uncorking a torrent of piss. Water running, then slow, heavy footsteps back down the hallway, the sound of a California redwood being felled as he tumbled back into bed, and then nothing, just faint sawing, for hours and hours thereafter.

A chinook had followed Marty down from the hills, and Sunday was a warm, springy day, a breeze alive with smells where the day before it had been cold and dead. By Sunday noon it was a beaut of a day, the sun at its full strength, the sound of water running off the roofs, everything slick. I could sit at my window and watch the snowbanks below melting like ice cubes in an empty glass. I'd opened the windows and was listening to CCR when Marty emerged from the second bedroom. I always listen to CCR when winter turns to spring, and even if this was a false beginning, I needed to feel good about things after the winter I'd had.

"What in the hell are you doing?" he asked me.

"Polishing my boots," I said. I was standing hunched over the table where I'd spread out newspapers, some spare rags, and an old shoebox containing my polish kit: a tin of polish, two brushes, and a shining rag.

"Look at you, your highness!"

"Sunday," I said. "Every Sunday I polish my boots. My dad used to do it."

"I see," he said, then looked around, sniffed, and rubbed his stomach. The smell of polish in his nose must have reminded him of the smell of food.

"Got any vittles here?" he asked.

"Sure, yeah. Cereal, toast . . ."

"Eggs? Bacon? Potatoes?"

"Yeah," I said, "though the potatoes might have sprouted."

"All right then, you do your thing, I'll cook." And he did. He went to work in my pathetic little kitchen, and with a cutting board, a dull knife, and a single fry pan he beavered away until he had made us a rich spread of eggs and bacon, toast, beans, warm stewed tomatoes. When my plate was empty he refilled it. Only once I was done did Marty sit down and eat. He had thirds, finished everything. I had forgotten this about Marty, that he loved to spend time in the kitchen, and that Eileen never had to cook.

By mid-afternoon, still full, we were sitting on the couch sharing my cigarettes, the sliding door to the patio wide open to let in the sweet warm breeze. CCR had given way to Rush in the five-disc changer: Marty's choice.

"What time do you work tomorrow?" Marty asked me.

"One," I said. "One 'til close."

"Good, then you can sleep in," he said, lighting another.

"Why do I need to sleep in?"

"There's a bar I think we should close tonight," he said. "Passed it on the way here."

And I thought, why not? What's the worst that could happen to me, in the company of this man who'd cooked me such a generous meal, on a Sunday night in the foothills with the warm breath of springtime upon me?

"Let's do that," I said.

We took my truck, the truck I drove out to Alberta from Kingston, the truck that I lived in for two weeks until I found an apartment. It occurred to me that there was no definite plan as to what we might do with the truck, how we might get back to my apartment or, failing that, where we would stay after this night of drinking. It's something I felt that we were actively not discussing, a thing floating between us. I kept returning to it in my head, but deciding that I shouldn't bring it up, because I felt like Marty was daring me to do just that, to be the responsible one, so that he could be proven, in a single chop, the opposite. Marty defined himself by these sorts of oppositions.

We drove west, straight toward the Rockies, which loomed purple and holy before us, an unreal painted backdrop. The last of the sun was honey oozing between the peaks, and through it we moved slowly, lazily. In the middle distance the foothills burped up from the prairie, little practice runs, junior topography. That's where we were headed, to a place called the Starlite, located nowhere in particular, just a sign, a parking lot, and a roadhouse.

We stood in the parking lot, Marty and I, feeling – what? Apprehension? Excitement? It's likely, given what transpired later, that we were not feeling the same thing at that moment, though it felt for all the world that we were comrades, men linked by uneven pasts and a hope that the near future, namely this night, would prove to be a kind one.

We leaned against the truck and did some damage to a six-pack liberated from my fridge. The light disappeared and the night came on and we watched two or three trucks pull in, their drivers making their way to the Starlite's steel door with their heads down.

My hair plastered down and my boots newly polished, I felt like a handsome devil. Maybe there'd be women inside, I thought. That's why I had come, for drinks and whatever interesting faces this evening might invite in. The usual things. I assumed that's why Marty had brought us out there, an assumption I'd find to be false in due time.

Marty specialized in broken women: those who'd known bad men, bad times, those who'd become familiar with the youth justice system. That's what drew him to my sister, of course. She hadn't yet gone off the rails, but he saw something in her. Marty would ride their momentum for a time, have some laughs, then jump off before things completely fell apart. He had a knack for it. When you were riding alongside Marty, you would meet women who quickly began to tell you all about themselves – everything, in one sitting – and you'd hear some crazy things. Then they'd want you to commend them on their strength, given all they'd endured. Sometimes I'd say something along the lines of, "Well, we've all got trouble, sweetness, but we don't necessarily go blabbing it to the first person we meet in a bar." This stance had, on more than one occasion, hurt Marty's chances with certain women, and he openly discouraged me from adopting it, or at least voicing it. I'd try to comply, if only because part of me felt that I owed Marty something.

An explanation on that one: while duck hunting with borrowed guns three years earlier, I broke my tibia galloping down a slope toward the spot we'd selected, on the rim of a broad marsh. Marty tied a stick to my leg and then put me on his shoulder and carried me three kilometres back to the truck. He let me drain the vodka from his flask while he drove me to the hospital. An episode like that can endear a person to you, even in the face of their obvious shortcomings.

I was remembering all this as we stood outside the Starlite.

I could hear the wind, which had taken on a coolness I didn't welcome, and I could hear the bar's sign buzzing. Far out in the night I could hear traffic on the highway, transports moving between Calgary and the mountains, and Vancouver beyond that, though at that moment the road in front of us was empty.

"Don't see his truck," Marty muttered, lifting his bottle to his lips.

"Whose truck?" I asked, but Marty was pitching his bottle across the gritty parking lot and striding toward the Starlite's front door. If he heard me he ignored the question.

Inside it was dark and musty with a checkerboard linoleum floor that might once have been black and white, but had gone grey and yellow many years ago. There were about a dozen patrons scattered about, most of them in high-backed booths, while three men in plaid shirts and leather vests slumped over the bar. The walls were wood panelled, but the chintzy variety of wood panelling, the kind your dad might have installed in your basement. It was warped in several spots. It had been a year or two since they'd got rid of smoking everywhere, but you could still smell the stale tobacco coming out of the Starlite's every plank and fibre. I imagined the bar stools' stuffing exhaling it every time another ass applied pressure to them.

Marty strode to the bar and took a stool, and I followed. The man behind the bar wasn't very interested in our being there. He was having a conversation with one of the other men sitting at the bar. But in a moment he came to us and we ordered beers. Above the bartender's head a small television perched on a wobbly looking shelf played a hockey game. The Flames were in L.A. The men at the bar were looking up at that through their eyebrows.

We slumped over the bar and half watched the hockey game and drank beer for an hour or so. There wasn't much conversation between us. Just quiet drinking. Then Marty stood up and excused himself to the men's.

I watched him go in the mirror over the bar. Then a moment later I watched that big steel door open and let in a blast of cool air. Riding it were a strange pair, a man and a woman, she taller than him, who nodded to the bartender, then walked past me to a booth in the corner. As they passed me I could smell them: she wore flowery perfume, and he smelled sour and pungently of pot. They took off their coats and hung them on hooks near the mouth of their booth. Then the man came to the bar, chatted with the keeper, and got them a pitcher of beer and a couple of glasses.

The man wore a knit Rastafarian hat, green, yellow, red, beneath which lay a long, dark ponytail. He wore an open plaid shirt with a black T-shirt beneath, from the front of which smiled Mr. Bob Marley.

The woman was tall and thin. If they were to make a movie about this whole incident they'd probably cast Katherine Heigl to play her, and that could work, but only if Katherine Heigl was falling apart a bit. The skin of her face was sagging a little, her elbows were bony, and her hair looked sort of like straw. But she was still pretty, there was no seeing around that. Probably as pretty or prettier a woman as either Marty or I would ever know again. She looked nice in her jeans, and she was a good three or four inches taller than Bob Marley. It was obvious to everyone present that our little Bob was punching well above his weight.

They settled into their booth and I more or less forgot about them. Marty was taking his sweet time, I thought, and a moment later I saw the light leak out from the bathroom door as it swung open. Marty's path back to our stools took him right by Bob and Broken Katherine, and on the way by he said, loud enough for the whole bar to hear, "Good to see you again, asshole!"

Why would he have done that? I wondered.

Marty fell down onto his stool and I could smell the drink on him. I realized that he'd lapped me several times over in terms of consumption. He was close to drunk; if he wasn't already there, he was on the outskirts. I thought maybe that had something to do with his greeting to Bob Marley.

"How do you feel tonight?" he boomed at me.

"I feel pretty good, Marty," I said.

"That's good. That's frickin' good," he said. "I gotta say, though, our evening might be about to change."

"How so, Marty?"

"I might have to beat that little guy to death," he said, and he was smiling broadly. His face was red, his ears and his neck. Something was racing through him.

"Why's that, Marty?"

"Oh, that don't frickin' matter now," he said, and he swivelled around to face the bar. He was finishing a beer and then he ordered a shot of vodka. Then a second.

"You want anything?" he asked me, but I just tilted my half-full beer glass to show its contents. "Fair enough," he said.

After a third shot he spun back around and faced the corner where the couple sat. He was looking at them over my shoulder and grinning. He watched them a moment and he moved his mouth like he was looking for something to say. He chuckled to himself.

"You need a ladder to kiss her?" he shouted.

"Fuck you," someone shouted back, but it didn't seem to me that it was Bob. He might have a defender in this, I remember thinking.

"How do *you* fuck *her*?" Marty shouted to the whole barroom.

I wished to hide then in my glass of beer. "Marty," I asked, "do you know those two?"

"I might've run into them before. Here." Then he laughed like a clown might before it touches you in the funhouse.

"On the way into town, am I right?" I asked.

"Sure, sure," Marty said. Then he shouted, "Look at him! Look at you! You look like her kid brother!" The couple was trying their best to ignore all of this. I don't imagine they were successful. Everyone else in the Starlite had gone quiet, like villagers waiting for a bombing run to end.

"You don't talk much," he said to me.

"I don't have much to say," I responded. "Not much important, anyway. I don't really know what's going on here."

"What's frickin' going on here is that I stopped by for a sip on Saturday afternoon, stopped right here at this establishment, and I was enjoying myself, talking to blondie there. Seemed to me we were getting on great. Then her fella there comes in and starts saying some unkind things, and I got agitated because it seemed to me that if he and I were laid out on a buffet, at best he'd be an appetizer, where I'd be the main course. I could see she might feel that way too, and I was about to do something about it when I was advised that the gentleman a few stools down was a police officer. That changed my plans somewhat. So I said I'd come back and we'd finish."

"And you brought me."

"You weren't busy, were you?"

"Suppose not."

After Marty's speech I decided I'd have a double Canadian Club, no ice, and as I ordered that I happened to glance in the mirror and notice their booth had gone empty.

Then I heard a microsecond of shouting. My jaw went electric and the stool I'd been sitting on was suddenly beside and above me. Marty's head was nearly staved in by the thick glass bottom of an empty pitcher, whereas I think Katherine Heigl had walloped me with a plate.

There were shattered bits of light in my eyes, on the floor. The linoleum down there smelled of winter and salt.

I was still trying to move my face when I heard Marty get to his feet and start to shuffle after our Bonnie and Clyde, who'd retreated to the other side of the room. Bob Marley was holding a stool in front of him and Marty, whose face was bloody, was headed over there with his fists loaded. But the bartender shouted, "Hey!" and when I could see over the bar I noticed the shotgun in his hands. There wasn't any doubting who it was pointed at. In fact the whole room of people was lined up against Marty and, to a lesser degree, me. Clearly the other two had thrown the first, but they were local and we weren't. We weren't even Albertans. And we probably didn't vote the same way either. They had their reasons is what I'm getting at.

"Christ!" Marty shouted, then reached down to yank me up. When we got to the truck it just worked out that I climbed into the driver's seat, though I had no business being there. I felt like someone had packed cotton balls into my skull. There was a sharp pain where my teeth ought to have been and I couldn't speak.

In my dreams of that happier life, things like this were securely in my past. They weren't adventures to me anymore; they caused my heart to ache. I'd look at myself and shake my head. That happier life – the hope of it, the possibility of it – came to me in sparing moments now, like when I'd eaten that breakfast Marty had made, or when we stood in the blue twilight in the Starlite's parking lot earlier and it seemed like maybe we had a good evening ahead of us. But every time one of those moments sprang up it was gone again just as fast, and that happy life got further and further away, like a thing you watch blow away in a storm.

It was full on night now, the roads bare but for my sweeping headlights. I didn't feel as though I was driving, but rather that the truck was driving me. I felt safe. That's why it was so surprising to me when that tree came up. I thought, who'd put a tree there? But of course it was that we'd left the road behind. The truck wasn't saving us, and Marty reached over for the steering wheel. He was saying something but I couldn't hear it because of the wind whistling in the hole where the windshield used to be.

There was an interval when I was aware of darkness, but not of anything else. I don't know if I was conscious or not, or just what state I was in. When I came to and tried to open my eyes there was a dazzling spray of light. What was interesting was that I couldn't be sure if the light originated inside my head or if it came from somewhere else. I knew there was a helicopter, and quickly reckoned that I was in it. The copter's blades sounded like a series of pops. Pop-pop-pop-pop, in a sort of fast slow motion. With each pop it felt as though my head might implode. I tried to look at myself but came to find that I was strapped down. I wanted then to throw up because my feet were above my head and the level earth was a distant memory.

I wondered about my truck, and in fact I must have asked aloud, because someone said it was gone. I thought that was too bad, because I felt a great sense of loyalty to that blue 1988 GMC, the truck that Marty had driven to the hospital after our ill-fated duck expedition, as I sat in the passenger seat and my head lolled around like a pinball and the pain felt like it had a centre and a million radiant arms. Our borrowed shotguns rattled around in the bed. It had been a good truck.

My blood felt milky. The helicopter rose and rose, as though it was going to take me over the mountains, or into the clouds. What happened then was that I had a flashback to the moment before we'd left the road, Marty and I, in my blue truck. I had been thinking that sometimes your life isn't the one you want to be living, even if it isn't terrible or dire. There was nothing I wouldn't mind seeing the end of, I had said to myself. That included Marty.

Now in the ascending helicopter, still going up, I didn't know if Marty was alive or dead, and I didn't want to ask. I knew he wasn't nearby, in my helicopter, but maybe he was in his own, thumping similarly heavenward. I wondered if we'd both wake up in the same ward, a mint-green curtain separating our mechanical beds, and laugh about all this. But I hoped not. I hoped I wouldn't see Marty on the other side of this. It was all his doing; I couldn't see any other way. My head was enduring a slow explosion and my eyes didn't seem to be working quite right. The rest of my body was at that moment either a rumour or a memory and I had to face the reality that Alberta wasn't really working out for me. And goddamn Marty, I thought. The mountains had sent him, and it was my great desire that the mountains should take him back.

OSSICLES

T he child had a thought like a nail through the sole of her foot, stuck. The hatted aunt with lips like scrambled egg looked at the child but could not see the thought; she saw only the child, staring into the corner at the floor where, the hatted aunt proved with a glance, there was nothing except off-yellow off-white smears six inches up from the floor, and dust.

Are you hungry at all, she said to the child.

But the staring seated child with the thought like a nail through the sole of her foot went sit, sit, sit.

So the hatted aunt with lips like scrambled egg and eyes like boiled eggs sat and watched the wall.

The uncle of the child came now tall and smear-coloured from the office halfway down the hall, and he said to the hatted aunt, Thank you for waiting. If we hurry we can make it there by seven. And the hatted aunt said, I wish we had gone to your – and the child could not hear what the hatted aunt said to the uncle after that, for she said it with her face hidden behind her hat and her mouth hidden up against the uncle's smear-coloured coat.

The uncle said, Come, Emily, and he reached his sallow fingers out at the child until she peered up from the thought she was having, and laid her hand in his fingers to hold. She followed the uncle into the elevator and the hatted aunt followed after them.

Outside it was all evening, and shadows rising like deep pooling water between the buildings, and the child was caught again on the thought like a nail. The uncle did not notice it so much except that now and again he had to tug the child by the hand when she forgot to walk. The hatted aunt did not notice it because she had her purse open in front of her as she walked and she was searching through it and saying, Herbert, where did I.

Meanwhile the child almost did not notice the dark rising purple from the storm drains, and she almost did not feel the uncle's fingers around her hand, and she almost forgot to cross her eyes at the yellow dog graffitied in the alley between the corner store and the hardware store, but at the last moment she did remember and the yellow dog did not try to follow them. But the thought like a nail caught and caught and caught, and she looked down at her hand, and wondered.

When they rounded the corner and there on the side of a building was the twenty-foot man, slick like wet soap and drinking a wet cold glass of milk and saying BONES NEED MILK©, the uncle did not feel what happened inside the child's thought. He only pushed open the door of a restaurant called Minelli's and held it for the hatted aunt as he said to her, I don't even think I spoke to him during the trip. And the hatted aunt might have replied, but the child did not hear her, because the thought like a nail through the sole of her foot went *twist*.

———

Marcus Lauzon has seven puppies.

I don't think he has seven puppies, Em.

He said he has, he has seven puppies now, and he named them Cleatus, Heatus, Hercules, Pinnochio, Tama-Tama, and Sam. And Le Dauphin.

Why did he name them after your ponies?

Why did he

Because I named them, I named them that.

He let you name his

Except also he has a brother named Le Dauphin and so that's, that's why he named that one that.

I really don't think he has seven puppies, Em. You like soup, right? Potato soup?

Except sorry, I forgot he named one Julius and the other he named, he named Max. And yeah actually I meant he has two puppies. Actually one is a kitten and he named it Harvey, and I think it's going to die soon, because it has lung cancer.

Did you hear me about the soup?

Em?

I'm fine.

Yes? Soup?

I'll have cereal, please.

You mean you'll have more of that candy.

Uncle Herbert said that

Uncle Herb spoiled you silly, thank you very much. That sugar is going to rot your teeth.

I have it with milk, though.

Sugar is sugar.

Please stop doing that, Em.

I said STOP that, Emily, or
they'll never heal.

Marcus Lauzon has
dissolving bones.

Go wash your hands. Dinner
is in ten minutes.

Marcus Lauzon has

GO

———

Here is how it happens:

You catch it from somebody.

Maybe because you're always sitting in a hospital where
people are sick sick, dying. Anyway. You catch it. It drifts into
your nose, probably, and then seeps through the soggy tissue-
paper skin in your sinuses and dissolves in your blood. Then
your blood goes blasting hot and happy through your skull and
your arms and your guts and your legs and this whole time it's
just floating along and waiting.

It has to wait. It's got to wait for a chance to get stuck inside
a tiny, tiny hole in one of your bones. It can wait seventy-five
years, sometimes.

But then, one night when you're lying dead asleep in your
bed in the dark with your bones dangling and your brain fiz-
zling, it catches at last in that tiny, tiny hole

like a tiny metal ball bearing careening finally into the
punched-out pore of a
plastic toy maze
and then it digs.

You won't notice at first. Nobody will notice. If a doctor X-rayed your skeleton she might not even notice unless she looked close, close, close at the film with a magnifying glass under a microscope, and then if she had one-hundred-per-cent perfect 20-20 vision then she would *maybe* see it, *aha*.

By the third month you can start to almost know. If you have an inkling, you can do this: turn on all the lights in a room that has a mirror. Make sure you can stand right up against the mirror, so this means bathrooms might be bad because the counter or the sink seems to get in the way unless you can climb up on them, which I recommend. You have to be able to hold your face about a centimetre from the glass.

Now if you have your face in the right position and the lights are on bright and your face isn't shading itself (be careful of that if the lights are behind you because the light will probably not be able to beam around your head) then if you roll your eyes down at the one-hundred-per-cent correct angle and look at your cheekbone reflected in the mirror

you will

see

honeycomb. Through the skin like yellow sponge candy dissolving under your pores and under your muscles and blood.

You understand that the lights must be bright bright bright and your face must be close close close or you will just see skin. Even then you have to keep turning your head and straining your eyes, and sometimes you'll think that maybe if you had a second hand-held mirror, or a kind of miniature periscope, or something, you would be able to see it better, or that of course if the skin weren't there and the flesh were gone then you would see it perfect, no problem.

And if you stretch the skin with your fingers a little bit that seems to help, but be careful not to do that too often, because eventually you start rubbing the skin off and getting pimples and little scabs and then everyone starts going *Emily there is something the matter with your face, are you sick*

And you can try saying
   take me to the regional specialist in acute juvenile osteoporosis and virulent pathological foramina for a probative bone biopsy and a regimen of aggressive biphosphonate administration
   and feed me exclusively on dairy products and broccoli
   and as a preventative measure have my body encased in porcelain and have my skeleton pre-emptively remodelled in titanium alloys
   and prepare the hip replacements knee replacements elbow replacements maxilla replacement rib replacements tarsal replacements mandible replacement cranium replacement et cetera et cetera
      to fill the spongy hollows left when my bones are cobweb rolls of nothing, someday

And you can try saying all that
   but you won't say it, not really
   because you are six years old and your father is dead of cancer
and it has been a strain even to hold *diagnosis* in your mind
   or *sarcoma*.

—

No one could see the child lying face-up under the altar. It was a poured concrete slab lain across two poured concrete pillars and the child's body beneath it crossed it midway like a small T. Chips and chinks in the poured concrete like hiero-glyphs and braille spoke down at her from the table's under-belly, spoke Joshua Samuel David Isaiah, spoke Hungry, spoke Camel Puppy Pony Elephant, spoke Jesus Christ Nazareth Nazareth, spoke Toothache and Daddy and Sleep. The child stuck her finger in her mouth and chewed it while her brain lay aching.

The purple frontal hung across the altar made the child invisible. The cloth made the grey purple, made the white-grey purple, made her skin purple and the shadows purple. Her feet poking out beyond the frontal, she knew, were not purple but somehow still invisible, for the men and the women out beyond it were going, He was so young and Thank you for coming, and never, There are his daughter's feet.

So the child with a hole in the middle of her middle made a purple duck come out from a purple concrete crack, waddled it across to the middle of the stone pavement hanging over her, and said to it, My bones hurt.

The duck said, Try drinking some milk.

She chewed her finger and told the duck that they were all out of milk and also that this was a church and a funeral. The duck said, Later, then. And she turned him into a mouse and then an airplane and then she made the whole altar into sponge candy in her mind and closed her eyes and dissolved it in dark.

Outside her cave there were men and women going Hum in a lake of sound. The child, behind her closed eyes, saw a white hand and then a smear-coloured curtain and a mouth that could not shut, but then she sent those things away into the dark where they could dissolve into nothing, into the nothing of nothing. In their place she left a yellow dog, shining.

After the mother with pearls lifted the purple cloth, the uncle who was with her reached underneath and took the child into his arms. He carried her sleeping past the nodding priest and the sad-eyed grandfather and the hatted aunt dabbing a hand-kerchief under her eyes and saying, Oh Herbert, dear Emily.

And the uncle took the child to his car where he spread her out sleeping on the back seat, and when the child awoke the uncle was sitting behind the wheel in the parking lot with the radio on. The uncle said something warm and handed her a cube of the yellow sponge candy.

She lay on her cheek and pressed the nougat between her palms until the sweat melted it into sugary glue, and the uncle hummed with the radio all the while weeping, Oh my love, my darling.

———

Caitlin Rhys's brother is allergic to pine trees.

Is that so.

He is so allergic to pine trees that if there is a pine tree five miles away from him he, he dies.

have announced that the funding for the facility will be cancelled through twenty fifteen the announcement was met with disappointment and outrage by the

I don't think that's true, Em.

Yes it is, it is true.

Where could he get that he would be five miles away from pine trees all the time? They live just across town. There are tons of pine trees around.

He wears a mask.

He wears a mask.

So he can't smell the pine trees, ever. It covers his whole face and his nose and his eyes and everything and he can go anywhere with his mask on but if he takes it off, he dies.

Hmm.

volunteer groups petitioning for improved access to resources in the downtown area they believe that the gordon centre provides a nexus for critical support services josie glieson reports protestors at the corner of houston and third avenue wave signs reading save the gordon centre save our city most of the protestors are volunteers with the social justice groups associated with the centre or beneficiaries of their services tammy sunwail is a retired librarian and volunteer at literart a non-profit group aimed

Except that he
maybe has to take
it off to eat but
then

Can you be
allergic to a
colour?

Like can you be
allergic to yellow?

Yes.

Except what if
it made you sick
sometimes to look
at a colour. And

Did you pick up
your room like I
asked you?

Em?

Did you hear what
I asked?

No. Did you pick
up your room?

Did you really?

Emily, I haven't
got time for this

at promoting adult
literacy there are
so many people
that benefit from
our services
and from all the
services provided
the gordon centre
is one of the best
things going for
our city if the
mayor can't see
that he's in trouble
he's in big trouble
another protestor
who asked not
to be named said
that she received
daycare services
through the
gordon centre for
two years i don't
know what i would
have done without
them i don't know
what anyone
would have done
meanwhile city
counsellors argue
that all essential

what if everything became that colour and it would be terrible.

And like maybe if you also became that colour and then you would be allergic to yourself and your body would start thinking it was a disease and eating itself and then maybe by the end there wouldn't be you anymore.

I'm going to die.

Still.

right now. I told you Sam and Ella are coming over tonight and I want you to clean up your toys before they get here. I don't have time to help you with everything right now, so will you please go finish tidying your room?

Stop scratching your face.

Not anytime soon, you're not.

services provided at the gordon centre will continue to be provided by official city programming throughout the downtown area chris repairs to the sutton island ferry pier destroyed a week ago in a ferry collision are nearly complete the metro transport authority announced this morning that the regular service schedule is set to resume on monday barring complications meanwhile ferry service to sutton island remains on a reduced provisional schedule doctors at rottmann memorial hospital believe their patients may have been

PHILIP HUYNH

GULLIVER'S WIFE

When her husband, Thuong, told Josephine that Vancouver was bilingual, that it was just as French as it was English – like the rest of Canada – she believed him. There was no need to go to Montréal, where some of her friends would end up. Vancouver would be as fine a place as any to continue life.

Until her last day in Saigon, Josephine taught French in primary school, refusing to admit that French would be useless to her students once the Communists took over. Her great regret was never getting to see any of them discover *The Stranger*. But at least she got to leave Vietnam in an airplane, not like her friends. She fled to Hong Kong with Thuong and his mother. Thuong returned to studying economics now that his military career was finished. In the year they spent in Hong Kong, while Thuong applied to universities all over the world, Josephine picked up more Cantonese than English, though all she could really do in Cantonese was haggle down the price of vegetables.

Two universities in the Vancouver area offered Thuong scholarships. All else being equal, Thuong chose the school located in the mountains because such a school is, naturally, more auspicious than a school by the sea. When they arrived, the only thing French about Vancouver was the bilingual grocery labels.

Now, seven years on, their son Christian set for kindergarten, the family rents a basement suite on Fleming Street in East Vancouver, and Thuong is still working on his PhD. Josephine's English is much improved, although she still prefers to read the grocery labels in French. She occasionally watches the French broadcast of the CBC, even though the Québécois accent will always sound foreign. Maybe it is just as well that they ended up in Vancouver instead of Montréal.

———

Josephine sits in with Christian for the first few classes, because he is a weeper when she leaves him alone. She doesn't like what she sees. She understands that in public school the children don't wear uniforms, but most boys here don't even wear collars. In Vietnam even the poor wore uniforms with stiff collars, even if they only had one shirt that their mothers had to iron each morning. And everything here is in English. Nothing is taught in French. Josephine pulls Christian out of kindergarten after only two weeks.

There is a Catholic school close to home. She had not considered St. Maurice's earlier because it charged tuition – a few hundred dollars and the cost of a uniform. They will have to budget better if Christian is to go. For dinner there will be fewer noodles in each bowl of *pho*. She will have to cut the beef into thinner slices. But it will be worth it. St. Maurice's teaches French.

The French language conjures up everything Josephine is fond of about Vietnam, of grey-green *margouillats* climbing the Doric columns of the school where she taught, of nuns chewing on betel leaves while tracing their sisters' steps across the court-yard, of ham and baguettes. What happens to wine when it is allowed to breathe in the open air? Josephine is not an expert on wines, but she imagines it is similar to the alchemy that occurs in her head when she inhales French. French takes her back home more than Vietnamese does, Vietnamese being, these days, the language of arguments over chores and the future.

————

No one notices them when they enter St. Maurice's. The teacher is writing on the chalkboard: "*le chat*," "*le chien*," "*au pays*," and other short words arranged like little *bon bons* on a plate. The teacher's back is turned to the pupils, who are scat-tered throughout the classroom amongst the books, toys, and cubbyholes.

Josephine sits on a popsicle-orange chair in the corner and Christian stands by her side, his hand on her shoulder. The teacher turns around and calls the children to attention, igno-rant of Josephine's presence.

There are many things here that remind Josephine of her classroom in Vietnam. There is, for example, the alphabet that snakes across the top of the walls, the various accent marks hanging over the vowels. There are familiar books, which seem beyond the grasp of five-year-olds, but which thrill her: *Tin Tin*, *Les Fables de La Fontaine*, *Le Petit Prince*.

But here class is held in a portable with the musty smell of plaster, wet wool, and rain-drenched wood. And here the pupils come in varying colours – brown, yellow, and white – though the squealing of children is the same everywhere.

All of this is to be expected. What is surprising is that the French teacher does not have a Québécois accent. It is Parisian, like the nuns who raised Josephine. And that the accent belongs to a man.

The kindergarten teacher is very tall and wears a yellow bow tie over a blue sweater-vest, both as bright as crayons, and a five o'clock shadow. He is like Gulliver as he tries to herd the children (dangling from window sills, buried in plastic toys) to the worn-out polka dot rug in the centre of the classroom.

Josephine hoped to simply drop Christian off, but already he is fidgeting with his clip-on tie. She knows Christian will start wailing the moment she leaves him.

"*Attention*," says the teacher, in French. No response, so he claps his hands. Nothing. He sucks in his breath to let out a holler, then sees Josephine sitting in the corner.

"You're a teacher?" he says.

"No. Not here."

"Oh, I see," he says. "The new boy. You can leave him."

"He will be a nuisance to you if I leave him alone." She says this in French, the first French she has uttered in seven years: "*Il sera une nuisance pour vous si je le laisse seul.*" She is not a smoker, but she can imagine the feeling of a long-awaited relapse. Blood rushes to her head.

Meanwhile the children have stopped in place and look over at Josephine. She claps her hands. "Over to the front," she says in French.

"I can . . ." says the teacher, then loses his train of thought as the children gather on the rug at the centre of the classroom for their morning alphabet lesson.

————

The copper statue of General Tran Hung Dao beside Thuong's desk is not the image that most are familiar with – that of Vietnam's great hero who fought off the Mongol invaders almost a millennia before Ho Chi Minh thwarted the French and Americans. It is not the General Tran struck in the tunic, cloak, and shoulder armour of full battle regalia, his dark beard in warring bristle, one finger pointing ahead – to a distant enemy or wind-swept oasis Thuong is not sure. In this version, which stands three feet tall, General Tran is dressed as a scholar king. His eyes are just as piercing, but tempered with sympathy. His beard is a pointed wisp in repose. He wears a turban, not his armoured helmet. His belt is a thin bolt wrapped around a scholar's gown, embroidered with a pattern of clouds. His sword rests in its sheath. In his hand is instead a rolled-up scroll. His victory over the Mongol oppressors is behind him, his fate as a deity lies ahead.

Thuong rescued the statue from the temple in his neighbourhood in Saigon. Who knows what the Communists would have done if they had gotten their hands on it. Thuong packed it in a huge steamer trunk that belongs to Josephine, swaddled in Josephine's silk dresses.

The statue stands in the corner of the study that doubles as their bedroom, the only space in the basement where there's room. When Thuong sits at his desk, he meets the General at eye level. It is still beautiful, although the copper is turning green-blue. Thuong isn't sure whether it is proper to regard the statue as an object of beauty. He is not sure if the look on the General's face is meant to instill awe, or fear, or devotion, or all of these things at once, and if so in what proportions. This is what he thinks about when he looks upon the General, when he should be working on his dissertation.

Sometimes he thinks the General speaks to him. The General has goaded him to study harder for his exams. He has commanded Thuong to settle on a dissertation topic, even though it may not be the perfect choice. Thuong knows that it is improper to pretend that an object of worship would stoop to be Thuong's personal academic mentor. But Thuong can't help himself.

Thuong wishes the statue wasn't such a distraction from his studies. Heaven knows, both the university and the Canadian government have given Thuong enough scholarships, stipends, and breaks to get him this far. They have even supplied him with his own IBM PC, which takes up most his desk, and a daisy wheel printer that rocks the walls when it runs.

But the General is always staring at him, unblinking.

Thuong gets so dizzy sometimes with all his thoughts that he has to stand up, stretch out. Get some fresh air. Call his friend Fred Wong, another economics student. See maybe if there's a card game he can join in Chinatown, just some penny ante table. Just to take his mind off things.

———

The students call the teacher Monsieur LaForge, though Josephine has learned that his first name is Paul. Against the walls of Paul's classroom are little framed pieces of paper containing pithy quotes in the French language:

"Happiness is beneficial for the body, but it is grief that develops the powers of the mind."

– Marcel Proust

"Solitary trees, if they grow at all, grow strong."

– Winston Churchill

"Be less curious about people and more curious about ideas."

– Marie Curie

Josephine can't help but to ask Paul about them.

"It's for the children to read," he says.

"You can't expect them to absorb all this wisdom," says Josephine.

"When I am done they should at least be able to mouth the words, if not understand them."

Josephine has attended the half-day kindergarten all week. Christian starts crying even if she gets up for the washroom, and has not improved.

Paul was at first annoyed by Josephine's presence. It was one thing for five-year-olds to judge him, it was another thing to have an adult's eyes on him as well. But Paul cannot deny the calming effect that Josephine has on all the children. When she is not in the room they not only fidget, as five-year-olds do, but cough, go glassy-eyed, snap at each other, droop, make a break for the Lego. Perhaps it has to do with Paul's deep, sonorous voice delivered at the pace of a metronome, a voice that could command the attention of a jury but which lies outside the register of young children. Josephine just barks across the room when there's defiance. She has a tone that corrals the children when they lose their focus on Paul.

It is during a usual rendition of "*Ballade à la lune*," when the children start laughing in the middle of the song, that Paul can smell sulphur. The children pinch their noses, then point fingers at each other, and then the fingers settle on a little red-headed girl with a sombre expression. The smell gathers strength. As the girl's pallor matches her hair and tears roll down her face, the children laugh harder and clear a radius around her.

Josephine comes to the girl, checks under her navy dress, and picks her up by the armpits.

"It's diarrhea," says Josephine.

"Oh dear," says Paul.

"I'll take her to the washroom. Can you bring a pair of pants?"

"How would I have an extra pair of pants?"

"The nuns must have supplies," says Josephine. "You must have a physical education department? An extra pair of shorts or sweatpants in a locker room? It doesn't have to be the perfect size."

"Of course," says Paul. "I'll be right back."

Paul does not realize that he has sweated through his dress shirt until class is done. The red-headed girl's mother shudders when she finds her daughter in baggy sweatpants.

"She had an accident," says Paul.

"You changed her?" says the mother accusingly. She hisses in relief when Paul points at Josephine.

Josephine stays after all the other children are gone, waiting for Christian who is so absorbed with a strange looking toy that she finally has to pull it away.

"Until tomorrow," she says.

"You know, I really teach fourth grade," says Paul. "Fourth grade and up."

"I understand."

"I'm just substituting for the term," says Paul. "Until a spot opens up in fourth grade. Or higher. Hopefully."

"We will see you tomorrow."

"Certainly."

———

Thuong's daydreams are as vivid as nighttime visions. Now, he is on a warship, looking for General Tran. The year is 1287. The Mongol naval fleet has settled at the mouth of the Bach Dang river, close to Hanoi.

Under General Tran's direction, the Vietnamese navy waits until high tide, and then its fleet engages the enemy's boats. When the tide ebbs, the Vietnamese boats retreat toward the ocean. The Mongol boats give chase, not realizing that the Vietnamese have laid metal spikes along the riverbed. The Mongols' heavier, sturdier boats become embedded in the spikes in low tide. Meanwhile, another cohort of the Vietnamese fleet have been laying in wait in the tributaries behind the Mongol boats. The Mongols are surrounded and skewered.

Thuong is on the deck of a ship, but General Tran is nowhere in view. In fact, Thuong is among Mongols, tall, burly, bearded men wearing looks of horror. They see through him, run right through him. The ship is sinking. In the distance he can hear the victory chants of his countrymen, while the Mongols around him are helplessly bailing out water with giant clam shells.

———

Once a year, on her birthday, Thuong cuts Josephine's hair outside in the old style. Not only is it his tradition to do it outdoors, but there is no room in the basement to properly cut hair. Outside there is an old apple tree, its protruding roots radiate through the backyard. There is a nail on the tree where Thuong hangs up a picture frame mirror. There are a fold-out wooden reclining chair and a lamp stand where he lays out his implements. Thuong does his barbering bare-chested, so that he does not soil a good shirt with her hair. He keeps a folded white towel over one shoulder.

It is unfortunate that Josephine's birthday is at the end of September, when, in Vancouver, the sunlight is spotty at best. At least today it's not raining. In the afternoon Josephine has set out *banh uot* in the kitchen when Thuong calls her outside. She knows what is coming. "I don't need a haircut," she says through the window, as she always does, and as always, Thuong leads her outside, arm held in arm, after Josephine puts on her blue-laced slippers to walk on the moist grass.

He ignores his mother, who croaks out the window, "Leave her alone."

Josephine wears her hair long and straight, cascading over her shoulders. Every year he takes off five inches. "You know this is my true calling," says Thuong, who is the son of a barber. "You thought you were going to marry a professor."

"I thought I was going to marry a Colonel." They regard each other through the mirror, the one time the whole year they make eye contact while talking. "I can settle for a professor," she says.

Every year, Thuong thinks, Josephine becomes more beautiful. Every year it becomes harder to hold her gaze.

"Wait," says Thuong. He calls Christian out from the basement. "Grab the sprayer." Christian mists Josephine's hair while Thuong pulls out the scissors from their plastic cover.

Next door is a barking Doberman. Around dinnertime it sticks its nose through the wooden fence posts and snarls at the apple tree. Now it is digging into one of the posts to loosen the soil around it. The dog's Cantonese owners have complained to Thuong's landlord, although it's been months since Christian threw fallen apples at the dog. Thuong's mother speculates that it's Josephine's cooking which sets the dog off. The dog gets this way no matter the dish, whether it's beef noodle soup, imperial rolls, or even her cold shrimp and papaya salad.

The barking usually doesn't bother Thuong, but now he nicks his little finger with the scissors.

"I'm fine."

"You've lost your focus," says Josephine. "Maybe it's the new incense." She means the joss sticks that he burns for his father's altar in their bedroom, the ones he got from Chinatown. "It keeps me awake too. It smells impure."

"There's nothing wrong with the incense."

"They are opening up a temple on Kingsway," she says. "You should get some proper joss sticks there."

"A temple in Vancouver? Buddhist? Vietnamese?"

"I think so. You should also take that statue of yours. Leave it with the monks. You've been distracted by it. I can tell."

"No, I haven't."

Josephine never complained when Thuong asked her to stow the statue in her trunk, never mentioned all the dresses she gave up, the farewell presents from her students that she had to leave behind. She had thought the statue was struck in pure gold, and was shocked when Thuong rubbed off the gold paint so it wouldn't be confiscated by the border guards. She thought Thuong did it for love of country, so there would be one less treasure the Communists could get their hands on. She didn't think Thuong actually worshiped the folk deity. After all, Thuong got baptized just before they got married. They go to church every Sunday.

"Why else can't you get your degree?"

Thuong taps her cheek with the scissors. "Please don't," he says. "Not today."

Josephine brushes the scissors off her face. "Does the General belong in a temple or in our bedroom?" she says. They stare at each other through the mirror.

It takes all of Thuong's power to peel his eyes away from her. When he is done cutting he takes the towel and wipes her hair off of his chest. The dog will not stop barking.

"Fish sauce," yells Thuong's mother through the window. "That's what makes the dog crazy." Fish sauce is the common ingredient in every dish Josephine makes.

———

There is one framed quotation Josephine had not noticed until today's class, because it hangs in the corner where the children are sent to be punished: "*La vérité, comme la lumière, aveugle.*"

The truth, as the light, makes blind. By Camus.

She loses focus the whole class. This is the guilt that Josephine cannot admit to: she has read *The Stranger* more times than any other book, except perhaps for the Bible. There is little that moves her, but she cannot keep her eyes from moistening when the protagonist Meursault drinks coffee idly in front of his mother's coffin. Nothing, nothing in the great Vietnamese romantic fables touches her as much as when, at Meursault's trial, he can blame only the sun for his shooting the motionless Arab those four times. Nothing even in the Book of Exodus moves her as when Meursault is asked if he loved his mother, and he answers yes, the same as anyone.

She cannot explain it. She is as much an existentialist as the crucifix she wears is made out of water.

Maybe she feels all the things Meursault is unable to. Each scene of the novel evokes in her the true Christian feelings that Meursault ought to have if he were Christian as well. Plus there is the added pity she feels for Camus, for only a writer who feels such sorrow for the world can create a figure of such tragic emptiness. And yet she cannot condemn Meursault. She comes back to the novel at least once a year, not truly convinced there is no place in paradise for such a man.

After class she tells Paul that *The Stranger* is her favourite novel. She has never admitted this to anyone. Paul wipes his face wearily, as if every one of his students has told him this.

"It's mine too," he says.

"But you must love God?"

"I do."

"Then isn't it difficult to reconcile?" she says.

"It is very difficult," he says, with furrowed eyebrows. "But we have to try, don't we? Even if we have to start over every day."

———

Josephine really does have a magic touch with the children. Those that fall off of their plastic chairs, or scrape their knees during recess, go to Josephine for ministrations. Paul is free to concentrate on his lesson.

Josephine's presence is based on a fib, and the fib is different depending on whom you ask. The nuns are told that Christian will break into tears and wet himself if Josephine leaves him for even a moment. The parents are told that she is a teacher in training. The children are told, for a laugh, that she is Gulliver's wife.

———

Among the toys is one the children don't know what to do with. It is the size of a tennis ball, but it doesn't bounce. Josephine cannot tell them what it is. She shows it to Paul.

"It's a heart," he says.

"It looks deformed."

"No. It's the real thing, more or less." It's a model of a five-year-old's heart, for medical school. The object looks like a toy, with the aorta, veins, and arteries rendered in a brightly-coloured plastic.

Some child fished it out from Paul's top desk drawer. It belonged to Paul's late father, once the chief of surgery at Mount Royal Hospital in Montréal. His specialty was mending the hearts of babies and little children. If you were a youngster in Montréal during the 1960s, and if you had heart troubles, then the chances were good that you knew Paul's father. He also taught in academies in Lyon and Paris, where Paul spent his childhood summers. Paul never thought his accent was Parisian, but if Josephine thinks so, then this was how he picked it up.

With a father like that, Paul became an engineer. Otherwise he would merely be a sparrow walking in the footprints of a bear. He thought he would actually design things the world had never seen, which was better. For what was a surgeon but a glorified mechanic, simply maintaining the designs of a greater creator?

Nobody told him when he dreamed of designing bridges, that Paul would end up stamping drawings for retaining walls in residential subdivisions. Nobody told him that the materials of his trade would be modest lengths of Allan Block and shotcrete over boulder stone, not miles of big bright steel.

If only he saw the potential of retaining walls, these modest structures. Because something small can fail just as spectacularly as something big. Nobody told Paul this either.

The day he left engineering was the day his father died, and he left Montréal soon after. If asked why he would trade Montréal for Vancouver, the Canadiens for the Canucks, Paul will never mention all the strangers he met in Montréal whose first question to him was whether he was his father's son. He will never mention the last straw, that woman he picked up at a bar in the Old Quarter, that night in his apartment when, in tearful gratitude, she lifted the floating bottom of her left breast to show Paul the scar that his father had left on her as a child. He will not speak of the odd satisfaction he gets for being paid in Vancouver to teach something that he never really had to learn.

And anyway, he still keeps his Canadiens key chain.

―――――

The statue of General Tran is light and hollow. Thuong could have carried it himself down Fleming Street to the bus stop on Kingsway, but got Christian to help him. It is time for the boy to taste labour.

Thuong and the boy carry the statue outside in repose facing skyward. The boy has the General by his heels while Thuong cradles his upper shoulders with his palms. The boy has to walk backwards. As soon as Christian turns his head behind him so that he can see the way ahead, Thuong stops.

"Don't lose your focus," says Thuong. "Keep your eyes on me."

Neighbours stare from their yards as the pair make their way gingerly down the sidewalk. Thuong has walked this path many times before, but now it feels much longer. He starts to count the number of blocks.

Sweat forms around the boy's temples. It's his mother's fault again, putting on so many layers of clothes. "Don't you dare drop it," says Thuong, and the boy nods. Four blocks, five blocks, six, and he sees the sweat come down the boy's face. Or is it tears?

At the bus stop they set the General back on his feet. Thuong strokes his son's ear. "Well done," he says, just in time to see the bus with the twin sparkles of its B.C. Hydro livery.

They get off after only a couple of stops. The outside of the temple looks like an auto-body shop, with its corrugated siding and flat rooftop. The inside smells otherworldly, but what Thuong first thinks is incense is actually plaster dust. The space was used briefly as a Tae Kwan Do *dojo*, but the business was unprofitable. The lowered rents have provided an opportunity for the Vietnamese community's first Buddhist temple.

The abbot greets Thuong with a hug. "We're still renovating," he says.

"It's already better than gathering to pray in someone's basement."

The monk laughs. "It has been too long," he says. "Are you here for a favour or a blessing?"

"Not a favour, but I could always use a blessing. I am here to make you an offering. General Tran Hung Dao."

"That is a gift no man can give."

Thuong takes the monk outside, where Christian is guarding the statue. The General looks no more out of place on this intersection with its gas stations than the monk in saffron robes.

"You'll agree he is entitled to a more suitable venue than my study."

"But we are making a house for Lord Buddha," says the monk.

"Of course. The temple won't be usurped from Buddha. Perhaps give General Tran a small space for people who want to make him an offering as well. You'll get more visitors."

The monk shuffles his sandals. "If we let the General in, then who's next? We'll open a floodgate to more statues of deities."

"You shouldn't worry."

"This is to be a serious place of contemplation and enlightenment."

"Of course."

"I don't want it to become a place where men go to make offerings to get rich, or where women go to light incense to get pregnant."

"It shouldn't come to that," says Thuong. "Besides, it's the deity Me Sanh that the women pray to in order to get pregnant, not Tran Hung Dao."

"I suppose you'd want a share of the offerings," says the monk.

This makes Thuong smile. "I could always use a blessing."

The monk agrees to reserve a small space to General Tran, perhaps near the front door to ward off evil spirits. Before leaving, he gives Thuong a box of joss sticks made out of the best aloeswood from the home country. Josephine should be relieved.

It is turning out to be a fine afternoon, and so Thuong walks home the whole way, carrying Christian on his shoulders.

———

"What would you do without me?" says Josephine. Today she has untangled two girls fighting over a toy, consoled another boy, wiped another tear, kissed another bruise, plugged, once again, the floodgate of hell.

"I don't know," says Paul.

"Maybe you can pay me a salary."

Paul smiles. "As if that was possible."

"Then private lessons, for my son?"

Paul nods. He has noticed how much further Christian has advanced than the other children. Josephine has been tutoring Christian at home. While the others are still learning single words, Christian is already making sentences with properly conjugated verbs.

"You're a teacher too," says Paul. "What could I offer?"

"Your voice," she says. "Your Parisian accent. Not my Vietnamese French."

"Your accent is fine," he says, but puts up only weak resistance.

Paul takes from his desk Sempé's *Le Petit Nicolas*. They find a booth in a White Spot down the street. Josephine orders all three of them mushroom burgers even though Paul didn't ask for one. He has a sandwich at home. But when he smells the mushrooms, he is silently grateful for it.

Paul gets Christian to read the Sempé. He has heard

Christian's voice rise above the others during class, but has never heard it alone in close quarters. Although Paul cannot take credit for the boy's sudden grasp of the language, he can hear in Christian faint echoes of his own street Joual, something he has been trying to purge since his first summer in Paris, the way he still runs his words together. Christian's voice is also layered with a wavering musicality – the Vietnamese accent that Josephine has imparted on her son and now wants to get rid of.

"He reads beautifully," says Paul.

"Then it's something worth working on?" says Josephine. Paul nods, and Josephine sees the little frays on Paul's collared shirt. If only she had the money, she would buy Paul a new one.

————

The Doberman breaks through the wooden fence post while Josephine is picking mint leaves in the backyard. The landlord forbids any garden, but has never noticed the mint grove that she planted. The dog heads straight for Josephine, who is on her knees with her back turned. She does not register the Doppler effect of the oncoming muzzle.

Thuong gets in the way just before the dog lunges. She has no idea where Thuong came from, but that's nothing new. He slams his thin bare arm lengthwise between the dog's open jaws, like a crow bar, to the back of the dog's mouth. The dog's teeth drip saliva, then blood. No longer barking, it wheezes like a broken flute and retreats back through the gap in the fence.

"Your arm."

"It's nothing," says Thuong. "It's the dog's blood. I broke its jaw." Still, there are teeth marks on Thuong's arm which Josephine has to clean up. The noodles she made are now waterlogged, wasted.

The problem is not Thuong's loyalty but his wisdom in exercising it. Like when Josephine had heard a loud clapping of thunder and climbed up to the rooftop of her school in Saigon to watch the firefight in the distant jungle. She had been up there so long, standing in the rain, that Thuong went after her and carried her back down, thinking that she was going to jump off. On the last flight of stairs he tripped and they both fell. He broke her fall and his arm in the process.

Or the time he came home with a broken thumb. He said he had just won them a flight to Hong Kong on a diplomatic carrier by beating a Colonel at cards. Later, Josephine was told not to pay attention to the rumours that Thuong had shot a private because the Colonel had ordered him to, and was sent away to shut him up. "Don't question fortune," Thuong said. He never explained how he broke his thumb.

Or that night in Hong Kong when Thuong had a crisis of conscience and jumped into the harbour to swim back to Vietnam to fight for his country. The Hong Kong coast guard fished him out and found nothing on him except for his toothbrush and a wallet with Josephine's picture.

———

It has become routine for them to convene after class at the White Spot. Paul looks forward to the post-classroom calm of listening to Christian's lone voice as he reads, helping to prune the boy's voice to a sharper, truer self.

On this day they do not meet after class. Josephine has to take Christian to the dentist. Paul, though, insists that they continue the lesson later in the day, so that Christian will not lose his momentum. In the meantime Paul naps in his studio apartment, right on the couch because he does not feel like pulling out the mattress, among the posters and knick-knacks taken from all the places he has been to: a Monet print from the Louvre, sand in a bottle from Mauritius, replica Lewis chessmen. Most of the travelling was done with his father. He hasn't done much since. Just hasn't had the time, or otherwise couldn't afford it.

The three of them meet, this time, in the late afternoon. He wears a freshly-ironed shirt. She wears, for the first time, lipstick. Christian seems more withdrawn. Everyone acts more gingerly around each other. It has to do with the break after the class, the change in the angle of sunlight.

Yet she can ask questions that she would not during the day. Like: "Are you a Roman Catholic?"

"Yes," says Paul, which is not a lie, because he was baptized.

"Which church do you attend?"

"The one at school, sometimes," he says, which is a lie.

"We usually go to St. Joseph's, but we'll try the school's. Then we'll see you this Sunday?"

"Sure," says Paul, then steers them back to the lesson. He pulls out from his vest pocket his paperback edition of *The Stranger*. "Christian can read from this."

"Oh no," says Josephine. Paul has never seen her blush before.

"I'm sorry. I didn't mean anything. Maybe he's too young."

Josephine takes a deep breath and smiles. "That's fine," she says. "He can try."

Christian puts his fingers on the page as if trying to find the words by touch. To help him along Josephine reads: *"Aujourd'hui, maman est morte. Ou peut-être hier, je ne sais pas."* She is more uncomfortable reading French out loud than just speaking it herself, feels that her instrument is too blunt for Camus' words, that she is tone deaf to his music. Paul nods and smiles. Christian repeats after his mother. Under Paul's forgiving gaze, Josephine finds it in her to continue to read and to wait for her son's echo.

They read until she looks up at the clock and gasps.

"I'm late for work."

"You work at night?"

"Yes, downtown. I have to take Christian home first."

"I can take him," says Paul.

"Are you sure?"

"No problem. Is someone at home?"

"His father and grandmother."

"Okay then."

Josephine darts off. Later, Christian leads Paul down Fleming Street, keeping two steps ahead, past stucco houses and wooden hydro poles. Paul sings *"Ballade à la lune"* to cut the silence. An oncoming car has its high beams on, dilating his eyes, and when he adjusts to the night again, Christian is gone.

Christian must have turned the corner into a side alley. Paul runs as if he is being chased. When he reaches the next turn to the back alley he sees Christian pumping his legs beneath the lamplight. He catches up, puts a hand on Christian's shoulder. They are both panting.

"This isn't a game," says Paul.

"This is my home," says Christian. Paul takes him down

concrete stairs to the back door. Thuong answers the door wearing an unfortunate wife-beater. He has to crane his neck to meet Paul eye-to-eye.

"Did Sonny send you?" says Thuong, then notices Christian. "Where did you find him?"

"I'm his French teacher," says Paul. Thuong smiles.

"I'm a teacher too. Well, almost. I study economics."

Thuong rubs the dressing on his arm. Paul had expected a drunk, but Thuong's eyes are too lucid. With the look of murder, but lucid.

"How is my son doing?"

"He's wonderful."

"I'm so relieved," says Thuong. "A good teacher is so important in a young man's life."

"I agree," says Paul.

Thuong seems to be staring at Paul's forehead, maybe trying to look him in the eyes.

"You need a haircut," says Thuong, "and a shave."

Paul brushes the back of his scruffy head. "Maybe so."

"Commanding respect begins with a good haircut and a close shave."

"You're right."

"Stay for tea."

"Thank you, but no," says Paul. He heads back to the alleyway.

————

Josephine works at the top of a thirty-storey building. Or at least that is where she starts, before making her way down one storey at a time, in her cleaner's uniform and with her cart with the dual mop bucket. Her luxury is a silk handkerchief that she wraps around her face; the same one that shielded her from the sun in Saigon, now spares her from dust.

The top floors are occupied by a law firm with varnished rosewood offices, its founders memorialized in oils hung on the walls. These offices are more lavishly appointed than any church she knows, yet they fall short of achieving the grace to which the firm no doubt aspires.

She lingers at a wall-length window facing north. She rests her chin on her mop, eye level with the lighted ski slopes of Grouse Mountain. The last building that she was this high up in was in Hong Kong, where she saw the New Year's fireworks. Gaudy dragons lighting up the night, which reminded her of the fire fight she saw on that rooftop in Saigon.

Up here her mind lingers on Paul and her son together, Paul's voice, his freckled hands around *The Stranger*. There is no way that heaven can be located in the sky, with what she has seen from this vantage point, with what she thinks of when she is up this high.

———

Professor Jennings calls Thuong into his office overlooking the North Shore Mountains, tells Thuong that his efforts to debunk Communist economics based on his application of game theory simply cannot be defended.

"I'll try again," says Thuong. "Another hypothesis."

"There's no point," says Jennings. "It's been five years. You're brilliant, in your own way, but you aren't meant for economics. I'm sorry it's taken so long to realize this. That is the Department's failing."

"I'll do anything," says Thuong. By the time they are finished both men are shaken. Thuong stares at the ground all the way to the bus stop. He will not head home. Not straight away. Somewhere is a card game to take his mind off things. Just penny ante fare.

———

On Sunday morning Josephine wakes up alone in bed, thinking that Thuong has been spirited away. When she gets up to look for him, opens the back door, and sees what stands before her, she does not hear herself shriek, does not feel her heels leave the ground as she trips over the loose threshold, her chin landing on a clay pot on the concrete step.

Outside stands the General. His expression, Josephine has finally decided, is of someone betrayed.

Thuong, as always, appears out of nowhere. "You're bleeding," he says. He pulls her off the floor. "You need a bandage."

"Why is he back?" she says. "I thought he had come for me."

"You have a guilty conscience."

"That's not an answer." Josephine goes into the kitchen for a white towel, which she presses to her chin.

"I went to the temple. I found him in storage. The monks never intended to give him an altar."

"What were you doing at the temple?"

"Praying."

"To whom?"

Thuong ignores her question. "I couldn't leave him there," he says. He carries the statue back to its corner.

"Wake up Christian. We should get ready for church."

"Go without me."

"Why?"

He smiles apologetically. "I have to study."

Josephine and Christian walk to St. Maurice under cloud cover. Its church has no bells to greet the parishioners, no steps to ascend to the nave. The service is in English and so Josephine has difficulty understanding much of it. Paul arrives during the prayer of absolution, in his Sunday best, although he is shaggy around the ears and sporting a two-week growth on his face. He kneels beside her. He hasn't knelt since he was a child. When they drop their chins in prayer he feels like they are play acting. Before the prayer is over Paul cheats, opens his eyes, and takes in Josephine's face while her eyes are closed. Her expression is beatific from this angle. He does not notice the welt on her chin until she raises her face to meet his.

"What happened to you?"

"Just an accident," she says. The blood has dried, but the bruise on her chin is still blooming.

"Your husband did this?"

"I fell."

"Let me see." Paul cannot help but touch her for the first time, two fingers on the boundary between white skin and violet. He tilts her bruise up like a jewel to the dim stained-glass light. It is a perfect oval. Nothing fashioned so precisely can be by accident.

They walk up together to receive communion, while Christian receives a blessing. Back in the pews they wish peace on their neighbours, many of whom are familiar children and parents, who smile among themselves, as if confirming a truth about Paul and Josephine that they had always known.

Afterwards, Paul offers to walk them home and, eventually, Josephine relents. Paul has one hand on Christian's shoulder and the other in a fist. Josephine walks by Paul's side. They take their sweet time in the Vancouver sunlight, which shines as shyly as they do.

When they reach her backyard they cannot see to the house because the clothesline from the apple tree to the fence is thick with her laundry, clothes that from afar look like dead birds strung upside down. Crows and pigeons, blue birds and red robins, seagulls and doves. Thuong has never done the laundry before.

There is the smell of lunch in the air. Behind the clothesline is Thuong. His shirt is off, showing his rack-thin ribs. He is urinating on Josephine's mint.

"Do you want me to talk to him?" says Paul to Josephine. She ignores him.

"What are you doing?" she says to Thuong.

"Fertilizing," says Thuong. He turns, zips up his khaki pants, and walks right up to Paul. "Eat with us," he says.

"I don't know," says Paul, but before he can finish his thought Thuong and Christian bring out the foldout table. Then they bring out chairs – some wooden, some plastic.

"You might as well," says Josephine.

Banh uot, vermicelli noodles, and prawns with their eyes still attached are doled out on paper plates. "We save them for special occasions," says Thuong of the plates and plastic cutlery. Everyone sits around the table and, after Josephine says grace, eats in silence. Paul has never tried Vietnamese food. His nostrils flare when he smells the fish sauce. The food feels strange when it touches his lips, never mind his tongue.

The *banh uot* has a squiggly consistency, and he is not sure if the filling is a ground meat or vegetable paste.

Thuong brings out a six-pack of Molson Canadian. "A friend gave me this gift but I just keep it under our bed." Thuong pours his beer in a glass full of ice. Paul would rather drink warm beer straight from the can. The fish sauce makes Paul thirsty and when he finishes one beer he accepts another. When the old lady offers Paul another helping of *banh uot*, he does not refuse. He had not known how hungry he is.

"I was supposed to be a teacher," Thuong says. "But I was really meant to cut hair."

"Being a teacher is so hard," says Paul.

Josephine pecks at her food and looks at the line of hanging clothes as if, at any moment, they will fly away. Christian doesn't want the day to end because when he sleeps, he always dreams his mother is missing. No one can protect her except for him.

When all the food and beer are gone, Thuong says something in Vietnamese and Christian gets up to clear the table. Thuong nudges Paul to get off his seat so he can put it away.

"Now, since you're my guest, you should let me cut your hair," says Thuong.

"No, that's okay," says Paul. He feels drowsy when he stands up.

"I insist," Thuong says. Then in Vietnamese he says: "I need the practice. That's my price if you want to take my family."

"You're being crazy," says Josephine.

"Am I?" says Thuong.

"What are you all saying?" says Paul.

"Now that he is on my property, he can't just leave," says Thuong.

Josephine throws her hands up the air and pulls out the reclining chair herself. "Have it your way," she says.

"What's going on?" says Paul. Josephine turns to him.

"The sooner you do this, the sooner we can move on," she says in French. "Trust me." Paul thinks about his dead father and realizes that Josephine is the only one left in this world he does trust.

"I don't understand you," says Thuong.

"You don't have to," says Josephine.

Paul sits on the chair under the apple tree. Meanwhile Thuong barks something at Christian, who goes to fetch a white towel and scissors. The mirror is already hung against the tree. The sprayer is at the ready on the lamp stand. The old lady is by the window, telling Thuong to leave the tall man alone. Thuong says something that makes her disappear from the windowsill.

Thuong gets Paul to remove his sports coat, uses a piece of a Glad garbage bag as a cutting cape, and starts snipping away. "Why is kindergarten your profession?" says Thuong.

"I didn't choose it," says Paul. "I'm waiting to teach older children."

Thuong puts a hand on Paul's shoulder. "A man becoming something is just as good as a man who already is something." Paul nods, though he doesn't really get it. Or maybe at some level he does get it, because all of sudden, he feels a little bit better about things.

Something about how Thuong turns the steel scissors into a butterfly, fluttering in the back, around the ears, an inch off the top, soothes Paul. When Thuong is done, he gives Paul a hand mirror, walks around Paul with the larger portrait mirror to show off his handiwork.

"It's perfect," says Paul. "Maybe you are on to something."

"I'm not done," says Thuong. He tilts the chair back so that Paul is facing the apple blossoms above. "You need a shave."

"I don't know," says Paul, but Thuong has, from somewhere, pulled out a brush and jar of shaving cream. Josephine is nowhere in sight.

"Relax," says Thuong. "I'm going to give you a real man's shave." Thuong applies the cream to Paul's beard. His son comes out with a paddle strop and a towel which Thuong's mother had steamed in a pot. The steaming towel that Thuong wraps around Paul's face is like a narcotic, and Paul almost falls asleep. When the towel is removed and Paul sees the straight razor in Thuong's hand, dripping sunlight, he does not panic. Maybe it's because his father used one, and taught Paul how to use it as well. Paul just closes his eyes, feels the razor brush against his cheeks, down to his Adam's apple, and gives himself to fate.

When Thuong is done he calls Josephine out, to show her his true talent, as much as to show Paul's face, unmasked, so that there is nothing for anyone to hide.

AMY JONES

TEAM NINJA

The day that Casey moved in across the hall from Lucas was the same day he decided to get rid of the bike. He was wheeling it out of his apartment when he ran into Pearl, his neighbour, who was on her way back from the store and carrying a bunch of plastic grocery bags. She looked messy, distracted. "I have the reusable ones," she said, smiling apologetically, "but I always forget them."

"Me too," said Lucas.

Lucas helped her with her door, and she told him her daughter and grandchildren were coming down from Kingston to stay with her. "Just for a few days," she said, although Lucas could tell by the way she looked past his head that she thought it was going to be much longer than that.

Lucas didn't know how to deal with messy and distracted people. "Maybe one of your grandchildren would like the bike," he said, because he couldn't think of anything else. Also because he couldn't think of anything else to do with the bike.

"Maybe." Pearl set the bags on the floor just inside the apartment. She patted her hair. "Oh, my. We're a pair, aren't we dear? I seem to be gaining people just as you are losing them."

"The balance of nature, I guess," Lucas said. He leaned the bike against the wall in the hallway, thinking that Pearl might just be getting warmed up. She was like that sometimes.

But she only patted her hair again. Then she said, "I've got to start baking," and absently closed the door in Lucas's face.

Lucas took the bike outside. There was a parking lot in back with an old, rusted out bike rack pushed up against the side of the building; Lucas thought maybe if he locked it up there someone would eventually come along and steal it. It wasn't like he could ever ride it himself, even if he took the basket off the handlebars. It wasn't a practical bike for a man. And then there was the whole Laure thing. Laure with her soft, dark hair curling around her green bike helmet, smile like a little kid's, all teeth and gums. It really wasn't a practical bike for a man.

After he had looped the flimsy lock through the front wheel to one of the rusting spikes of the bike rack, he leaned against the wall and pulled out a Belmont Mild. He rarely smoked anymore, since Laure left, but he had ten minutes to kill before his shift and thought the occasion called for it. He was just finishing when the red Civic pulled into the parking lot, one headlight busted out, plastic storage tubs from Canadian Tire bungeed to the roof rack. The driver was a woman in her forties, a bottle blonde with an expensive looking tan, looking almost too classy for the car. In the passenger seat there was a younger girl, obviously a daughter: same blonde hair as her mother, only natural. She opened the door. She was wearing an oversized Canucks jersey belted at her waist like a dress, a pair of Heelys, and a plastic tiara on her head. She smiled and waved at Lucas, but her mother swatted her hand down.

"God, Casey, you'd think you just fell off the turnip wagon," she said. She grabbed Casey's hand and dragged her toward the door of the building. Casey turned around and stared at Lucas until the door closed behind them.

Lucas had never even owned a blender before he moved to the little apartment above World Famous Comics. He had never owned a television or a set of tea towels printed with pictures of various herbs. Stuff had just somehow come to him over the years, left behind by various roommates: a vase carved with the image of Mayahuel, the Aztec goddess of fertility; pens from Canadian Blood Services; a shower curtain with a map of the world on it. Lucas had always just assumed that these things belonged to somebody else until one day he woke up and realized there was no one else there but him.

Laure had been the last one to leave. Dave and his girlfriend, Julie, had moved out maybe three months earlier, and Lucas and Laure had never bothered to get anyone to take over their room. Before that, there must have been at least a dozen roommates. Lucas couldn't be bothered to keep track. Pearl used to call them orphans.

"Where'd your latest orphans take off to?" she'd ask every time one of the roommates moved out.

"Adopted," Lucas would always answer.

Aside from being his neighbour, Pearl was also his landlady and technically his boss, although according to the other employees at World Famous she hadn't been down to the store since her husband died. That was ten years ago. "Nate is in every single one of those silly comic books," she told Lucas once. "And I just can't stand to see him reduced to that." Lucas wondered if the things his roommates left behind contained pieces of them. He pulled a Canadian Blood Services pen out of his pocket and stared at it, trying to see Kurt or Angela or Dave or whomever else it had belonged to. But it was pretty much still just a pen.

And his apartment was still *his* apartment, no matter who else lived there. His name was on the lease and had been for the past five years, since he'd been a graduate student in the English department at York. Lucas had never thought about moving. The rent was good, the noise from the intersection below didn't bother him, and his job was right downstairs.

Laure used to complain about this all the time. "Your world is supposed to get bigger as you grow up, Lucas. Not smaller," she'd say. But Lucas liked things to be contained. The grocery store, the library, the bar, a decent souvlaki: they were all within a block of World Famous, and this was as far into Toronto as Lucas was willing to go.

Lucas came on his shift just as Mel was leaving. There was never more than one person working at World Famous at one time, except on Saturday afternoons or right before Christmas. Mel was sitting behind the counter writing in a Hilroy scribbler like the ones that Lucas used to use in elementary school. Lucas thought she was some kind of writer, although she didn't ever talk about it. But Kyle, the kid who worked the weekends, had found some of her poetry online. Kyle liked to tell people he could find anything online. The poetry was all about crows and was on a website for a magazine that only published poetry by lesbians. Mel had never told Lucas that she was a lesbian, but she did have very short hair. Kyle and Lucas had had a good laugh over those poems, and sometimes Lucas felt as though Mel somehow knew about it.

"Slow morning?" he asked, dropping his bag behind the counter.

Mel nodded. "A couple of online orders came in about an hour ago," she said without looking up from the scribbler. "I haven't done anything with them."

"Okay," said Lucas. They usually left the online orders for Kyle anyway. Lucas liked to think of it as a punishment for always bragging about his computer skills. Mel left without saying anything more to Lucas. Lucas sat on the stool behind the counter, which was still warm from Mel sitting on it. He put his elbows up and cupped his head in his hands. This was how he usually spent the first half hour or so of his shift, but today his head felt heavier. He would never admit it to anyone, but he hadn't really been sleeping well since Laure left. He felt his eyes begin to close.

He woke to something tickling his face. Opened his eyes to Casey drawing on him with a tube of bright pink lipstick. He reached up and grabbed something off the top of his head. The plastic tiara.

"Aww, you looked so pretty," Casey said.

Lucas put the tiara down on the counter. He turned around and checked himself in the Silver Surfer mirror hanging on the back wall. Whiskers. Casey had made him into a cat. "Please tell me this comes off," he said.

Casey reached down and pulled a tissue out of one of her Heelys. "God," she said, pushing it across the counter. "You'd think someone who worked in a comic book store would be a little more fun."

"You obviously haven't been in a lot of comic book stores," Lucas said, wiping at his nose. The lipstick left a faint pink stain on his skin.

Casey put the tiara on her head. "Dude, I've *never* been in a comic book store," she said. "My sister says that comic books are for losers."

Lucas sat back on the stool. "Well, I am a pretty big loser," he said.

"Me too," said Casey. "I mean, that's what my sister says."

"Uh huh," said Lucas. He wondered how long he would have to ignore Casey before she went away. He pretended to be occupied with something on the computer. When he finally looked up, Casey was still looking at him. "What?" he asked.

"What's your name?" Casey asked.

Lucas pressed some buttons with what he hoped looked like urgency. "Lucas," he said.

"My name's Casey," she said.

"I know," said Lucas. "I saw you outside with your mom."

"She's not my mom," Casey said, with noticeable venom. Lucas looked at her, surprised. Casey sighed. "Okay. She *is* my mom. But I like to pretend she's not. That's what Dylan told me to do, if she ever makes me mad." She paused. Lucas didn't say anything. "Dylan's my sister, you know."

"Cool," said Lucas.

"Don't you want to know where she is?"

"No."

"She died." Casey paused dramatically. "In a helicopter crash." She dropped her voice to a whisper. "She was on her way to the South Pole to catch a penguin. There was this penguin, see, it was blue. And the scientists, they wanted to figure out why it was blue, but they couldn't catch it cause the blue penguin kept outsmarting them. But Dylan, she had this ability. With animals. She made them feel safe. So they sent her to the North Pole in a helicopter, but the guy driving the helicopter had just had a fight with his wife, and he drank a whole bunch of alcohol until he was drunk and then the plane crashed." Casey rested her head on the edge of the counter and looked at him. "And now the scientists will never know why the penguin was blue."

"Maybe he was cold," Lucas said.

Casey pouted. "Aren't you going to tell me you're sad for me 'cause my sister's dead?"

"I would," Lucas said, "if I thought she really was dead."

"Whatever," said Casey. "She went to live with my dad. In *Saskatoon*." She straightened up and wandered over to the nearest shelf and ran her fingers along the book spines. "So she might as well be dead." She pulled out a book. It was a graphic novel called *Red Angels* and Lucas knew it was anything but appropriate for a kid Casey's age. But he didn't say anything. She flipped it over, reading the back. Then she looked up. "I live upstairs, you know."

"So do I," Lucas said.

"Well, that makes us neighbours. And that means you have to be nice to me." She sat on the floor in front of the counter then opened the book and started to read. Lucas turned back to the computer and opened *Solitaire*.

Five hours later, Lucas was ready to close the store and Casey had finished *Red Angels*. Lucas had almost forgotten she was there. He had filed away two more online orders for Kyle to fill on Saturday, talked to a regular on the phone who wanted to know when the new *Siege* was coming in, and sent an email to his friend Mike in Alberta. And Casey had finished a book.

"Can I ask you a question?" she asked Lucas.

"No," Lucas said.

She kept talking anyway. "I know what a hand job is," she said. "But I'm not sure what a blow job is. And the picture didn't really make any sense."

"No," said Lucas. "I'm not answering that. Ask your mom or something."

"My *mom*?" Casey threw the book on the counter. "My mom doesn't know." She narrowed her eyes at Lucas, who was counting up the deposit for the night. "Maybe I'll ask Nana. I'll tell her I read about it in a book you gave me."

"Christ," said Lucas. He ripped the top off the deposit bag and stuffed it in an envelope. "Fine. A blow job is like a hand job, but with your mouth. Understand?" He banged open the back cupboard where they kept the safe, and started fumbling with his keys.

"Yeah, I understand." Casey was quiet for a few moments. Lucas stuffed the deposit bag in the safe and locked the door. He turned around. Casey was still staring at him. "But why do they call them 'blow jobs'? Do you actually blow?"

Lucas stared back. "How old are you?" he asked.

"How old are *you*?"

Silence. They both answered at the same time.

"Thirty-four."

"Twelve."

Twelve. Lucas could hardly remember twelve, and he saw

on Casey's face that she could hardly picture thirty-four. He grabbed his bag and started walking around the store, switching off power bars. Casey followed him silently. When he got to the door, he flicked off the lights. The store was dark except for the neon glow of the Green Lantern lantern hanging on the wall. He looked at Casey. In the green light, she looked like a little alien.

"You don't really blow," Lucas said. "It's more like you suck. So I don't know why they call it that."

"Have you ever had one?" Casey asked.

Lucas had a momentary flash of Laure on her knees, looking up at him. He shook it off. "I'm definitely not answering that," he said. He opened the door and gave Casey a push outside.

On the way upstairs, Casey ran ahead of him. When she got to the top of the stairs, she turned around and said, "Can I come over?" She slid back and forth across the hall on her Heelys, pulling at a piece of her hair.

"I'm going out," Lucas lied. "Besides, don't you think your mother is wondering where you are?"

Casey's face darkened. "My mother's *gone out*," she said. Then she rolled inside Pearl's apartment and slammed the door.

Four of the things Laure left in the apartment: a bottle of Bath and Body Works Vanilla Noir shower gel, a set of Egyptian cotton sheets, a copy of *The Royal Tenenbaums* on DVD, and the bike. The shower gel Lucas threw out. He never told Laure, but the smell of it always made him sick. The sheets were on their bed and hadn't been washed since the last time Laure had done the laundry. The DVD, Lucas figured, was partially his anyway. But the bike really bothered him. He had bought it for her, after all, at a yard sale down the block the spring that she moved in. It was pink and green and had a basket attached to the handlebars with a plastic flower in the middle of it. It was exactly the type of thing Laure loved, and Lucas felt she should have been more sentimental about it.

Laure's father had been a hockey player in the nineties, a fourth-line journeyman who had played for twelve teams in eight years. Name a city with a hockey team and Laure had lived there, if only for a few months. Toronto had been her favourite, or so she had said. In every other city they had lived in downtown condos fifteen storeys above the street, but in Toronto they had a rented house near the university and Laure remembered backyard cookouts, neighbours with dogs, kids on bikes everywhere. When she came back, after finishing her undergrad in some isolated New England college town, she ended up renting one of Lucas's rooms above World Famous. She ended up sharing Lucas's own room, too, but that came later. There were no dogs, no cookouts. Just a comic book store and some IKEA furniture.

One afternoon, just after Laure moved out, Pearl came across the hall with muffins. She liked to bake for Lucas, even though he'd told her a dozen times he didn't like sweet things. "Where'd this orphan run off to?" she asked. She eyed the bike in the corner behind the sofa.

"She didn't run," Lucas answered without thinking about it. "I mean, she didn't run, because she was adopted." He laughed. Pearl must have seen something in his face, because she left the muffins and went home without even asking him, the way she did sometimes, for a cup of tea from the teapot shaped like a rooster that, obviously, someone had left behind.

For some reason, Casey only ever came into the store when Lucas was working. As far as Lucas could tell, Mel had never even met her. On the weekends, Kyle teased him, called Casey his "girlfriend" until Lucas punched him in the arm, hard. Casey's mom, Lucas had never seen again, although he'd hear her sometimes, coming home late at night, stumbling through the hallway and scraping her key against the lock across the hall while Lucas was playing *Call of Duty* with the sound off so he wouldn't wake Pearl. Whenever her mom came up in conversation, Casey would make up some elaborate lie.

"She's quarantined in one of Nana's rooms," she said once. "She caught malaria when we were in Southeast Asia."

"Don't they have medicine for that nowadays?" Lucas asked.

"Not for the type she has." Casey dropped her voice to a whisper, the way she always did. She rolled up the sleeves of her cardigan, which was bright yellow, to reveal rows and rows of shiny metal bracelets crawling up her arm. "She was a ninja, you know. The three of us were. Team Ninja. That's what the natives called us. We crept through the jungles of Tibet, searching for the evil warlord who was holding the princess hostage in a castle built out of vines high up in the trees. My sister nearly caught him, once, near the end. But then she had to choose between killing the warlord and saving my mom's life. And here we are."

"There is so much wrong with that story," Lucas said, "that I don't even know where to begin."

"God, Lucas!" Casey slammed her little fists against the counter, and her bracelets sounded like breaking glass. "You have no *imagination*!"

Lucas turned back to the computer. "You are not the first person to tell me that," he said.

"Well, you should have listened." Casey rolled over to a box of books at the side of the counter. It was a shipment of the latest issue of *Blood Ring*. She pulled one out and started flipping through it. "Didn't you ever want to do anything else?"

Lucas grabbed the book from Casey and threw it back in the box. "Who are you, my mother?" He lifted the box up onto the counter. "I have to price these." He went back to the computer and pulled up the inventory screen. Casey kept watching him while he loaded the printer with labels. The machine started up, a rhythmic whirr and hiss as it spat out the price tags.

"Wouldn't you rather be, like, *making* a comic book than *pricing* a comic book?" she asked after a while. She pulled on a piece of her hair.

"Nope," said Lucas.

"Why not?"

The labels spilled out over the edge of the printer in a long loop down to the floor. Lucas picked it up. "Can we not have this conversation?"

"You never want to have *any* conversation."

Lucas slammed the labels down on the counter. "Casey, I'm working," he said, a little too loudly. Casey stared at him. Then she rolled away on her Heelys. He could hear her bracelets clinking down one of the aisles.

Lucas sighed. He walked over to a shelf along the back wall and pulled a book out of one of the bins. He followed the sound of the clinking to the giant Iron Man cutout by the stairs midway through the store. Casey was sitting behind it reading a copy of *Techno Wars 3*.

"You're not much of a ninja with those bracelets on," he said. Casey didn't say anything. He held the book out to her. "*Kaleidogirl*," he said. "She's a kid who can see through time. Might be more your kind of thing."

Casey put down *Techno Wars 3* and took the book from Lucas without looking at him. "See through time?" she asked.

"Yeah." Lucas sat on the bottom step. "Like, if she was looking at you, she could see you doing what you were doing now, but she could also see all the other things that had happened in this spot, all at the same time, all whirled together like a kaleidoscope."

Casey opened the book. "I wonder what she'd see."

Lucas shrugged. "Probably me, vacuuming the carpet or something."

"Maybe my grandfather," Casey said.

"Maybe."

She looked at Lucas, closing the book. "Was he nice?" she asked.

"I don't know," said Lucas. "I never met him." He paused. "Maybe you could ask your mother."

"My mother . . ." Casey stopped. "Yeah, maybe. Whatever." She opened the book and started reading. Lucas sat on the step, watching her. After a minute, she looked up. "Um, I'm reading here," she said.

"Right," Lucas said. He went back to the counter, picked up the labels and started sticking them, one by one, on the backs of the books.

—

"God, Lucas, for someone who works with superheroes all day, you have no imagination." That was Laure, during a game of Pictionary against Dave and Julie one Saturday night the previous winter. The subject was SpongeBob SquarePants. Lucas had spent the whole time drawing an exact, detailed replica of SpongeBob, who apparently Laure had never even heard of and thought that Lucas *should have known* that she wouldn't have heard of him, and because of this he should have taken the drawing in a more abstract direction. Later, in their bedroom, the fight ballooned, and suddenly it wasn't just his approach to Pictionary that lacked vision, but his entire life.

"Why are we at home on a Saturday night playing Pictionary with Dumb and Dumber, anyway?" Lucas asked. "It's like we're fucking retired." Even before Laure said anything, Lucas knew he had made a mistake. A tub of moisturizer flew past his face.

"Because you didn't want to go anywhere!" she screamed. "You *never* want to go anywhere!"

"Laure," Lucas said. He tried to wrap his arms around her while she pummelled him against his chest. "Where do you want to go?"

She wrenched herself away and stared at him, wet-faced and angry. "Spain," she said. "I want to go to Spain."

Lucas, who had been expecting a "somewhere fun" or "away from here" or something like that, was thrown off by her specificity. "Uh, okay," he said. "Why . . . what's in Spain?"

Laure sat on the bed with her back turned to him, wiping at her face with the palms of her hands. "Nothing," she said. "Forget it. Just go get ready for bed." She lay down and curled herself into a ball. She still wouldn't look at him.

While he was brushing his teeth, Lucas tried to imagine himself surprising Laure with two plane tickets. She would probably think it was romantic. He tried to think of what airline would fly to Spain. Would there be direct flights from Toronto? Or would they have to switch planes in London? What if they had a long stopover there? Would they have to change their money to pounds, and then to whatever kind of money they used in Spain? What kind of money *did* they use in Spain? The whole thing just seemed so complicated. Later, when he had crawled into bed next to Laure, he decided maybe he'd just take her to a Spanish restaurant. Or Mexican, even. Yes. Mexican would probably be the best idea.

A few weeks after Casey and her mom had moved in, Lucas opened the apartment door to find Pearl scrubbing vomit out of the carpet in the hall. He got down on his knees to help her, the stench curdling his earlier cup of coffee in his stomach.

"She's going through a rough time right now," Pearl said. "The divorce was bad enough, but when Dylan chose to live with her father . . ." Pearl stopped. "I'm sorry, dear. You don't want to hear this."

"It's fine," Lucas said, breathing in through his mouth.

Pearl looked at him. "I know Casey's been hanging around the store all the time, Lucas. I'm sorry if it's been a burden."

Lucas dropped a paper towel into the Loblaws bag Pearl had brought out for garbage. "Pearl, don't even worry about it. I barely notice her."

"I just – I don't know what to do with her." Pearl stopped scrubbing and Lucas saw that she was crying. He started picking up the rest of the paper towels and stuffing them in the bag, slowly moving away from her. Pearl took a piece of paper towel and blew her nose. "She's just so much like . . . Nate . . ." She sat back on her knees and looked at Lucas. "You're a good boy, Lucas," she said. "That girl of yours is a fool for leaving."

Lucas stood up. "I'm going to, I mean, I'm on my way to Falucci's for some milk," he said. "Do you, uh, need anything?"

"No, no, go, it's fine." Pearl dabbed at her eyes. "I'm just going to . . ."

"Yeah," said Lucas. "Okay." He turned around and walked down the hallway as fast as he could without looking like he was running away.

At Falucci's he thought about buying something for Pearl, some chocolate maybe, or a bag of cookies. But he didn't even know what kind of cookies she liked. She probably knew everything about him, but he didn't even know what kind of goddamn cookies she liked.

On the way back from Falucci's, Lucas stopped to check on the bike, which, after three weeks, was still there. Lucas supposed he wasn't surprised. Most bike thieves, he guessed, were men, and it wasn't a practical bike for a man. Probably not a practical bike for a woman, either. He really thought Laure had liked it, though. She liked flowers, and girlie things. And she seemed so appreciative, when he brought it home, riding it around the parking lot, posing with it for pictures to put up on her blog. "And you can stop taking the subway all the time," Lucas had told her. "Ride it to school, get some fresh air. You know."

"And I can put my books in the basket, just like a European," she had said, wrapping her arms around him. But she never did ride it to school. It just sat in the corner behind the couch gathering dust. When people would come over to the apartment, she would show it to them, brag about Lucas's amazing yard sale find, and wasn't it so cool and vintage? Like it was a decoration, Lucas thought.

"What are you doing?" Casey came up behind him, startling him so much he almost dropped his milk.

"Why are you always around?" he asked.

Casey, preoccupied with a Fudgsicle, ignored him. "Is that your bike?" she asked.

"No," he said. "It belongs to a friend of mine."

She walked over to the bike and prodded it with chocolate-sticky fingers. "It's cool," she said. "Kind of useless, though. There's not even any speeds."

Lucas leaned against the wall. "Yeah. I guess she thought so, too."

Casey slid the end of her Fudgsicle off of the stick with her teeth and threw the stick on the ground. "Can I try it?" she asked.

"I guess," said Lucas. "The key's upstairs, I can . . ." But Casey had already pulled a bobby pin out of her hair and was jamming it in the lock, and within a couple of seconds it popped open. "Nice work," said Lucas.

"Thanks," said Casey. "You know, Dylan was a professional bike thief. She used to take me on runs with her some nights in Kingston, until one night she stole the bike of the son of the leader of the Russian mafia and they put a hit out on her . . ."

"Yeah, yeah," said Lucas.

Casey jumped on the bike and started pedalling around the parking lot. ". . . In the middle of the night," she called back over her shoulder, "we had to fleeeeeeeeeeee . . ." Her face was still covered in chocolate, and she had something green stuck in her teeth, but she was smiling. Lucas found himself wishing he was twelve again, that he had the time to do it all over again. The thought surprised and scared him. Up until that moment, he hadn't thought he *had* anything to do all over.

Casey brought the bike to a stop in front of him. "Yeah," she said. "This bike sucks."

"Sorry," said Lucas. "Maybe some other little brat will come steal it."

They walked the bike back over to the rack together. Lucas picked up Casey's Fudgsicle stick and handed it to her. "Put this in the garbage," he said.

"Okay," Casey said, taking it from him. "So, what was her name?"

Lucas looped the lock back around the front wheel of the bike. "Who?" he asked.

"Your friend. The bike chick."

"Oh." Lucas stood up. "Laure. Her name was Laure."

"Weird." Casey popped the end of the dirty stick in her mouth. Lucas cringed. "Where is she?"

Lucas leaned against the bike rack and brushed his hands against his jeans. "Well," he said. He looked at Casey. "We had been living together for two years, and I thought we were madly in love. She was a cellist. She had been recording herself playing and posting it on the internet. One day, this guy, a famous underground DJ from Ibiza named Isoceles Jones, found her site. Apparently he liked her stuff and wanted to sample it. So they started emailing each other, and talking on the phone, and then one day she just up and went to Spain to be with him." He paused, rubbing his hands over his face.

"Since then, they've recorded a single together that went to number 17 on the U.K. dance charts, and they're going on tour opening for a German digital hardcore group called STV Suicide. All of which I found out from her Wikipedia page." He grabbed one of the bike handles. "So I guess she doesn't really need this." He gave the bike a shake, then pushed it over. It clanged against the rack, but the lock kept it from falling.

"Holy crap." Casey took the stick out of her mouth, staring at him. "Dude, I am sorry I said you had no imagination. That was the best story *I ever heard!*"

"Yeah," said Lucas. "It's a pretty good one." He started walking toward the door.

Casey trotted behind him. "Seriously," she said, waving the stick through the air. "That could be a movie or something. Can I use that one sometime? About Dylan, I mean?"

"Yup. Sure." Lucas ran up the stairs, Casey at his heels.

"I'd have to change all that love stuff . . ."

"Whatever you want." Lucas stopped at his apartment. "Milk's getting warm," he said. Casey opened her mouth again, but Lucas closed the door before she could get anything out.

She had left him a note.

A note. Even the insignificant roommates, the ones whose names he *didn't* have plastered across his fucking heart, had managed better than that.

Later, she had called him, crying. "Just tell me you want me to come back," she whispered through the phone. She sounded so far away. "Just tell me you can't live without me, that I mean everything to you, that you'll come to Ibiza to get me if you have to."

But he couldn't. "I'm keeping your sheets," he said instead. "And your DVD." He hung up, the phone shaking in his hand.

That night, Lucas woke up to the smell of something burning. His first thought was that he was having a seizure. "Dr. Penfield," he remembered the thick-accented woman in the Historica minute saying. "I smell burnt toast." When he woke up enough to realize he was okay, he turned the light on and saw smoke pouring in from outside through the open bedroom window. Holding his breath, he closed the window and then threw on a T-shirt and headed downstairs to check it out.

The bike was on fire. It seemed impossible, but it was true. Someone had taken stacks of paper – comic books, Lucas realized – and stuffed them around the bike rack and set them ablaze. Bright orange flames were licking the side of the building, illuminating the thick black plumes of smoke that were rising straight from the pile up to Lucas's apartment. And off to the side, holding a can of WD-40, was Casey.

"What the fuck are you doing?" Lucas snatched the can from her hand. She just kept staring straight ahead, watching the flames. "Casey!" He grabbed her shoulders and shook her.

Slowly, she looked at him. "It was true, wasn't it? Your story."

He dropped his hands. In the distance, he could hear sirens. "Yeah. It was true."

Casey kept staring at him. "I wish mine was," she whispered.

Lucas looked around, then threw the empty can on the fire. It exploded in a bright burst of flame. "Come on," he said.

Casey looked down at her hands. "People will find us," she said.

"No, they won't," said Lucas, giving her a push. "You're a ninja, remember? Be a ninja."

They started walking. Behind them, they could hear voices, and the sirens getting closer, but they didn't turn around. After about a block, Lucas realized Casey didn't have any shoes on, so he bent down and let her climb on his back. He wasn't sure where he was going, so he just kept walking, past Falucci's, past the library, past the souvlaki place, into the unknown.

"*Perfect Storm*," he said after a while.

Casey, who had been nearly asleep against his shoulder, raised her head. "Huh?"

"*Perfect Storm*. It was the comic book I used to write. Well, tried to. I sent an issue to a publisher, but he said it was stupid."

Casey put her head back against his shoulder and was quiet for so long he thought she had fallen back asleep. Finally, she whispered "What was it about?"

Lucas stopped. There was a small park ahead, and he bent over, sliding Casey off his back and onto a bench. The sun was just coming up. Across the street there was a Tim Hortons, and Lucas wished he had brought some change with him. He sat down on the bench next to Casey. "A super-intelligent tornado," he said.

Casey yawned. "That *is* stupid," she said. She leaned over and put her head down on the bench, curling up into a little ball. Lucas stretched his legs out in front of him and waited for the sun to rise.

MARNIE LAMB

MRS. FUJIMOTO'S
WEDNESDAY AFTERNOONS

Mrs. Fujimoto takes her powdered green tea on the balcony at three o'clock on Wednesday afternoons from April to October. She has a standing appointment at one for a rinse and set. Her hair, a delicate helmet of curls, has retained the softness and lustre of youth. On leaving the stylist, she strides to the florist's, designer two-inch heels clicking, turquoise coat (a small, as always) swaying. Older men smile as she passes, younger ones open doors.

At the florist's, she chooses the freshest flowers, yellow chrysanthemums perhaps. Back home, she arranges them asymmetrically in the two-headed porcelain vase and places the arrangement on the mahogany dining table. She boils water and opens the tin with the powder. She adds two jade-coloured scoops to a cup, stirs the mixture with a bamboo whisk, and brings the cup out to the balcony.

The balcony faces a box-like building populated by low-level salarymen and foreigners, a view that is usually uninteresting to Mrs. Fujimoto. Instead she cranes her neck to the north, pinpointing the spot behind the NTT and Panasonic spires where she knows the temple garden lies. The honking of car horns and the yelling of schoolchildren below fade away as she imagines the winding pathway enclosed by azaleas, the spark of meeting a patch of irises in full bloom. Her face becomes slack. This slackening occurs only when no one else is present.

One Wednesday in May 2005, two things attract her notice. The first is a white camellia petal which has blown onto the balcony and lies at her feet, waiting. She caresses the flower, its texture soft and vulnerable as wet paper, and inhales the aroma. The second is a flicker from the opposite balcony. A new foreigner, a young woman, is bending over a washing machine. She peers around the side, lifts up the top, and looks inside. She steps back and stares at the machine. From the way the foreign woman coils her copper hair behind her ear and stands with one leg slightly bent, Mrs. Fujimoto concludes that she is shyly aware of her good looks.

When the foreign woman goes inside, Mrs. Fujimoto appraises the machine. She has excellent eyesight and can see that the machine is dirty and the hose to connect machine and tap is missing. The foreign woman comes out with a pile of clothes and begins stuffing them in the washing machine. Surely she realizes . . . but she pours detergent on the clothes, replaces the top, and reaches for the tap. Water sloshes onto the floor, and a rogue jet shoots into her eye. She leaps back. The corners of Mrs. Fujimoto's lips twitch.

The foreign woman grabs the clothes out of the machine. She stamps into the apartment and hurls the door shut, leaving Mrs. Fujimoto amused. What did she expect? Has she never done laundry? Mrs. Fujimoto hasn't noticed the washing machine before and, later, discreet inquiries will reveal that the apartment was recently rented by an English-language school, which supplied the furniture. It isn't entirely the foreign woman's fault, then. She probably expected to find electric lipstick here, and they leave her with this ancient contraption? What stories will she take home to her country about Japan? *I thought it would be so modern, but they don't even have automatic washing machines.* Mrs. Fujimoto rubs the petal into shreds.

Sixty-four years earlier in a neighbouring prefecture, she plays on the beach with her friend Sakina after school on Wednesdays. Wednesday is Mayuko's day off. The other days are spent helping her mother, perhaps by shaving the dried bonito and stirring the flakes into the stock her mother is cooking.

But Wednesdays she and Sakina race each other to the beach, down the alleys crowded with hawkers shouting to bargain seekers, past the stench emitting from the cartloads of freshly caught yellowtails. The beach has sand the texture of ash. Savage little waves snap against the shore, spitting their juice onto her bare feet. To Mayuko, it is paradise.

This Wednesday, the wind pulls at Mayuko's hair and buffets the terns in their path across the grey autumn sky. Nearby, a group of boys are playing soldiers. The taller, more muscular boys are the Japanese army, while the younger, weaker ones are the Chinese resistance. Mayuko and Sakina do not want to play, despite being offered the role of Chinese girlfriends. They have rejected the Japanese army's gift of shiny stones.

The girls prefer the oddly shaped shells they collected last week, the prizes for this round of *jankempo*. "One, two, three," says Sakina. She points two outstretched fingers at Mayuko, who shows a flat open hand. "Ha!" Sakina exclaims as she snatches a shell. She looks at the boys, who are whooping and spearing each other with willow branches. "Soon we'll have a war with the Americans. Because they won't let us have oil."

Mayuko considers. "My dad says war is bad. He says we should leave China and make peace with the United States. He says we should build things other countries want and sell those things. That's how Japan will advance." She emphasizes this last, new word, which leaves a glow in her mouth.

"Your dad's stupid. He shouldn't keep saying bad things about war. He's going to get in trouble. That's what my dad says."

"My dad is not stupid."

"Yes, he is." Sakina turns to look at the boy soldiers.

"Can we play my game now?" Mayuko asks. A few days ago, she invented a game. She and Sakina would collect wildflowers and use them, with the shells and sand, to make ikebana on the beach. Mayuko has been thinking all week about the kinds of flowers she will use, how she will position them between the shells.

"Your game's not a real game. Real games have winners and losers."

Mayuko blinks away tears. "Race you to the big willow tree!" Sakina says. She leaps up and runs away, her foot crushing a small pink shell. Mayuko picks up the pieces and cradles them in her palm.

That night, Mayuko dreams of storms. The snapping waves become giant green monsters, thumping onto the beach, swallowing everything in their circumference. Shells, branches, children. Thump. Thump. Thump. Mayuko is awake and the thumping is coming from inside the house. She slides open her bedroom screen and walks down the hallway, stopping at the living-room screen.

Through the glow of a lamp, two figures are silhouetted against the screen. One is crouched on the floor like a rock. The other bends over the rock like a tree twisted by the wind.

"You insult the emperor. Why do you speak against the Japanese way?" the tree demands. The voice is unfamiliar.

The rock answers. The words are indecipherable, but the tone, low and measured, is her father's.

The tree raises a branch and strikes the rock. A shrill cry from across the room reveals a group of three figures, one struggling to free itself from the grasp of the others, like a sheep caught in a thicket. Her mother.

Mayuko's body trembles, but she knows she must remain still. Though she wants to burst through the screen, wielding a sword, and pierce the tree so that sap runs to the floor, she must stay here. If she does that, the men will leave and every-thing will be all right.

"We know you studied at a university in Boston for three years. Are you a spy? Are you spying for the Americans?" Thump.

The low voice, laced with panic Mayuko has never heard.

"You will help the war effort. You will manufacture your lenses, and they will all be sold to the navy for radar. No more microscopes, no more cameras. Say that you will do this!"

"I will do it." Her father's voice is like the edge of a stone chip, hard and jagged.

The tree straightens and waves a branch. The sheep, freed, tumbles across the room to the rock. The screen is yanked open, and two soldiers stomp out the front door. The tree pauses to pull his khaki jacket taut over his waist, the gold buttons jiggling.

Mayuko shrinks into the shadows, but he turns and sees her. She feels a circle being drawn around her body, feels the force of the wave in his eyes, black as forest pools. He snaps his head forward and stalks out.

The Wednesday after the camellia petal, the foreign woman takes another pile of laundry out to the machine. Wednesday must be her day off, Mrs. Fujimoto thinks. Her eyes narrow as she peers over the top of her teacup. It seems she will no longer be alone in her contemplations. Yet this fledgling routine suggests a steadiness she would not have attributed to a foreigner.

Sometime between one and four on Monday, the washing machine was connected. Mrs. Fujimoto cannot tell the exact time, because she was at her ikebana class all afternoon. She has been studying at the innovative Ichiyo School for twenty years. Long ago she passed the advanced course. The next step would be to take instructors' training. But she cannot abide the thought of blandishing neophytes into crafting inferior arrangements. So she remains in the advanced class, creating original, sometimes wild, flower sculptures, to the amazement of the other students and muted respect of the headmaster.

Namika cannot understand this interest. "Why fiddle around with a bunch of dead twigs?" she always says. She thinks her grandmother should undertake something zestier, like photography. "Photography! I don't need to take photos. I prefer my memories," Mrs. Fujimoto says. But then it's hardly surprising that Namika does not appreciate the art. She prefers the flashy style of flowers popular with the Hollywood celebrities whose weddings she reads about. Roses, hydrangeas, carnations, with their shameless profusion of large red petals.

Mrs. Fujimoto's eyes follow the foreign woman. Yes, she will grant that certain physical similarities exist between this woman and Namika. The fine shoulder-length hair, the curve of the hips in tight-fitting jeans, the giddy way the foreign woman claps her hands when the washing machine finally starts to fill.

The foreign woman begins to dance. A crazy dance like a woman in a cup ramen commercial. Heels kicking her behind, arms crossing over each other as she punches an imaginary target. Then she stops, makes a fist, and pulls her right arm back and forth, a victory salute.

Mrs. Fujimoto glances around, wondering if anyone else is witnessing this display. That the foreign woman would dance by herself in a public place where anyone could see, all over a washing machine . . . Such imprudence. Such wantonness. Such joy.

Mrs. Fujimoto sips her cold green tea.

The sun sparks off the newsstand's metallic sign. The date on the *Yomiuri* reads Wednesday, June 6, 1951. It is noon and Mayuko, along with two new friends, is strolling the main street of the city in that neighbouring prefecture. All three sport trendy polka-dot dresses with full skirts, but while the friends have opted for slim belts that cinch in their waists, Mayuko has wrapped a wide sash, obi-style, just under her breasts. The three swing handbags, coil hair behind ears, dash across the street to the record store.

On the empty lot beside the store, two American soldiers slouch against a shrivelled willow tree. Whiffs of smoke drift from the cigarettes between their stubby fingers, and reckless laughs flee their throats. Mayuko's friends whisper excitedly. She catches the words "Frank Sinatra." But to Mayuko these men do not resemble Sinatra. One has the spotty yellow skin and bloated belly of a *fugu*, the poisonous blowfish. The other resembles a crab, with his sunburnt face and gangly limbs.

Is it because of them that all this has happened, Mayuko wonders. That her father was beaten that night a decade ago? That, weary and dispirited, he recently sold his company to wealthy Mr. Hampton of Rhode Island? That her mother, weakened from post-war diphtheria, no longer has the strength to lift the big pitcher to water her irises?

A third man joins the others. He is not like anyone Mayuko has ever seen. His skin is pale and luminous as that of a peach, his blond hair soft and wavy. His uniform hugs his slim, slightly muscular frame. From the tips of his long fingers dangles a three-inch wooden amulet. An amulet from a Buddhist temple. He speaks – his voice is low and sonorous as the murmur of the ocean in a seashell.

Fugu grabs the amulet, hangs it from his nose, and waddles around the tree. Crab cracks up. The third man smiles but his eyes cloud over. He grabs the amulet and cups it in his hand. The others guffaw.

She feels a poke in the ribs. "Go talk to them, Mayu." Mayuko shakes her head.

"Yes," says the second friend. "Didn't your father used to teach you English? Talk to them in English. Ask them their names."

"Ask them if they have girlfriends," says the first. The two giggle.

Mayuko looks down. "That was a long time ago. I don't remember any English."

"Con-itchy-wall!" Fugu shouts. He and Crab beckon the girls. Mayuko's friends titter, then scamper over. She follows, careful to remain behind them.

Fugu and Crab make several embarrassing attempts at Japanese, to the tinkly delight of the friends. The third man gazes at the amulet. Then Fugu notices Mayuko. "Geisha!" he exclaims, pointing to her sash. He and Crab look past the other girls to Mayuko, their eyes moving over her body like snakes slithering up and down hills. She looks at the pavement.

The other girls exchange looks. One fumbles in her hand-bag, pulling out a camera and gesturing to it. Fugu claps and shouts, and the girl shoves the camera into Mayuko's hands. "Here, you take the picture."

Mayuko retreats several paces and when she looks up, a tableau is in place: Crab in the middle, beside the tree, one drooping branch looking as if it is sprouting from his ear. Fugu slouching on the right. The girls in front, faces stupid with shy giddiness. The third man to the left, a couple of paces away, his eyes like blue topaz. Mayuko holds the camera to her face. His gaze intensifies through the prism of the lens. She names him Romeo. Romeo from Massachusetts.

Fugu shouts. Her friends exhort her to hurry up. She positions her finger on the button. At the last second, she shifts the camera so that Romeo is the focal point, cutting off her friends' legs and slicing Fugu's body in half. Click.

Her friends are upon her, their boldness evaporated, and

she is pulled toward the record store. Nails claw into her tingly skin, bubbly voices hammer at the shell encasing her ears.

Two weeks later, the friend with the camera moves away. Mayuko never sees the picture.

The last week in June, the husband is in Switzerland on business, so Mrs. Fujimoto invites Mrs. Okada and Mrs. Inoue over to drink tea, eat dinner, and watch the foreign woman. It will be a pleasure to linger over dinner, to not bother preparing a plate for the husband when he stumbles in from his after-work socializing.

She chooses her jewellery carefully, selecting the platinum chain with the emerald crane pendant. She will pair the pendant with her green suit. The jacket's scoop neck will allow the pendant to rest against her bare skin. As a young woman, she learned about the seven ages of women's skin from a magazine: silk, satin, cotton, linen, wool, crepe, and leather. While most of her contemporaries have reached the crepe stage, she remains at the linen.

Mrs. Okada and Mrs. Inoue arrive precisely at three. After so many years of friendship, they know better than to be early. They are not what their hostess would call cultured women, but they are docile and amiable, and at her age Mrs. Fujimoto cannot be bothered cultivating new friends. It takes too long to become accustomed to the rhythm of another's existence, the unchanging complaints, the irritating habits.

She shows the two women her latest arrangement, birds of paradise bent to resemble a bird taking flight, placed on a triangular plate. As usual, they ooh softly but ask no questions about the inspiration or technique. Mrs. Fujimoto presses her lips together and offers tea.

On the balcony, Mrs. Okada talks about her new English school; she changes them faster than most people change chopsticks. Today she is raving about the handsome Londoner who teaches her, his Pierce Brosnan looks and alluring accent. But this is nothing new. She poured out dithyrambs about a vegan with celiac disease who taught spelling by having the students form their bodies into letters.

Mrs. Fujimoto does not study English. As a child, she listened ravenously to the fairy tales her father read her. "Beauty and the Beast," "Rapunzel," "Cinderella." But when the war came, her father returned late at night, thin, haggard, with no time for stories, no motivation to speak the enemy language. As a teenager, she learned a little English, through grammar workbooks at school and at the movies with friends, giggling over the dulcet tones of the latest Hollywood heartthrob.

As an adult, forty years ago, she returned home after her father's death from a heart attack, to help her mother pack up the house. Her mother was preparing to move in with a widowed sister in Kyushu. The bookshelves contained hundreds of books, many of them English. "Take them," her mother urged. "He wanted you to have them." But when Mayuko looked at the nicked leather, she saw only the khaki of the soldier's jacket. She donated the books to a local library and never looked back.

Today, Mrs. Okada and Mrs. Inoue are fascinated by the foreign woman. She turns on the tap and then, as if responding to a sudden sound, dashes into the apartment. The telephone, perhaps. As the three women watch, the tap continues to run until streams cascade down the sides of the machine. The foreign woman runs out, shuts the tap, and stomps in a puddle of water. Mrs. Okada and Mrs. Inoue tsk. Mrs. Fujimoto suppresses a sigh. It seems the foreign woman is not so steady after all.

Mrs. Fujimoto recounts the time the husband did the laundry, when she was pregnant with their first. He hung the clothes outside overnight – in January. The result was predictable. His face was almost as frozen as the tie he cradled. He had an important meeting that morning. Following her suggestion, he held the tie over the kettle on the gas burner she was heating for the breakfast tea. The ice melted and the steam straightened the wrinkles. "He obtained a promotion that day," Mrs. Fujimoto says with a conclusive smile.

The two women nod perfunctorily, then look across the street. "Why leave her with one of those awful old things? Surely they could have found an automatic one," says Mrs. Okada.

Mrs. Fujimoto coughs. She has several coughs, which vary in volume from a leaf rustling to a branch snapping in two. This one is a twig being stepped on, cracking a little.

Mrs. Okada's eyes dip down briefly. "Has anyone been to the movies lately?"

"Yes, I saw that new American film about Pearl Harbour. The lead actor, the one who plays the American general, is so handsome," says Mrs. Inoue.

Mrs. Fujimoto bristles. "Why do people continue to be interested in that? The war ended a long time ago."

The others study the painted twigs on their teacups. Mrs. Fujimoto inhales sharply. Why does she expect empathy from these women? What do they know about birds of paradise, nicked leather, frozen ties? She wants to slap them.

"More tea?" she asks.

—

"It is a good match for you, Mayu-chan. Just think about it."
Her father's voice is worn, like a stone eroded by centuries
of pounding surf. Her mother's is that of someone who has
tripped over the stone. "Put a little effort into your hair,
Mayuko. Don't you know how many young men were killed
in the war and the tuberculosis epidemic? You might not get
another opportunity like this." These voices overlay Nat King
Cole's sensuous baritone, which emanates from the radio in
the café opened last month.

On this Wednesday night, Mayuko waits at the table as the
young man with the earnest grin and fuzzy eyebrows stands
at the counter ordering coffee. Across the street is the record
store. It has been two years since the photo, and Romeo has
surely departed with the rest of the soldiers. She imagines his
long fingers buttoning his olive shirt, combing through the
pale waves of his hair, the dark fields of hers, unbuttoning
her blouse . . .

A splat of coffee scalds her wrist. She swallows her irrita-
tion and smiles at the young man, who apologizes and sets the
cups down on the table. That evening he came to the house
with zinnias (a symbol of loyalty, her mother indiscreetly
noted), a business degree fresh from the local university, and a
junior position in a new electronics firm. Never mind that the
zinnias are orange, her least favourite colour, or that spittle
foams at the corners of his mouth when he talks about his
favourite baseball team. He is a nice boy with prospects. She
should be grateful.

Mayuko and the young man sip their coffee, exchange
pleasantries, and fall silent. His hands begin to shake, coffee
staining the white tablecloth, his white shirt cuffs. His voice

trips over itself, a series of compliments tumbling out, the most memorable of which is "You have very beautiful eyelashes." Mayuko could smile or nod, but she does not. As he stutters, she looks at the willow tree, which has shrivelled further. She wonders how much more it can shrivel before it dies.

She thinks of blond men from Massachusetts, a place where people surely have never needed to subsist on rationed gruel. A place of creature comforts beyond even nylons and lipstick. She sees a clapboard cottage, inhales the aroma of the purple irises outside the doorstep, hears the rumble of his laugh as he steps toward her.

She looks across the table and sees a young man with fuzzy eyebrows and prospects, smells his blend of sweat and cologne. If she reaches her hand out only inches, she will feel his moist palm. The seconds pass with an almost audible click.

"Yes. I will marry you," she says.

It is late July. A film of grey haze enshrouds the surrounding buildings. The air is broken only by the buzz of cicadas. The days melt into one another, and Mrs. Fujimoto imagines the black numbers and lines on the living-room calendar dissolving into the white.

Mrs. Okada and Mrs. Inoue left to visit out-of-town daughters and will not return until September. Mrs. Fujimoto's children, always busy with their own lives, are vacationing in Okinawa and Australia. The husband stays out later than usual after work. By the time he returns, Mrs. Fujimoto has withdrawn to her room, so they see little of one another. He is long past retirement age, but as a vice-president, he is indispensable to his company; this is what they tell each other. Even the foreign woman spends little time on her balcony. She has mastered the washing machine and emerges only briefly to drain the machine or change loads.

Mrs. Fujimoto knows that, like other housewives, she should be preparing for the festival of *Obon*, which celebrates the return of the ancestral ghosts. But this year she is irritated by the niggling details of finding the best incense for the family altar, or airing out extra futons in preparation for her children and grandchildren's visit.

She thinks of Namika. Namika wants her grandmother to climb Mt. Fuji, to become a tourist astronaut, to do something huge that will disrupt her life, like a careless footprint on raked sand. Yet Namika is the only grandchild who notices her after the new year's money has been doled out. The others are all too busy with soccer, hip hop lessons, manga. To Mrs. Fujimoto, Namika is a red poppy: sweet, bright, a little wild. She will attend university, Waseda hopefully.

A horn sounds. On the street, a young Japanese man leans out the window of a white Honda. A Japanese woman is at the wheel, trying to manoeuvre the car into a parking spot. The foreign woman appears on the balcony, shouts to the couple, and disappears into the apartment. Two minutes later, she reappears in front of the building and hops into the back seat. The car speeds off.

Mrs. Fujimoto sets down the teacup with a rattle. She begins to pace the length of the balcony.

She wants to talk to the foreign woman, to tell her things it will take her months, if not years, to figure out. Where to go to experience the best tea ceremony in the city. (The ceramics museum, not the lotus temple, it's too crowded and touristy.)

How you should never open the door to a man in a cable company uniform. (These "salesmen" have been known to be disguised *yakuza*.) How to deal with groping men on subway trains. (Embarrass them. Grab their hand, look them in the eye, and say "no.") The foreign woman won't stay longer than a year, two at most. They never do. Mrs. Fujimoto feels an urgency to impart these pieces of wisdom before it is too late.

She continues to pace.

One Wednesday night, a few months after her father's death, she perches at the edge of the futon, watching her husband in the mirror as he fumbles with his tie. A small velvet box sits beside her. Outside, a drunken man hollers. She waits for the echo to fade before speaking.

"Why are you giving me this? It's not my birthday."

His eyes rise to meet hers but dip at the last second, like a wave that cannot gather the strength to crash against the shore. "You deserve something special."

She remains still, breathing shallowly. He turns. Their eyes meet, then his sink. He runs a hand through his oily hair. She waits. "I've done something," he says. "With another woman. It was a few times only. I'm very sorry."

A cry escapes her throat. She throws the velvet box at him, but it hits the edge of the dressing table and bounces to the tatami. A moan from beyond the papery walls, followed by the thump of someone turning over in sleep. One of the children.

She forces herself to whisper. "I've given you a son and a daughter. I cook, I keep this apartment clean, I don't question your decisions –"

"It's nothing you've done."

"I buy the best clothing we can afford. I try to make myself . . ."

"You are beautiful. But you're cold. I feel I cannot touch you. In any way." She squares her shoulders. His voice hardens. "Most of my colleagues have done it at least once. It happens."

She places a hand against her mouth, the satin of her robe tickling her chin, mocking. "My father would never have –"

"Your father was a different type of man. Look where it got him." She turns away, swallows the bile rising in her throat. After a moment, he picks up the box, creeps across the room, and sits beside her.

"I'm sorry I hurt you. Will you forgive me?" He holds out the box. "Will you accept this?"

The topaz bracelet is stark against its white pillow. Four stones. Four people in the apartment. She holds out her hand, and he fastens the bracelet to her wrist.

Later, she places the bracelet in her lacquered box, where it will be joined by other pieces. Three strands of Mikimoto black pearls, a rhodium watch with a diamond-studded face, an emerald pendant and platinum chain, among others. Each given with the same look of eyes rising and falling, each received with the same wave of bile rising and subsiding.

The first Wednesday in August, Mrs. Fujimoto realizes that she has run out of the powdered tea. Why didn't she notice this last week, so that she could have picked some up before now? She cannot be bothered walking to the back-alley tea shop in the stickiness of the afternoon heat. Instead, she takes the mail out to the balcony.

Two things are about to slice through the stickiness. The first is a brochure from the foreign woman's school. Bright blue lettering on glossy paper proclaims in Japanese, "Come learn with us at the Edelweiss School. We can teach you to speak English with confidence and ease." Mrs. Fujimoto's heart begins to pound as she looks at the smiling faces of the students and the foreign woman. Her name is Cheryl. Cheryl from Philadelphia.

The second is a flicker from the opposite balcony. Cheryl is standing at the edge, her hand shading her eyes as she gazes in the direction of the temple garden. Her face is slack. She turns and looks directly at Mrs. Fujimoto. They stare at one another. Then Cheryl waves.

Mrs. Fujimoto feels light and cool, as if she is hovering weightless above the sea. Seconds pass. Her body begins to sag. She tries to raise her arm but it is heavy as a sandbag. A fly lands on her elbow. She does not have the strength to shoo it away. Cheryl's arm slowly drops. Mrs. Fujimoto is pulled under by the sea.

A minute later, she resurfaces, and by the time she reaches land she has made a list of twenty things she must buy for *Obon*. With only days to go, she can complete the preparations, but not to her satisfaction. She has wasted too much time.

STEVEN BENSTEAD

MEGAN'S BUS

said to Adele when we had a quiet moment together, I told her, "Reggie Thompson and his wife – Nancy." I smiled at the casual way I tossed off the woman's name. Just thinking about her filled me with a thousand contradictions. I had not met her before, but I was not likely to forget her. She was a practical one, cool, all common sense, cut and dried. "They came by the shop today. With their little girl. Sophie."

Reggie I knew from the shop. He had been a good customer, ever since he and his family had moved into the neighbourhood a few years ago. I had a Petro-Can on the corner of Nathaniel and Grant. Gas pumps and two bays offering complete Certigard Service. We'd chat briefly when he came in for gas – longer when he brought the car in for maintenance. Now he stopped by almost every day. We would compare notes, repeat stories we'd heard, share bits of news, scraps of gossip.

It wasn't as if I had any business to do. We would lean elbows on our respective sides of the counter and visit over a cup of coffee. I used to keep a fresh pot constantly on the go for my customers, when I had customers. But my coffee supply was not going to last forever, and when the day came to tell him I only had enough for one more pot, he misunderstood. His face went white. "You're not pulling out too, Frank," he stared, his eyes filled with fear, "are you?" Without waiting for a reply, he said, "Where you gonna go? What you gonna do?"

Half the houses on Reggie's street were empty, mine the same. People packing up. The lucky ones had carts or wheelbarrows, the rest simply walked out with what they could carry. Seeing me – me and Adele and our two kids (Megan was eight, Joel was almost seventeen) – seeing us go, another family, might have shaken his resolve.

"There's nothing out there," he insisted. "Nothing. Those rumours about the camps? That's all they are, rumours. People are dying out there, Frank, getting preyed upon. You'd be a fool . . ."

By this time I was laughing, and Reggie realized he had jumped to the wrong conclusion.

Not so long ago if I needed more coffee – or anything: automobile parts, oil – all I had to do was pick up the phone. I had deliveries every day all day.

Used to have a tanker truck deliver gasoline too, regular as clockwork. I had managed to salvage half a dozen jerry cans of gas from my storage tanks using a hand pump. The level was so low by then the retail pumps were sucking fumes. But I got broken into early on. Someone jimmied the back door, wiped me out, took the gas, my last two cases of oil, all my filters, spark plugs. But they didn't get the sugar. Reggie and I drank our coffee black, and I had taken the box of sugar packs home to Adele a few days earlier. The thieves would have made off with that, I'm sure of it, lickety-split. A practical bunch, I took them for, serious scavengers, the holy-roller types that were coming out of the woodwork, because they didn't take the coffee that was sitting in plain sight, coffee being just coffee after all, with no real value to it except to keep you awake at night.

Running out of it proved to be something of a moot point, however. Not long after Reggie and I drank our last cup, the power went off and stayed off.

———

By then Joel had us storing water at the house in every possible container we could find. And collecting firewood (we were lucky enough to have a fireplace) and candles and batteries. I went along with his precautions, but he pursued them more earnestly than I did. He seemed to think the idea that things would eventually return to normal not worth considering, whereas I held out hope that they might.

For me, normal meant going into the shop every day, if only for a few hours. I hung on to what was left of that routine, I clung to it. It was my way back. Chatting with Reggie over the counter, and anyone else who might pop in. Sometimes I found myself listening for the sound of a train – the CN mainline was only a few blocks away – or gazing down the street hoping to see a Hydro repair truck working to get the power back on. There hadn't been anything in the sky since the helicopters stopped flying. Where they went nobody seemed to know. Sometimes I even hoped for a convoy of army trucks to go by, but I never said as much, not even to Reggie. Because for one thing, if the army had to take over we were in really bad shape.

For another, I was afraid he'd tell me to quit dreaming: there was no army, there was nothing, we were on our own.

But we were not by ourselves. At dusk you could see the bonfires burning on the bridges that led into the downtown, lines of demarcation tended by pockets of men, women, and children, the ones who had gathered in the city's core at the start of all this. They were as desperate as we were, but maybe more organized than we were. Everyone I talked to suspected that a growing band of warlords was recruiting the gangs from these dispossessed souls, dispatching groups of young men to roam our neighbourhoods nightly in search of abandoned houses to loot. I worried about a time when we might find those fires burning at the end of our street, and what that might mean.

Almost from the start, Adele had not let Megan go out to play without one of us being with her. Her friends were gone, left when their parents pulled out. A more ominous reason had to do with the rumours about kids being abducted, snatched right out of their own front yards – by the gangs, we all presumed, but maybe not. The idea that someone might appear suddenly in broad daylight and run away with a child seemed alarmingly possible. What they did with these children was what worried me. No one, not Adele, not Reggie, seemed to want to talk about that. Reggie's scoffing, "What do you think?" came as close to confirming my worst fears without defining them.

Food was an issue. A drought the year before had left little local produce. In the spring, the rains had been welcomed at first, but then the rain never stopped long enough for the farmers to get a crop in, and those who did were hit by a severe frost in June. Then twenty centimetres of snow fell in July, the skies turned grey, and the snow did not melt completely until August, when the weather turned unusually hot, forty degrees for days on end, if I was to believe my thermometer at the shop. By then the grocery stores were cleaned out. People had started walking in and taking what they could, me among them, and nobody tried to stop us. TV was off the air, we hadn't seen a newspaper in weeks, but we heard sporadic reports on the radio – Joel searching the dial for a broadcast, any broadcast, sometimes we didn't even know what city it was coming from – of people fighting over a can of beans, for instance, an apple. In the more disturbing of these broadcasts, you could hear gunfire in the background and people screaming.

Then the power went off. We had a wind-up radio so we didn't have to waste our batteries, but after that, Joel couldn't raise a signal on any band no matter how slowly he searched the dial.

And without power, of course, our freezer went, and we had to eat up whatever perishables we had left – the pound of hamburger, the half a package of fish sticks, our one chicken – before they spoiled. A brief, unwanted feast to no good purpose.

———

Reggie and I were still drinking coffee, which meant we still had power, when I started taking Megan to the shop. Adele realized she couldn't keep the girl cooped up all the time. She was eight years old, she needed to run and play, at least a little. The shop was only a twenty-minute walk from the house. I thought the risk worth taking, for Megan's sake. In fact, the risk seemed very low. I had never felt threatened on my way there or back. I had not been confronted by anyone, and certainly not by the mythical gangs of roaming young men.

Megan played in the service bays or out front where I could keep an eye on her. Her favourite game seemed to be something she called "bus driver," in which she drove an imaginary bus around the lot, picking up and dropping off imaginary passengers. Upon one occasion, I noticed she had come to a stop at the edge of her route between the gas pumps and the air hose. She remained fixed to the spot, and I grew concerned that she had seen something down the road, something unusual enough to rivet her attention for what had become a considerable amount of time. Reggie had his back to her and was going on about a rumoured shipment of corn coming up from Mexico, though how it was going to get here was anybody's guess. I excused myself.

Reggie's voice trailed off as I hurried away. "What's up, Frank?" he said, suddenly nervous.

I shared his concern. "Megan? Honey?" I stood beside her. I looked where she was looking and saw nothing but the empty street winding up toward the railroad tracks.

"We have to wait," she explained.

I nodded as if I understood. Then, "What for?"

"The train," she said. "It's a long one." Though she had no watch, she looked at her wrist as if to check the time. She peered to her right and craned her neck. Drawn by her gesture I peered in sympathy, looking for the end of the train. For a brief moment I was with her, standing at the front of her bus, an enquiring passenger anxious to get home or to work, watching a whole string of freight cars trundle by. I could've sworn I heard them creak and groan. I even glanced the other way and saw the thin plumes of exhaust making the air shimmer as the engines disappeared down the line.

And then with a word from Megan – "Here we go." – the train had passed, the warning bells had stopped, the barrier arms came up, and we were on our way. She let me off at the next stop, and as I turned back to the office, I felt an odd surge of happiness. I was almost surprised to see Reggie standing in the doorway, his face grim, his eyes on Megan.

"Everything okay?" he said before he realized it was. His face relaxed; he offered a smile.

I shrugged, "Kids," as if that explained everything, and maybe it went a long way toward doing just that. They didn't see the world the way we did. "You've got a daughter, doncha, Reggie?" Back inside the office, I refilled our cups. "I recall you saying. What's her name again? Sophie? You should bring her next time. She and Megan could play together. They'd be good company for each other. They're about the same age, aren't they?"

"About," Reggie conceded, but he was reluctant to pursue the subject.

He could have had a hundred reasons not to want to bring her along on his daily trek, and I didn't press him. "I'm only saying," and left it at that.

But we had fallen into a bit of a funk, which only deepened when he said, "We are the blind leading the blind, Frank. We are the blind leading the blind." Then he tapped the counter, "Better get going," and he abruptly left.

"See you tomorrow," I called after him, something I didn't normally do.

He waved, but I only saw his back and in that there was no promise.

He did not, in fact, return the next day, but he did stop by the day after, when we pretty much found ourselves back to normal. I didn't mention Sophie, and neither did he – not until several weeks later, long after the power had gone out. To me it seemed as if he had chosen to talk about her out of the blue. "Would you like to meet her?" He stood with his head back and his chest out in a formal gesture of pride that was undercut by a stiff smile and the uncertainty in his eyes, as if I might say no.

I clapped him on the back. "Of course, of course. Bring her around. Anytime."

He brought her the next day, he and his wife, Nancy. They were waiting for us outside the shop. Reggie did the introductions and then stepped back, out of fear, I couldn't help thinking, out of shame. He let his wife do the talking. I was hoping the girls might run off and play together, and although Megan looked on with some interest, Sophie seemed to know that was not why she was here, and so I scooted Megan into the service bays to play on her own.

It was the middle of October. In the morning the windows were rimed with frost. To save on firewood, we had started gathering in the living room and sleeping in our sleeping bags. And we had been rationing our food, of course, for a long time, and growing gaunt in the process, taking in a morsel of anxiety with each mouthful we consumed. The shelves of every grocery store, in as wide a radius as we dared to make, were empty, though we continued to search in hopes of finding something, anything. Scavenging had become part of our routine. Joel and I took turns, one of us going out and one of us staying home. A man, we reasoned, we hoped, at least for the time being, was almost as good as a dog at keeping intruders away. And we didn't have a dog. No one did. They either ran wild in packs or their bones had been picked clean.

By then I was opening the shop just long enough to give Reggie a chance to drop in, and long enough to let Megan drive her bus. She usually had the same route, though sometimes there were detours, she explained to me, due to roadwork or a parade. It was a tough job being a bus driver, making her way through all that traffic, but she soldiered on for the sake of her passengers. She took great delight in having a full bus, calling out, "Move to the back, please," when all the seats were taken and the aisle was crowded. When I boarded her bus and dropped my imaginary ticket in the fare box, she did her best to treat me as if I were any other passenger, regular or otherwise. She took her driving seriously, waiting for the traffic lights, checking her mirrors as we pulled away.

Sometimes I would be waiting on her route, other times I would be a few seconds late and have to flag her down. I invariably stood at the front of the bus hanging onto the pole and we would chat about the world through which we made our way. She told me all sorts of stories about her regular passengers. There was Martha who worked at the Tim Hortons, there was Sam who worked at the airport, there was Mrs. Jones who went downtown every Wednesday to get her hair done, and on like that. I didn't know where they came from, all these people and names, all these stories. When I got off that bus and watched her pull away, the desolation in which I found myself – the abandoned houses, the stores with their windows broken, the empty streets – seemed, if only for a little while, the illusion, and not the other way round.

But Megan wasn't playing "bus driver" the day Reggie and

Nancy brought their Sophie to my shop. Facing them – that woman with her fingers digging into her daughter's shoulders and her hard, calculating eyes fixed on me – I wanted to order them out. Whatever they had to say I didn't want to hear. Instead, with a heartiness I did not feel, I said, "So what's up?"

Nancy pushed Sophie forward, leaving her to teeter. "She's a good girl. She won't be any trouble. Will you, Sweetie?"

Reggie could not contain his agitation. He began to pace, throwing himself from one end of the office to the other.

"She's in perfect health," Nancy continued. "She hasn't had so much as the sniffles since all this started. Has she, Reg?"

"What?" He was running both hands through his hair, and with his fingertips still fixed to his scalp, he shook his head. "No." He stopped as if to reflect. "No." He laughed. Then he bent forward. I thought he was going to burst into tears.

We stood in rigid silence, staring at each other for all of thirty seconds.

"I told you this wouldn't work." Reggie jerked his whole body toward the door. "I told you." He came back, grabbed his daughter's hand and hauled her outside.

Nancy followed hard on their heels. "Reg, Reg," she sniped. "You promised. We agreed."

He kept marching, head down, toward the road, their little Sophie struggling to keep pace. They had a house several blocks from us over on Queenston.

Later that night as our walls creaked with a sudden drop in temperature, I told Adele about Reggie and Nancy, how they had come by the shop with Sophie, and the peculiar mood they were in. I tried to make light of it, but I couldn't help but wonder if she was thinking what I was thinking.

One of the wilder rumours going around in a world full of wild rumours, an old wives' tale really, was that parents were trading children. Hurried and clandestine exchanges were taking place on the principle that the idea of eating your own child was abhorrent, but in circumstances dire enough you might at least consider eating the child of another.

———

The change in the weather was sudden – from a frost that disappeared with the rising sun to a cold so dry we woke up the next day to find the windows deceptively clear. The visit from Reggie and his wife, however, had a much more dramatic effect on me. Their showing up with their daughter the way they did had changed my thinking. The shop was now off-limits, opening it every day, no matter how briefly, a link to the past that I finally had to admit had no future, at least not one that pursued a commerce I wanted to entertain. What if they brought their Sophie around again, and wouldn't take no for an answer, simply took what they wanted, and over my dead body if it came to that? The shop was simply one more thing I would have to leave behind in a world where it seemed we were leaving behind more than we had ever thought possible.

The cold was a good enough excuse to forestall any questions Adele might have about our not going to the shop that day. Indeed, when I told her Megan and I were going to stay put, she barely raised an eyebrow.

Joel announced that if I was going to be around, he was heading out to see what he could find. The cold worried him, presaged worse weather to come. But he was gone less than an hour, though he did not return empty-handed. "Mom?" he called from the back door. "Mom?" There was enough of a strain in his voice to make me lift my head.

I was reading to Megan, snuggled up with her on the couch.

After a long pause, I heard Adele say, "Who's this?"

"This," Joel replied, "is Sophie."

He had found her bundled up in a parka outside the shop.

"Frank?" Adele called out. "Frank. Come here for a sec."

I was already on my way. Joel had no idea of the bargain he might have entered us into, no idea. When I arrived at the back door, I half expected to find Reggie and Nancy waiting. Did they really think we were going to turn Megan over just like that? But Sophie was by herself.

Adele said to me, "Is this . . . the girl?" When I said yes, she told Joel to bring her in, quickly, and quickly she went to the door and locked it.

Megan had followed me into the kitchen. With a mixture of surprise and delight on her face, she said softly, "Can Sophie come and play?"

Adele was crouched in front of the little girl. She was holding Sophie by the shoulders. She shook her ever so slightly, "Where's your mommy and daddy?"

———

We found out a couple of days later.

By then Sophie and Megan had become inseparable. Sophie would not let Megan out of her sight. It was a pleasure to hear their whispers turn into bursts of laughter and their shouts of glee accompany them as they ran upstairs to play.

Adele, as aware of all the various rumours as I was, had speculated that Reggie and Nancy might have gone for help, packed what they could carry and set off on foot, heading south, where some said the government had set up camps. Leaving Sophie with us served two purposes: on the one hand it allowed them to travel more freely, on the other it was a promise that they intended to come back.

Perhaps.

I didn't need to remind Adele that Sophie was another mouth to feed. I tried not to think about that as I selected five small potatoes from our dwindling pile in the cellar. Potatoes were one of the staples we had sought out in the early days of the crisis, when we thought we might have to hold out for a couple of weeks. Joel and I had nailed some scrap lumber together to build the walls of what we thought at the time was an enormous crib. Now, six months later, I could see the pallet we had used for the crib's floor. The pile had resolved itself into a collection of individual potatoes; soon I'd be able to count on the fingers of one hand how many we had left, and the crib would be good for nothing except to augment our little pile of firewood.

I returned from the basement to find Adele sitting at the kitchen table. She seemed puzzled. "Look what Sophie gave me." She opened her fist to reveal a key. "She and Megan walked up just now and handed it to me, said I was supposed to have it. What is it, Frank?"

"A house key by the look of it."

"But what does it mean?"

The next day, with the key in my pocket, I set off for Sophie's house hoping for an answer. The day after Joel had brought Sophie home, a snowstorm had swept through, and now I found myself mired in snow up to my knees in places.

There were few fresh tracks, however. The snow and then the cold that had come in behind it was keeping everyone holed up, the gangs included.

Reggie's house was an ordinary house on a street of ordinary houses. How many had been abandoned I couldn't have said. The ones with the broken-in doors for sure, but the whole block might have been deserted for all I knew.

I went around back, knocked a few times, then pulled out the key. I could see immediately it wasn't going to fit, and I berated myself for coming out on a fool's errand, exhausting myself for nothing. But what was the point of the key?

I experienced a prolonged moment of frustration before I thought of the garage.

It had a side door entrance that was secured by a deadbolt, and sure enough the key fit. I opened the door and peered into the darkness. A single window allowed some light in, and slowly my eyes adjusted to the gloom. But it was not until I stepped inside that I saw them hanging from the rafters, Reggie and Nancy, their bodies at the far end of the garage, and my heart sank.

As I got closer I could see the chairs they had stepped off. Did they go together, holding hands? Or did one go first, leaving the other no recourse but to follow?

Suicide was not something Adele and I ever talked about, but it had crossed my mind more than once, and hers too I had no doubt.

I cut them down. Their bodies were already frozen and they fell like pieces of stone, despite my efforts to let them down gently.

What was I going to tell Sophie? What was I going to tell Adele? Only when I imagined the conversation with Joel, that I was going to need his help, did a prospect I had not previously considered enter my mind.

And at this I wept, wishing there was a God to save us, wishing that some did not have to die so that others may live, and wondering what I would do given the circumstances, wondering how willingly I would give up my life so that others may live – and I realized I had been wrong about Nancy.

I thought of Reggie saying how we were the blind leading the blind. Now we were the dead leading the dead.

I thought of Megan and Sophie.

I thought of Megan's bus.

NABEN RUTHNUM

CINEMA REX

T he Cinema Rex sign was completed long before the rest of the theatre. A quick whitewash of the exterior shell of the building had elevated it into heavenly brilliance, and when the sign was attached, it seemed to be hinged to a low-hanging cloud that was too pure for the Mauritian sky to produce. It was a sign that suggested great things inside.

Instead, there were only the unfleshed bones of a movie house. During the months of construction, market labourers and sugar-cane workers who had got drunk after work and tried to pass out in the cool high halls of the unborn cinema did not have to be ejected. They breathed in the billowing sawdust that their loose, dragging footsteps had kicked up, noted the stray nails and dark gaps that took up more floor-space than the floor itself did, then walked to their tiny homes and the screaming wife, mother, or father they had been trying to avoid.

Vik's tutor, Reynolds, had taught his Friday afternoon students the word "marquee." Its letters encompassed the towering bulbs

that spelled out and outlined "REX," and the slick, neighbouring blankness that would soon be filled by ever-changing titles.
It stirred anticipation among the three thirteen-year-old boys
who comprised the tutorial group, and who paid obeisance to
the marquee after each weekly meeting.

"Man, fuck Royal Cinema, I say fuck it right now," said
Siva, who insisted that the best way to integrate English into
daily life was to master the swear words, which made the
sounds of the language more exciting. "It's already been a dead
place for what, since we were in primary. They been showing
that same *Chori Chori* shit thing for six months, and we all just
keep going. Snacks rubbish too."

"*The* snacks *are* rubbish too," said Renga, not letting go of
his role as the tutor's apprentice.[1] Reynolds, who had formerly
worked at a bank in Australia, was now making his living on an
ancient third in English he'd received from Queen's College.
He assigned the assistant's role every class, giving it to the boy
who had achieved the highest marks on the take-home quiz.
The competition was always between Vik and Renga, each
of whom suffered the threat of a beating at home if he could
not affirm that he'd won the temporary privilege. Siva was

---

1 Renga's prickliness over his friend's *Chori Chori* comment was sub-
limated into a grammatical nitpick, but it was rooted in his deep,
abiding love for that film, which he had seen eleven times over its run
at the Royal. He went alone, by arrangement with his music tutor, M.
Bouillhet. The tutor allowed Renga to skip every second piano lesson
if he could replicate a new piece of music from Shankar Jaikishan's
soundtrack at the next lesson. Bouillhet was a hardline but affable racist
who reasoned that it was easier to train a coloured boy to use his natural
ear for rhythm and melody than it was to drill him on Bach.

convinced that Reynolds had fled Australia in order to avoid a criminal charge, a theory that agreed with his idea of that country as a land populated solely by consistent lawbreakers.[2]

The boys took in the Cinema Rex sign and the men labouring beneath it. The builders had their shirts off, and steel flasks of tea lay at their feet. Several times in the past weeks, Vik had witnessed a man pick up a flask that wasn't his own and take a drink, then screw the top on and let it drop to the ground next to its rightful owner, who seemed unperturbed. Eventually Vik realized the workmen shared these containers, swigging indiscriminately, backwashing tea and saliva into a collective brew-up of fluids.

The interior of the theatre was almost complete; the boys had been carrying on this ritual of staring at the marquee for months. "This one's going to be better, that's for sure," Vik said, speaking in French, his eyes fixed on the sign. Vik felt a premature nostalgia, understanding that the act of staring up at these lights would decline in importance once the movies were actually showing. He spent a moment in peaceful reverence before Siva hit him in the balls with the side of his fist. Siva used a unique blow that he'd perfected – it was halfway

---

2 Twenty-nine years after the opening of the Rex, Siva would take his inappropriately young son to a screening of George Miller's *Mad Max 2: The Road Warrior*, the Australian Mel Gibson film whose relentless action style would go on to dominate 1980s blockbuster cinema. Siva, now a nurse at the second-best hospital on the island, found an accurate visual depiction of his absurd childhood vision of Australian life. The film, in its joyful ridiculousness, served to confirm that his notion of Australia had been pure fiction. He enjoyed *The Road Warrior*, except the bit when Max's dog dies, which he felt was an unnecessarily cruel touch.

between a graze and a punch. A gasp, a numbness, and an ache that would last about fifteen minutes succeeded the impact, but nothing as incapacitating as the aftermath of a real testicular mash. Vik folded into the dirt and the workmen laughed, laughing even more when Vik's mother, Devi, appeared at the door of their house – just across the street from the Rex – and hauled her fallen son home with an utter lack of sympathy.

"That's what happens when you spend time around those apes," Devi said, gesturing at the cackling construction workers. Devi was already notorious at the cinema, having lodged her first complaint just after the sign was erected. The workmen had been laying down a sea of jade-green tiles in the lobby and as a sort of hard carpet leading out of the doorway into the dirt street. The theatre owner had purchased a gross of the tiles at a very low price, he explained to Devi, and the workers knew this. It was perhaps why they were shattering so many, creating the shards that Vik's mother was complaining about, waving her shrapnel-pierced sandal. The workmen flanked the boy and the woman, crowding in to absorb the sight of their boss being scolded. They hovered with their buckets and cheered Devi's tirade, shuffling tiles like ceramic jacks and aces. The theatre owner shot his employees amused glances while Devi loosed her fury; her eyes followed his as though she could hunt down his gaze itself. She left with enough rupees from the theatre owner's pocket to buy a dozen pairs of sandals, and with a promise that her family was welcome to come to the theatre, free of charge, forever.

Vik, who had come to the tile confrontation against his will, returned home that day with a sense of elation as high as his current deflated-testicle state was low.

"I see you talking with those men," Devi said, releasing her son's arm as soon as they were in their open courtyard. A large white dog – dubbed "White," which wasn't as boring a name as it could have been, because the English word had been used – ate the innards of chickens that had been slaughtered for the stew simmering in the kitchen. White could occasionally be trusted to receive some affectionate stroking, on the condition that the person doing the stroking was a very fast adult that the dog knew well. Anyone else was at risk of a serious mauling. A mutt-breeder had supposedly given White to Vik's father in exchange for the erasure of an outstanding balance on a parcel of low-grade meat. This was a story that Vik had never quite believed, but he did believe many rumours about the breeder himself. The man was said to cultivate viciousness in his dogs by starving them for days, then throwing them honeycombs active with bees. The stings made them nearly insane with fury, and they learned the value of regular meals. The theory behind that process was that it produced an angry beast that would only serve the hand that fed it. All other hands would be bitten off. Vik had never tried to pet White, and he noticed an ember of contentment in the chained beast's eye as it watched Vik walk past, clutching his nuts.

"Stop grabbing that everywhere," Devi said. "You think it looks nice to people on the street?"

"But it hurts."

"Holding it won't make it hurt any less," Devi said. Vik saw the logic in this. He let go of himself as his mother herded him inside.

Darkness. Devi treasured cool darkness in a country where the sun was absolute. She passed this philosophy on to the housekeeper, who was an unmarried aunt of Vik's. She wasn't actually paid or obligated to serve by any tangible means, but took on the upkeep of the house as another component of the suffering that she believed constituted her entire life.[3] All windows were perpetually curtained, except for the small one over the kitchen basin and stove. This allowed some light to be admitted, in order to prevent burns and cuts. Devi pointed her son to one of the kitchen chairs, and continued to stress the importance of never exchanging a single word with the workmen, lest they take that dialogue as an invitation to enter/ steal from/otherwise pillage the family home. Devi silently stared her sister out of the kitchen and began to tend to the various dishes on the range. Vik watched her through the single beam of light, trying to decide whether the visual effect was intimate or aquatic.[4]

---

3 This aunt, Roshi, was to become Cinema Rex's most beloved customer. The boys and older men who worked as ushers all referred to her as Auntie, and offered her free Coca-Cola every time she came in. She drank gallons of it every week, and died of complications from diabetes in 1973. Devi, who outlived her by almost two decades, didn't know her sister's precise age, but knew that she had died too young. She never drank any sort of carbonated soft drink after 1965, but continued to take four sugars in her tea.

4 Cinematographer Gordon Willis would indirectly answer this question for Vik. In 1972, Vik sat in a packed theatre in London, watching *The Godfather*. The lighting in Brando's study precisely replicated the kitchen's light on the day he had watched his mother prepare stew. The effect was intimate, not aquatic, and notable for how much of the darkness it made visible.

—

A week after Vik finished his plate of stew, Cinema Rex's opening day arrived. The first film shown would be an American one: *The Night of the Hunter*, dubbed into French to make it comprehensible to the islanders. After school on opening Friday, the boys walked to their tutorial to find Reynolds slumped over his desk. The fake brocade cloth that usually covered the desk had slipped to the floor, revealing it to be a door with its handle broken off. Four boards nailed to the corners served as legs. Reynolds was not dead; he was snoring drunkenly. Renga pointed to the puddle of urine beneath their tutor's chair.

"The fuck we do?" Siva said, delighting in the opportunity to drop an English swear in front of the man who personified the language to him.

"We leave, quick," said Renga, already heading for the door.

"Wait," said Vik, reaching into his schoolbag for a loose piece of paper. He grabbed the pen stuck in the front pocket of Renga's short-sleeved shirt and scrawled out a note on Reynolds's door-desk. He stuck the thing to the outer wall of the shabby dwelling as they left. *Boys all sick today. Sorry, pay still coming*, it read, signed in an illegible geometric flourish that could have been the mark of any of their less literate parents. Siva thought that Reynolds might try to verify the note, until Renga reminded him of the pee.

"Right, yes," Siva said. "So now what? I can't bloody go home."

"Yes, me neither," Vik said, switching the language of the conversation to proper French, navigating away from Siva's buccaneer English and the Creole that Renga favoured outside of the classroom. "We do need to get inside. Or in shade." The heat was severe, a lapping humid organ that clung to anyone who stayed in the sun for more than a few minutes, depleting energy and the will to do anything other than sleep. A four p.m. nap might lead to grogginess at the seven o'clock showing of *The Night of the Hunter.*

"Let's go to market," Renga suggested.

"You joking? My dad's got another two hours there, one of his guys will spot me for sure," said Vik.

"No, under the market, I mean," Renga said. The market was located on two extended piers in the main port – one pier was all fish and meat, the water beneath it rank with carcasses and offal. The neighbouring pier, though, the one where fruits and vegetables were sold, was walled off from its tamasic neighbour in order to spare the vegetarian Hindus who shopped there from the sights and odours of animal decay. Depending on where the wind was on a particular day, the separation almost worked. The rocky slope beneath the vegetable pier was usually cool and clean enough, and often occupied only by scavenging gulls and drunks.

Once the boys were encamped in the shade, gathered on an old sheet that they'd stolen from Reynolds's front garden, Renga volunteered to go to the surface for a round of cold alouda, if Vik was willing to finance the mission. It was known that Vik was usually rife with pocket money; what was less known is that he had built his stock of cents and rupees by strategically spending time with his father during the man's Saturday lunches. Vik's father would come home drunk from that morning's deal-closing whiskies with the twenty-odd boat captains he traded with. Devi or her sister prepared a sauce in the hour leading up to his arrival, and he'd have a gutted and scaled fish in hand, ready to be fried and flavoured. He had installed a cushioned burgundy couch in the kitchen, in defiance of his wife's open rage. It had absorbed the odours of a thousand meals, and the pore-filtered effluvium of gallons of Johnnie Walker. Vik's father would present the fish, strip to the waist, and nap on the couch for twenty minutes, until the table was laid. Unfailingly, the contents of his pockets would transfer themselves to the gaps between the couch cushions; every safety pin, every wadded receipt, and every coin would find its way into Vik's pilfering hands. Along with the coins, he gathered the trash to lessen his feelings of guilt. Removing rubbish was worthy of some recompense, and if that recompense was to be found among the rubbish itself, so much the better.

Vik handed a few cents to Renga, who scurried up the slope with enough speed and forward lean to avoid slipping backwards. When he was in reaching distance of the pier, he used his long fingers and the developing muscles in his shoulders to pull himself into the invisible above.[5] Siva and Vik were left in uncomfortable silence; their friendship only functioned when Renga was present.

"So you going to the show tonight?" Vik asked.

---

5 Renga would later develop his corded strength with a set of exercises described in a Charles Atlas kit that was mistakenly delivered to his house six months after the opening of the Cinema Rex. The parcel was addressed to Raj Ghany, the silent fat boy who lived across the street, but Renga chose to accept it as a gift from beyond. The physique that he constructed and maintained was partially responsible for securing the respect of a curiously flabby and middle-aged Tamil action star named Arvind, who gave Renga his first major scoring job, on an explosion-heavy, 1983 rip-off of *E.T.*

"Fucking yes, man, of course I am," said Siva, relieved to fall back on ridicule, "Saved one rupee twenty-five, so first-class seat for me."

"Oh. How much for the other classes?"

"What do you care? You're first class, full-time, man."

"I don't know. My family, we get in free, so I don't know –"

"What? You, free? Fuck is that, man, you're the richest!"

"Can we speak in French, Creole?" asked Vik, hoping that shifting to a different language would lessen Siva's hostility.

"Sure, boss."

"My mom yelled at the manager, so yeah, free for us."

"Sure," Siva said.

"What else have you heard about the opening? I don't know anything," Vik said, attempting to place Siva in a superior position.

"Yeah, I guess you haven't gotten permission from Mummy to check it out. Yesterday I heard something pretty good."

"What?" asked Vik, and Siva pointed upwards.

"All the best market vendors? They're going to be posted at the cinema, for the breaks between movies. Right after market close, they go home, right, but then they hitch the carts to lorries, haul everything to the Rex for that break. Poori, peanuts, corn, pineapple with chili chutney. You know, all of it."

"Man," Vik said. Siva was skinny, but spoke of food with a fat man's relish, slurping his syllables as his eyes filled with lust.[6] The next part of their exchange was silent; Siva squeezed

---

6 In the early 1990s, Siva realized how obese he had become at a screening of *In the Line of Fire*. He'd come alone, as he had a bond with Clint Eastwood that had nothing to do with his children or married life. The

the pockets of his thin shorts for a moment and looked at the ground. Vik palmed the seventy cents that remained after his alouda expense, and placed it on Siva's lap. The money disappeared.

Just as rapidly, the drinks appeared. Renga dangled upside down from the pier and shouted for Vik to come up the slope and grab the cups. He was holding them with his right thumb and two fingers, which were each stuck a joint deep into the liquid. Vik noticed a scummy aureole of dirt spreading around each digit in the sweetened iced milk, with its delicious jellied strips. He shook the cups to disperse the filth as he descended, also jostling the image out of his mind so he could enjoy the drink.

Vik was home earlier than usual, but Devi made no comment. He told her the story he'd prepared anyway, an undetailed concoction about an argument with Siva that had caused him to walk home instead of dallying with his two friends for the usual post-tutorial half-hour. Devi relished these tales of disagreement, as Vik had noticed long ago; she was waiting for

---

new owners of the Rex had installed rigid plastic armrests the previous week. Siva placed his large Coke in the cupholder of his favourite seat [27A] and sat, only to find that the armrests chafed his sidefat dreadfully. He came out of the film dented and numbed. As obesity problems had spread over the island in the past decade, the management found Siva's petition for a row without armrests to be reasonable. Row 27 was soon stripped of the offending plastic projections, and cupholders were attached to the seatbacks of Row 26.

Siva widened into the neighbouring seats until he suffered a massive heart attack in 2005 while attending to a patient who had been admitted after a heart attack of his own.

her son to outgrow his friends and to find new ones, ones that suited her idea of his future.

"Soon, you'll understand," Devi said, her voice lugubrious and laden with the wisdom of suffering. She was sitting on the kitchen couch, allowing her sister to attend to dinner. Aunt Roshi's contribution to the conversation was the soft plosion of vegetables and meat plunging into boiling oil; she always dropped raw food in from a height, a risk illustrated by the lashing of white scars on her forearms.

"Understand what?" Vik asked, doing up the top button of his shirt when he noticed his mother's eyes resting on his exposed chest.

"Why you and those boys are different."

"I already know," Vik said. In reply, Devi kicked off her left sandal – part of the haul of footwear she'd purchased with the theatre owner's payout – and sailed it across the kitchen, where it lightly footprinted her son's stomach.

"Don't think you *know* anything, little one," Devi said. Her mood seemed to have changed in the moment between hurling the shoe and its impact; she smiled indulgently and waved him to his room.

Vik parcelled out the small amount of change he had remaining, easing it out of the hiding place in the sliding joint of his bottom dresser drawer. A cockroach skittered over some dropped coins and Vik crushed it reflexively, using one of Siva's English curses when he saw the mess it had made on his money. He cleaned and examined his haul: twenty-six cents. A small sum, but more than enough for some snacks at the interval.

Vik's father didn't return from the market at closing time, so the family ate without him. Aunt Roshi had improvised a sort of servant's table in the darkest corner of the kitchen; it consisted of a tall stool facing a piece of scrap lumber that bridged two separate sections of the countertop. She ate with her back to Vik and Devi, her open-mouthed chewing loudly emphasizing the silence at the proper dining table. Devi wasn't talkative when her husband was this late. That extra half-hour meant that he had decided to have a drink after work, and that drink implied a half-dozen more after it. After three gateaux-piments and five minutes, Vik spoke.

"Do you think we can reserve seats at the Rex?"

"Rex? What? The cinema?" Devi replied. "We're not going to that tonight, too crowded. We'll wait at home for your father. He likes it when we're waiting."

Vik bit his fork, grinding the metal against his teeth in despair. Devi was punishing him. This wouldn't have happened if his father had come home on time.

"But we're expected, Ma. We have to go."

"Who's expecting you, like you're the king making a tour? We're not going." Devi would have yelled at Vik for neglecting the rest of the food on his loaded plate, but she had stopped eating as well. She waited for the boy to leave the table and then called her sister to clean everything up. Roshi disposed of the vegetables, and loaded meat into White's bowl.

The marquee seemed to glow even brighter through the pane of glass in Vik's window, a cruel illusion. Vik's attendance was required, not optional. Escape from the house was possible from at least three doors leading into the courtyard, but his absence would be noticed within a half-hour. He decided to leave a note explaining where he was and when he would return, and to accept the consequences. Showtime was thirty minutes away, and already audience members were pacing outside what must have been the third-class-ticket window, passing bottles back and forth, arguing and laughing. A few vendor carts had already arrived, and Vik could smell the hot peanuts that the men outside were washing down with rum.

Roshi was massaging the monstrous veins in her calves when Vik crept past her door. She looked at him without any interest, then returned to her task. Devi was still in the kitchen, so Vik exited through one of the side doors. White was tearing into a gristly piece of curry lamb on the bone, which Vik recognized as one that he had left behind on his plate. The dog looked at the boy no differently than he looked at his dinner, but did not bark or shake his chain. Vik struck out toward the Rex in time to see Renga and Siva enter the first-class doors. The highest-paying segment of the audience was entitled to early entry, it seemed.

"Hey!" called Vik. He was almost sure that Renga had heard him, that he had held the door from drifting shut behind him for an extra moment, but the boys vanished behind all of the other bodies entering the Rex. Vik rushed the doors, only to have a purple-costumed usher seize the front of his shirt, just above the print that Devi's shoe had left.

"No. No," said the usher. He was short, only a bit taller than Vik, and about twenty years old, with a brushy-looking mustache that belonged in a colder climate. When he spoke, Vik saw that he'd grown it out to obscure the stained stumps that had once been a top row of teeth.

"I get in free," Vik explained, graciously tolerating the hand on his shirt, holding his own palms upward in a peaceful, explaining gesture. The usher laughed.

"Free, free for this one," he said, talking over his shoulder to someone he thought was there. The colleague he had been turning to was gone, and the usher turned back to Vik with all the humour leeched out of his face.

"Go to third with the rest of the garbage, beg some money off one of them. Don't mess up my entryway, got it? Ticket inspector will throw you out, then fire me."

The third-class queue had none of the characteristic features of a lineup. It was a roughly circular press of humanity that stank of sweat, liquor, and worse. Vik tried to will the money he'd so casually given to Siva back into his pocket, because it would have been enough to get him to the second-class entryway. He was pushed through the heaving mass of men, feet barely on the ground, eased forward by the damp movement around him. He was able to progress by not shoving back; men would propel him forward in order to yell at the people that had been standing at either side of him. As far as Vik could see, there were no women waiting to be let into the third-class seats. He paid for his ticket and threw his two leftover cents on the ground in a useless gesture of anger. In ten minutes, the film would start.

The tiles were brilliant under the countless bulbs in the lobby, and the walls were covered by paintings of movie stars, some of whom were so famous and Western that Vik didn't recognize their names, only their faces. Robert Mitchum was depicted in one, his skin the colour of a banana peel and the lines of his cowboy hat trickily painted to make it project from the wall. Lacking the time to make any further observations, Vik made for the entry that led into the balcony for third-class ticketholders. He walked to the front row, where a man had passed out across two seats. With the experience he'd gained from many stealthy afternoons of manoeuvring his sleeping father on the couch without causing him to wake, Vik cleared the drunk's drooping limbs from one of the two seats and sat down. Holding his place with a foot on the seat, Vik leaned over the railing to see if he could spot Renga and Siva in the dark.

His foot was violently slapped off the seat and he lost his balance, falling backward instead of over the balcony. The damp hands of the front row quickly had the boy upright. The ticket inspector's relief at Vik's survival was quickly covered by a mask of business. He extended his hand for Vik's ticket, which he gave back after a suspicious once-over.

Bottles clinked behind and around Vik as the lights went down. The projector whirred alive before barking out its beam. The movie was in black and white, but the suggested spectrum of colours on the scratched film was limitless. There were children in the film, a grand surprise for Vik, as they seemed to be principal characters in a grown-up story. No songs. A flickering knife. Mitchum's eyes, barely open most of the time, occasionally flaring in malicious passion. Talk of money. Tattooed knuckles. Mocking songs about the children's dead father swinging at the end of a hangman's rope.[7]

---

7 Vik was to write many of his major papers at the London Film School on *The Night of the Hunter*, actor Charles Laughton's sole directorial outing. Instead of tiring of "actor Charles Laughton's sole directorial outing," Vik began to love that string of words, thinking of it as his own personal cliché, a coded signature that appeared in all his work on his favourite film. When the editor of *Cahiers du Cinema* excised the French iteration of the phrase from Vik's fourth article for the journal, without first asking permission, Vik swore to never publish in it again. Unfortunately, maintaining that

There was movement in the first-class section. Vik's eyes panned down from a bedroom scene between Mitchum and Shelley Winters that didn't bore him in the slightest, despite being beyond his comprehension.[8] A smooth and forceful ripple that originated in a back row of the centre aisle was moving forward in a succession of turning, irritated heads. The source of the ripple was Devi, now a black silhouette against the simulated Virginian sky behind Mitchum, the lines of her figure so sharp she might have been scissored from the

---

promise to himself would only have been possible if he had succeeded in chucking his journalistic and academic career in favour of screenwriting and directing, a dream that failed to materialize after seven drafts of a screenplay and a humiliating internship at the BBC in his mid-thirties. *CdC* accepted his proposal for a long feature in which he would interview five important directors on their own poignant and career-influencing early failures. The piece was well-regarded, but Vik failed to attain the encouraging sense of recognition that he was looking for in these conversations with great figures of cinema; their failures had been experiments in learning and fortitude, while his own taught him that there were things he would never be able to do.

8 While pre-code Hollywood films had made selective appearances on the island, *The Night of the Hunter*'s unsensational portrayal of a new wife's normal sexual drive and Mitchum's psychopathic distaste for regular intercourse was so unusual that it didn't register as subversive. The audience seemed to look through the screen, a fact that Vik had noted before he was distracted and that he would later expand upon in his dissertation, a reception-theory piece that would eventually be resurrected as the centerpiece of his first volume of essays, *Hollywood in the Colonies*. This publication, more than anything else in his career, was responsible for his tenured position in UCLA's film studies department, an appointment that he took up in 1984 and held until his retirement in 2011.

screen. She was whispering to the person at the end of each row, then craning to examine each incredulous face. If she continued to move forward, she would spot Renga and Siva, and the real noise would start.

The gnawing immediately beside Vik stopped, and he felt something arc past his ear. A whirling cylinder was twice arrested in the projector beam; once as it travelled upward, and once more during its plunge.[9]

The list of expletives from the row where the stripped corncob turned missile had landed began with "Bastard pimp motherfucker" in Creole and ended in angry shushing. Devi recoiled from the language, which came from a seat uncomfortably close to her, and ran back up the aisle to the lobby.

"Ah well," said a soft voice beside Vik. "Almost got her. You think she'll come up here to look?"

Vik faced the gnawing drunk, scared for a moment that he had sat beside his own father without noticing. The face that looked back at him was half-covered by a thick beard, but the skin that was visible was ochre-dark, the kind of pigmentation that would have prevented him from being the favourite of his mother, or of any mother on the island. Vik checked the man's knuckles to see if he had Mitchum's LOVE/HATE tattoos, but only whorls of hair were visible in the darkness of the theatre.

"Vikram. You know me?" asked the bearded man. "From stories your mother tells, maybe?"

---

9 Vik used an altered, depersonalized recounting of this incident in the opening chapter of his second major academic book, *Rabelais at the Drive-In: Carnivalesque Interrogations of Class Structure in Colonial Cinema(s)*.

"No," said Vik. "Please, can I just watch?"

"Sure," said the man, smiling. "We can talk after. Don't leave too quick."

But Vik did leave quickly. He didn't watch the movie as he timed his run. He only counted minutes, watching the pops of light and sound at the edge of the screen, seeing the lines of wear overlaying the picture, which had developed as the film travelled across continents and through foreign projectors to reach the Rex. Even a failed film like *The Night of the Hunter* had to make a tour of the first world before it reached the gutter screens of the colonies, and the battering the reels took was as visible and audible as the movie itself. Vik counted minutes. He hopped over the knees on his left as soon as minute five came around, leaving by way of the balcony exit that led to the drink stand. If the bearded man thought he was going for a Coke, he wouldn't follow. Vik could linger in the bathroom, then perhaps come in and find another seat.[10]

Siva was peeing in the steel urinal trough when Vik entered. "Hey," Siva said, before concentrating on hastening his stream, urging his pee out with frightening rapidity. He still took the time to amuse himself by directing it into different

---

10 Vik was not to see the rest of *The Night of the Hunter* during its run at Cinema Rex. His mother was so relieved to recover him that she limited his punishment to a ban of the film, which counted as a light penalty to her, but was crushing for Vik. His long essay *On Interruption*, which caused one critic to call him "the othered Barthes," begins with the author's broken first viewing of Laughton's film. "So did my career," Vik said during an interview with that same critic, an instructor from the American University of Paris who managed to simultaneously condescend and flatter.

areas of the trough, achieving a marimba-like musical effect. Vik could have hugged him, but even terror of the bearded man couldn't bring him to violate an ancient code by touching his urinating friend.

"Where's your family sitting?" asked Siva, when he had shaken off. "Fucking noisy in there, animals can't shut up for ten seconds."

"I'm in the third class, alone," Vik said, pretending to pee as Siva washed his hands.

"Third? First full up, yeah? Boring film anyway. I'll see you after."

Siva ran for the door, eager to get back to the film, boring as it might be. Vik didn't let himself beg his friend to stay. But he wished he had when he made his way to the sinks and the bearded man entered.

"Thought you had run away," he said. In the caustic light of the bathroom, Vik was able to see that the rest of the man matched his face; hairy and bloated. The arms were too long, and there were ancient liquor stains on his rough cotton shirt. His zipper was undone.

"You don't know me?" The man made no move to the toilets. "I guess mother Devi doesn't tell stories about the people she used to go with before she classed up, first class all the way. I could be your dad, you know, if you were a couple of years older. Me and a lot of guys I know, we could have been your dad."

Vik said nothing. He wished he had peed in the urinal, because there was now a real risk that it would happen in his pants.

"I'm not first class all the way, no. But your dad drinks the same whiskey I do, so maybe the smell, maybe that, reminds your mother of me." The man's pants were undone, held up solely by a leather belt. "You don't like sitting with me?"

"No," said Vik. He didn't know if this was a bold reply or a safe one, but it was the word that leaked out of his mouth.

"Of course you don't, because you're your mother's boy. So go home." The man ambled over to the urinal and dropped his pants entirely, exposing ape-strong legs and a coating of fur that looked thicker than the pants around his ankles. When he saw that Vik hadn't moved, he turned and waggled his penis at the boy. It was as wrinkled and pouched as an elephant's trunk, but thankfully not as long, or the piss would have reached Vik. The boy backed up; the man held out a placating hand and turned back to the trough to finish up. He was laughing, but without the cackling note this time. He was all avuncular chumminess, and when he fastened up and spoke again, his tone was as placid as the green of the tiles snaking from the entryway and through the lobby into this bathroom, where the supply had finally been depleted. About two feet, at the perimeter of the room, was done in ill-matched purple tiles of different dimensions, probably to the rage of the theatre owner, who would remember all those discarded, shattered tiles stuck into the sandals of a complaining woman.

"Bizou taught us all that trick. Not really a trick, but show me a man who doesn't back away from someone whipping himself around like that, and I'll show you a man who *you* should be running away from." Vik didn't answer, but he also didn't leave.

"Bizou, that's what we call your dad at the card game. No one calls him that at home?" The heavy man walked to the sink and turned the tap on, letting it run without wetting his hands. He wiped them on his pants after he turned the stream of water off. "I thought maybe your mother might still call him Bizou, no?"

"No. She doesn't call him anything but 'your father' when I'm around."

The furred man laughed at this. A rounded tuft of hair protruded from his collar and encircled his neck, like the ruff worn by one of the old British courtiers that Vik had seen in schoolbooks. This ruff was coarse and black.

"Your dad's game is still on. You want to go inside and grab my boy, we can all go and pick up Bizou? Maybe he'll want to take you for the late showing, you can watch the rest of the movie without worrying about Devi popping around."

"I don't know your boy," Vik said.

The man eased Vik to the side and went into the lobby, where he just as casually displaced the lean, reeking usher and made his way toward the first-class seats. Vik watched him walk into the altered darkness,[11] heard him bark a name: Renga. The boy was propelled outward on a wave of disgusted jeers at this latest disturbance. Renga looked in distaste at his father, and then in horror at Vik.[12]

---

11 When Vik did watch the film all the way through, he was able to place the moment when the man had walked into the theatre: it was during the moonlit boat ride that the children take down the river, where every shot foregrounds an animal that looms massively over the drifting boat in the background. A lunatic masterstroke on Laughton's part, a sequence that Vik never dared unpack in the confines of one of his academic studies of the film, for fear of damaging its place in his memories and his sense of film.

12 Renga had never allowed the other boys to come to his house for a number of reasons, the most significant of which was that he did not

"Take us home," Renga's father said. "I want to sleep. And your little friend here is running away from my old girlfriend, so let's get him to Daddy."

The trio walked out of the Rex, into the splashed field of illumination produced by the marquee, which outdid the shine of the pale butcher's moon. Renga's father, who had seemed sturdy inside, went legless in the ocean-heavy air, and the boys had to carry him. For the first of many times to come, Vik extracted himself from present discomfort by presenting reality to himself as cinema, watching himself from a gracefully positioned, neutral camera. He saw Renga and himself as the opposite ends of an uneven, three-headed entity that veered across the dirt street in a waltzing rhythm of balance and momentum,

---

want them to see his piano and begin to ask questions. After the events that took place on the opening night of Cinema Rex, which included Vik seeing his home and the piano it contained, Renga dropped his English lessons with Reynolds in order to take on additional musical training at the conservatory on the eastern side of the island. This allowed him to see less of Vik, and to focus on the skill that would get him off the island two years before anyone else of his age, with his admission to the Royal College of Music in London. He ran into Vik at an early Pink Floyd concert in Camden (they would often, separately, boast that anyone who hadn't seen the band perform with Syd Barett could never understand what popular art lost in his disappearance). The conversation they had that night was their longest since the night they had been pulled away from Robert Mitchum's pursuit of two celluloid children and a cash-stuffed doll. Their friendship began again, quickly and simply, with Renga purchasing two lagers at the bar with pound notes passed to him by Vik as heavy psychedelic noise interrupted their talk. When Vik took his beer from Renga, he saw that the spindly pianist's finger was stuck a half-inch into the liquid. He noted the sight nostalgically, then forgot it in order to enjoy his drink. They both agreed that drinking felt safer off the island.

juddering over a curb, slipping over patches of tile, arriving at the driver's door of a delivery lorry where it continued to twitch and fumble, a crippled spider in the shadows, delineated as the forms of two boys supporting a semi-conscious drunk when a passing car bounced light toward them.

"This your dad's?" Vik asked, referring to the vehicle. He decided to be all business, to speak in the clipped, efficient language of a heist man from one of the too-few gangster films that the Royal had shown, in order to compress the awkward minutes that awaited Renga and him.

"It's your dad's," Renga said. Giving a signal and a shrug, he allowed his own father to slide to the dirt in a kneeling position. Renga grabbed at the outside of the man's pockets until he found the hot metal clump that he was looking for. He keyed open the back door and Vik helped him pour the man onto the narrow back bench, which was covered in cabbage leaves that clung to the torn leather like much-needed patches. Renga's father grunted when an exposed spring pulled at his shirt and scratched the fat projecting out from his waist. The heat of the man's body and its liquor-perfumed slickness was familiar to Vik, who often rolled his father onto his side at Devi's behest.

Renga got into the driver's seat of what Vik had finally recognized as one of the three vehicles in his father's small fleet. Most of the vehicles in Mauritius were just like this one, smoke-belching conveyances that carried vegetables and meat to hotels and Chinese grocery stores. His father's were the only ones with green steering wheels. Vik had painted all three wheels himself one afternoon. When the bucket of paint that his father had found in the back shed had run out, so had his father's interest in having a uniquely done-up fleet. The anonymous bucket had been filled with an impressively low-grade variety of house paint, which stuck to skin better than it stuck to whatever surface it was applied to. Renga gripped the wheel beneath this crumbling, unfinished decoration.

"You can drive?" Vik asked.

"Sure, I drive. Maybe you should just go home now? I don't think my dad really wants you to come over, you know, he just talks like that when he's drunk. Gets hospitable." Renga laboured over this last word, and Vik suddenly realized from the effort the boy was making that he was speaking in English. They had both been speaking in English, from the moment that Vik delivered his tough-guy question about the lorry's ownership. It was a way of excluding the drunken father from their discussion, a decision that became conscious when Renga stuttered over "hospitable." Renga brushed hair off his forehead, and flecks of dry paint clung to the strands.

"Siva's in there. Take my ticket stub, join up with him."

"Sitting next to him without having to talk sounds good, but your dad is right about my mom. She's real angry, waiting for me at home. Maybe if I come with my father, she'll worry about him instead, let me off."

Renga reflected. The scenario was beginning to align itself with Vik's brisk gangster tone; they were scheming. A small boy ran past the driver's side door and kicked the front tire, laughing and distracting Renga. Renga leaned out of the window and spat hard, far, and clean, an expectoration that Siva would have applauded. The wad landed on the back of the child's neck. The kid paused and then shuddered forward, bucking the slick saliva off his neck before starting to cry, running into one of the nearby houses. Renga and Vik laughed, and the timing was too perfect for Renga to do anything but turn the key in the ignition and set off, more unsteadily than either boy would have liked, toward his home.

Renga was tall for his age, and Vik noted that most of that extra length was in the legs that worked the creaking, resistant pedals of the lorry, and in the fingers that urged obedience from the gearshift. The roads approaching Renga's home were more hole than surface, and it seemed miraculous that the man in the back was able to sleep through the jouncing. He wasn't properly on the backseat anymore, but lodged between the bench and the backs of the front seats. A cabbage leaf covered the top half of his face: a poorly conceived villain's mask. Craning his head around the back of his seat to look at the paralytic drunk, Vik wanted to pull the leaf off, but was afraid that a slight, sensuous touch might wake him, even though all the violent juddering of the vehicle hadn't.

"Didn't know your dad worked for mine," Vik said.

"Doesn't," Renga said, with more insistence than necessary. "They play cards together after market. Sometimes in the office behind your dad's stall, sometimes at my house if it goes late. They taught me to drive so I can go pick up whiskey, cigarettes. That's why my dad had the lorry."

"But he was at the movies."

"Sometimes he forgets where he's going when he's drunk," Renga said, braking to let a pack of dogs cross. The headlights picked out the snarl of the head dog, yellow teeth in a dark face, pink sores blossoming in its fur. The pack loped into one of the patches of jungle that the city had so far forgotten to eat.

"He forgets he went for cigarettes, goes to the movies instead?" Vik laughed.

"Yeah," said Renga. "That's why they send me. I don't get distracted by a bright sign. I get the cigarettes and I bring them back, and your dad gives me some of his fucking money." Vik twitched at hearing Siva's word in Renga's mouth.

"That's good. Extra money, always good."

"Yeah." Renga pushed his hair back again, this time striking it off his forehead with impact, leaving more flakes of alien dandruff in the strands. Without slowing down, he stopped the lorry all at once, hard enough to unwedge his father in the back and roll him back onto the bench proper.

Renga left friend and father behind, walking through a courtyard that was between the parked vehicle and a small home that he soon entered. Before long, Vik saw him come out, signaling his friend to come in.

There were no outdoor lights of any sort, this far from the centre of the city. Electricity in homes, yes, but bulbs were extinguished early in the evening or jealously curtained off, to avoid sharing illumination with the rest of the neighbourhood. Thinking of the pack of dogs, Vik scanned the street before opening the passenger door and running toward Renga.

"Slow down, idiot," Renga said, conducting him through the courtyard and into a tiny front room, which seemed to be both a kitchen and a general living area. It was clean, but intensely crowded. Renga paused in front of a cheap piano of the upright variety, similar to the ones Vik had seen in Westerns. He pointed to a man sleeping beneath the abandoned card table, next to the stove. Vik's father.

"The other player went out the back. Getting a cab to come back here for you two. Let's haul him out front," said Renga. The boys leaned Vik's unconscious father against one of the gate pillars at the front of the house. In the lorry, Renga's father briefly surfaced from sleep and gave the waiting boys a curious look, looking entirely sober for a moment, before passing out again. Soon, the loud rock-on-steel scraping of an approaching car brought Renga and Vik the welcome news that their night together was almost over. It seemed the best time to venture a last question, Vik thought, as he wouldn't risk getting too thorough an answer, or one that was so well thought out that it was false.

"Your dad called my mother his old girlfriend. You know why?"

"He was drunk."

"I know, yeah, drunk. But why did he say that?"

Renga saw the cab's lights cresting the incline that their own lorry had struggled over minutes before. In his relief, he released the brief truth.

"She was his old girlfriend. She used to do what I did, get cigarettes and whiskey for all of them at the card game, back before either of us was born. Your dad met her here."

The boys again shared the dead weight of an unconscious man as they shovelled Vik's father into the back of the elaborately dented cab. The driver seemed the type to have hand tattoos. Vik checked for them when he got into the front seat for the ride back, but there were none. Vik gave Cinema Rex as the destination address, reaching into the backseat toward his father, removing the wallet from the inside breast pocket. The driver noted the thick wedge of paper in the leather and started to drive.

Vik's return coincided with the emergence of the Rex audience, which was released into a delightful miasma of frying oil and the treats it birthed. The vendor carts were so thronged that it made it difficult for the taxi to park, a problem Vik solved by telling the driver to drive straight into his family courtyard. He paid the man from his father's stack of bills. Devi emerged from the house, swathed in a fresh sari unmarked by the traces of hurled corncobs. When she saw Vik pulling his father's feet out of the backseat of the cab, she came over to help, first breaking the dignity of her bearing by screaming at the dog in authoritative French, which devolved into Creole when it became clear that the barking, snarling animal wouldn't subside into peace unless she used words it understood.

"Bouche to fesse," she said, lending the words a Gallic crispness that could have been pulled from the lips of one of the dubbing actresses that Vik had heard in the few minutes of film he'd seen that night. The dog was silent, and Vik and his mother pulled his father out of the cab and onto a pile of empty rice sacks. First-class-audience members, overdressed in suits now flecked with grease and flavoured salt, began to filter into the courtyard. With them came a foodcart stink and the ecstasy of a great and mysterious film. They were clamouring for the cab, which Devi thumped brutally until it reversed off her property.

The crowd followed the car, except for a hunched figure traversing the tiled carpet at the Rex's exit. She hovered at the edge of the pale light dripping from the open kitchen door, staring at Vik: Aunt Roshi. She was even more tranquil than usual, calmed by a massive ingestion of sugar that had come in the form of three Cokes and a sackful of licorice, the remnants of which she was loosening from the generous gaps between her teeth.

Devi pointed to the inert form of her husband, and Roshi trundled over to help, after carefully setting down her final, half-full Coke. Vik was waved away. He sat on the vacated stack of rice sacks and watched White walk to the end of his chain, which was long enough to allow him to nose the bottle of Coke onto its side. The dog licked up the spill, and the boy waited for the rest of his family to go to bed. Renga's father had been right; bringing his own whiskey-sodden patriarch home had deflected, even defused Devi's anger. The routine she entered each time she ushered Vik's father out of a binge and into the recovery cycle from late night to early morning, a period in which she always maintained an utter speechlessness, provoked an emotion in her that was quite different from the light, hot rage she would have otherwise flung at her son.

Vik avoided going out for the rest of the weekend, cutting off his mother's flare-up before it could begin. He watched crowds enter and exit Cinema Rex from his bedroom window, saw Roshi patronize the establishment twice more before Monday. He felt he had a tacit agreement with Renga to avoid discussing the events of Cinema Rex's opening night with Siva, but wasn't able to verify this when the school week began. Renga was absent, an absence that stretched into the rest of the week. On Thursday, their teacher (a slender Frenchman who refused to give top marks to any prose that wasn't as polished as Flaubert's) told the class that Renga's father had died.

"When?" asked Vik, forgetting to use any respectful niceties of address.

"The weekend. That is all I know, and all you should know. Renga will perhaps be back on Monday, and I expect you all to have written eight hundred words on de Maupassant's 'The Necklace' by then."

"Is it due on Monday for sure, or just whenever Renga gets back?" asked Siva.

After the news, Siva and Vik felt comfortable around each other for the first time that week, bonded by the invisible presence of tragedy. Vik was sure that Renga's father had choked to death in the back of the lorry later that Friday night, his throat filling with vomit. This fatal possibility was one of Devi's most frequently voiced fears, the genesis of the standing command that called for Vik to rotate his own father onto his side during the drunken naps that consistently laid the man on his back.

"How you think it happened?" Siva asked. "Shot? Maybe by robbers?" Vik nearly shared the vomit-aspiration theory, but decided to hold onto it.

"Don't know, but probably something a lot more boring. Heart attack, maybe."

"Still sad that way. Sadder, maybe. No story with it."

The lorry never returned to Vik's father's fleet, which seemed to confirm Vik's theory.[13] While Renga never returned to their lessons with Reynolds, he did eventually return to school. The three boys used their daily breaks to discuss the movies screening at the Rex, a routine that continued until the year that Siva convinced his mother to let him drop out of school and take up a job as a hospital porter.

---

13 At that concert in Camden, just after having bought a large blended scotch for an unappreciative and very-ugly-up-close David Gilmour, Renga confirmed Vik's theory. "Wanker guitarists everywhere favour the brand that strangled my dad, it seems."

Renga was soon to leave the school as well, accepting his early scholarship to the Royal College of Music. He ran into Vik at the Cinema Rex one week before his flight departed the island. Vik had taken to carrying a notepad into the movies with him, which he'd fill with scrawls legible only to himself as he went to see even the most trivial films three, four, five times. Renga was a repeat attendee as well because he had to watch any film at least twice before he could stop being distracted by the plot and could concentrate solely on the way the images aligned with the music. He explained this to Vik, who seemed slightly awed.[14]

---

14 At a retirement event, when he was asked what he thought his greatest contribution to film had been, Vik replied that it was the minor role he had played in installing Renga in Hollywood, twenty-five years earlier.

Renga had lopped off his unwieldy last name as soon as he started appearing in the credit sequences of Bollywood films, and it was as Renga that he was known to Vik's friends and colleagues. Vik pinpointed Renga's Hollywood launch as the first handshake between his friend and Bobby Gopal, who had been hailed as a new Satiyajit Ray in the international press and was utterly ignored in his native India. Renga was crashing in Vik's Westwood guest room, writing incidental music for daytime TV shows as he attempted to break into the real scoring game. "We're two bachelors in our forties," said Vik, after two months of this arrangement. "Living together. In California. And not even one of us has the dignity to be homosexual." When Renga had failed to laugh or return a comment, Vik realized something new about his oldest friend.

It may have been part of the reason that Bobby Gopal had established an immediate sympathy with Renga at the UCLA reception following Gopal's lecture on the hidden racial complexities of *Indiana Jones and the Temple of Doom*. The talk had been elaborate and fascinating, and became even more interesting when Gopal tossed his blank papers aside to declare that he'd improvised the whole thing and didn't believe a word of it. Still trim in his fifties, his physical grace shamed the spider-bodied

"And why do you watch these things so many times?" Renga asked.

"I sit in the different sections, see how the movie comes at me when I'm sitting with different people."

"Is it any different?"

"Sometimes."

"Seems like a waste of money, no?" Renga asked, smiling to dampen any potential sense of insult. Social gestures like this were important now; they were both a little older, he needed to practice politeness for Europe, and he'd grown to know Vik much less in the two years since his father's death and the opening of Cinema Rex.

"Waste? I get in for free."

Vik, whose bulging abdomen had put an end to the useful life of his favourite jeans earlier that year.

After the lecture, Gopal directed his answers to Vik's questions toward Renga, whose slender muscularity complemented the director's well-kept form. "My next one is going to be a gangster film about colonialism. Well, not about *colonialism*, per se, but you know, cultural rape." Renga asked if there was a composer attached to the project. Bobby replied with an interested "No," and Vik silently peeled himself away from the conversing men, returning to a conversation he'd engaged in earlier with a scarecrow-haired screenwriting professor whose dryer-mutilated sweater displayed more wrist than neck. Renga appeared at his side a few minutes later to request the car keys, so he could play a tape of his music for Bobby. When Vik walked toward his Camry at the end of the reception, he saw Renga and the new Satiyajit Ray kissing in the back seat. Vik called himself a taxi. When Bobby Gopal's *Mother of Slums* swept the Oscars two years later, Vik told his new wife, who had once been married to that wrist-flashing screenwriting professor, that he should have received some sort of producing credit for ushering Renga's Academy Award–winning score into existence, however indirectly.

Renga was about to reply that it seemed like a waste of time, at least, but he remembered his politeness. He said something else instead, and they talked about nothing in particular until the projector awakened and allowed them to be silent.

JAY BROWN

THE EGYPTIANS

t's a photograph of a famous snowstorm in 1974 when the city shut down and the world shrank to a single neighbourhood, and the shape of everything was soft and simple for three days.

It was taken in Windsor, from the concrete porch steps of the home where Clive grew up. The boxwood hedge is a column of white with its bare branch tips breaking through the snow like insectoidal cilia. Across Ray Street the bricks and glass of St. Bart's rise above the snow and out of frame. The hood of the car in the driveway is buried completely by roof-fall and serves as the top of a giant mound that slopes inwards toward the front of the house. The two bodies on the slope: Clive and Carl, both ten, in their parkas, hoods zipped to full power so that their faces are sunk back into furry tunnels clouded with breath. They are lying still, arms and legs straight, like King Tut's faithful guardian mummies.

Clive pulled it from the album earlier today, the fibres from its shedded matting were tufted on the back corners. He looked at it for several minutes, and pressed it between the pages of an *Architectural Digest* on his desk-side table with the letter from Carl folded around it.

Now, as Clive stands on a new brick path that follows the natural contours of Victoria's inner harbour, surrounding the Industry, Clive's development, he's got a million things on his mind but Carl's letter keeps surfacing like a toxic Old Faithful. The timing could not be worse. Clive does not need this right now. This afternoon, in two short hours in fact, the ribbon for The Industry will be cut. It's an actual ribbon – "ribbon cutting" is not metaphorical. The ribbon is green and will stretch between the two iron lampposts that frame The Industry's waterside promenade. There will be photographers. Clive's son will hand the brass scissors to Bob Naussman. His wife and daughter will join with the members of the ARC Development board and lead the first set of unit owners onto the unblemished blacktop of the walkway. Everybody will merge at the berm by the street entrance, where the sidewalk veers under an iron arch, for the unveiling of Jacob Klosterman's expensive soaring wire heron.

Everything has to be perfect. If the clouds over the Juan de Fuca Strait bring rain and there is consequent drizzle pooling in the subtle warp of The Industry's fresh asphalt pathways, even that will annoy him. Asshole crows clustering around the brushed steel Industry garbage bins along the promenade will annoy him.

Even the sight of his own son monkeying in his suit with the kayak stands, right goddamned now, when he could be thinking over what Clive has said about his simple role in today's pomp, is driving Clive's pulse through his body in what feels like cartoonish lumps in a hose.

And his daughter's arms are a nightmare of scabbed eczema that she's refused to cover up with the silk sweater he bought her, and has instead stuffed into her reeking canvas purse. That purse will go or so help him. Her long hair is dankly straight and parted by her ears so there's a visible swath of angry pink skin down to the neck of her T-shirt. She emanates a dissatisfaction that seems complete and irrevocable.

His wife, at least, is trying to pull Brandon out from his position behind the kayaks, to impress upon his skittering eight-year-old brain the importance of the occasion and the need, for just a little while, to speak like a regular human being and not forever regurgitate the same tired, shrill, yuk-yuks of his pull-string SpongeBob SquarePants doll. His wife, at least, is lending the occasion some appropriate gravity and decorum. This is millions of dollars. This is eight *years* of work. Everybody who counts will be here today. He's satisfied that she's working hard to make sure he's not embarrassed in front of the members of the ARC board and Bob Naussmann, the small-time Harper wannabe whose office stamp of municipal permission cost ARC hundreds of thousands in wheedling concessions and design changes. And he appreciates her very much. Though it's always hard to forget that there's something about the way she holds her mouth when she's talking to attractive men. That there's something about the way they lean into her ear and the way she gently brushes their hands away that goads him into long fantasies of certainty and revenge.

Things are precarious. Clive is already set to explode, like a solar system–consuming star just about to absorb the last of its fuel.

Goddamned fucking Carl Chellapinko, thinks Clive, I banish you from this world. I put you into the trunk of a rusty Pinto and have it compacted into a square of metal so tight and shiny it could be a piece of modern art.

Workers have been on hand for the last seventy-two hours doing touch-ups and checks at the direction of a hulking contractor who's rarely seen outside of his van. The event coordinator is on her cellphone, her laughter carries on the wind. Clive must shoulder everything himself. Everybody forgets their job the moment it's almost, but not quite, finished. Some union loafer has left a bucket of white paint by the kayak stands and Brandon's buffed Timberlands are just missing knocking it into the water as he swings around the bars. "We've been smackldorfed, Squidward!" says Brandon SquarePants. "And then I took a shit!" Because everything is funnier when you say that afterwards.

Goddamn it! Goddamn it, Brandon! says Clive to himself. Fiona, control him! Control control, Fiona. Just for today. So help me. – "Honey," he yells, "watch the paint there."

Looking around for a tradesman – "Can somebody do something about that paint?"

The letter from Carl came to Clive's office, return address some apartment building in Windsor. The Excelsior. It's neatly written and lucid, though strewn with scribbles in the margin – as though it is of two minds.

Dear Clive,
    We ran into each other after high school in the Mountain Mall once, remember? Right in front of

Japan Camera. You and Kathy Iverson had bags with new tennis things in them. You guys were sweethearts, I think. You were going to play together down at Lawnson Green. And you were late for the time she'd chalked you down for. Remember now? You said to give you a call sometime.

Well, sorry for taking so long to get back to you. Ha ha. More than twenty years maybe, eh?

You know, this letter, the idea to write this letter, came to me about a month ago when I was riding my bike behind a guy and we were both stopped at a red light on the street. (I don't have a car.) He turns to me and – so what's up with what happened last night – he says – what's up with all of that dancing you were doing – never seen you like that and all. And I was thinking, you know, what? to myself, and said to him – sorry? And he was laughing and said to me – "getting on a bit to be so deep in the sauce" – and then he narrowed his eyes and pushed up his helmet and said – I thought you were a friend of mine. I thought you were somebody else who's always riding behind me on the way to work.

That little bit of talk was pretty much all I'd had in almost four months. Proper talk, anyway. I felt bad thinking of it like that, especially since it was an accident and all. It made me think, you know, what kind of person does that make me?

Which is to say what? We haven't spoken in so long, but god you were easy to find. Your name and so much about you is all over the internet. You've really made something of yourself and you must be a busy person.

I haven't had the same kind of success, but I don't begrudge you yours.

I've been thinking of Nelson Derrick and that snow-storm when we were kids. I think it's time to

Naked, Clive fills a room like a football tackle pad. He's smooth and a bit rubbery like Stretch Armstrong left in the sun. Swathed in his navy overcoat with a tufting cravat and fresh black crew cut, Fiona's told him he could be a doorman at a strip club. Just waiting for someone to give him a little lip. He likes to wear leather gloves even in warm weather. He likes the bulge and their slight creak of give when he makes fists in the air.

The Industry is the last parcel of riverside development on the grounds of the old Jenn Cola bottling factory all owned now by ARC, the company Clive started from scratch. Every Industry unit is two narrow floors. The centrepiece bay window is triple-glazed, framed by steel inset cedar planks with prominent ingot work around the corners. The floors are polished mocha concrete, intentionally distressed then resined. Starting at $375,000 you can have your oatmeal in view of the waterway and the metal recycling plant on the other bank only 150 feet away. It's not a terrible ugly view. It's a wonderful show. The jaws of the crane plummet into a pile of steel and rise, drooling bumpers and rebar, furry with metal around the mouth. It drops the steel into a crusher while all day long, six days a week, trucks arrive through the chain link bringing garbage, hauling away giant wrinkled cubes of faded wreckage.

It's a stroke of genius. That's what it is. What's objectionable becomes the attraction itself. Part of The Industry's appeal is: *the industry*. The way the angle of the promenade – a wooden dock with a slanted stainless steel roof and faux girder columns – points directly across the water was Clive's idea. A separate sister dock, slender and inviting, is anchored by two sunken posts and the tip of it, holding the kayak stands, floats on clean white pontoons right on the water. It's the stairs to the theatre. The front row to the show. Clive feels great ownership. Anything is beautiful framed by glass and steel and concrete. It's all about the frame, he keeps telling himself.

Though. Every weekend for the last month a watchman has had to sit nights on the water because some young scumbag keeps tagging the great curve of lacquered spruce that supports the stainless steel roof. "SeXriTe" or some such bullshit. And there are seventeen more units that need to sell before a dime of profit can be realized – and the Americans stopped buying, stopped even looking, over two years ago. And there's the columnist from the basically communist local weekly who's making whatever stink he can about the statistics on a soil sample taken from the neighbouring lot almost twenty years ago. Twenty years ago Jenn Cola was a toppled factory, a condemned ruin that people drove up to in the night to dump their old refrigerators. It was a rat paradise and an eyesore and ARC took it off the city's hands, removed everything, including the first six feet of earth, and buried the ugly past in new exotic materials that rise now like the realized dream it is, so handsomely in the brown, green, and red tones of the designer's selected Scandinavian theme.

So handsome and yet there were some who had the audacity to complain, to suggest that the polluted rubble of some forgotten industry was preferable in some demented sense to this. Who waited until thirty million dollars of investment had already been sunk into equipment rentals, materials securing, labour – waited for that moment to convene the "town hall" and to raise their concerns about heritage and safety with the ARC board in attendance. Dear people, Clive wanted to say, have you never seen the clawed bucket of a giant backhoe break through a crust of ancient cement and not felt some inner sigh of relief? Will you forever save the broken thing just because it reminds you of some imagined rosy, honest past? You life-ruining, bead-curtain-hanging potheads. You foot-dragging crybabies. You lead-fucking-buckets. I do what I can to make this life more ergonomic and pleasing. Jenn Cola is gone, but the world is still full of abandoned wooden warehouses filled with broken glass and stained with industrial lubricant. Go and see them. Enjoy. Let me get your bus fare.

Dear Carl, he'd write. Dear Carl. I often think of you and wonder how you're getting along in the world. I see you're still in Windsor. How are your mother and Stephen? I seem to recall something about a hip problem for her. She tripped and fell in front of Lazenby's, right? You see? I've kept track a little myself. I hope you sued them for the lifetime of trouble that a hip operation can be. Believe me. I've got problems all over this body of mine and your mom's got years on me! I don't mean to impose, but could you use a little money? If so, how much? I'm enclosing a cheque for five hundred dollars. I've done well for myself. I hope this is not presumptuous.

or:

Dear Carl, Any good student of biology knows that we're rebuilt every seven years in every cell of the body. You must have run up against a little biology at some point in your life, I suppose? So think of it just like a building whose boards and mortar and tile are replaced slowly but completely. Since the events you speak of we've been renewed, made over, in every cell of our bodies almost five times: can it even be said that we're the same people at all?

or:

Dear Carl, Fuck off.

The first of the attendees are arriving. Unit owners parking their Subarus and Volkswagens on a Superseal coated Industry lot. A woman is the first person to emerge from her car. She's got a light green scarf fashionably bundled around her black hair. She steps out of the open door and unfurls her long slim body. Her shoes gleam dully and the scarf catches the breeze and departs like a ghost of mist through the air. Not so fast that she can't catch it in three steps, but she looks great, really great. She's a taste of what Clive has hoped for. It could be a telecom commercial. If one was imaginative one might even hear the moan of some synthetic opera duet to complement the moment. The event coordinator appears stage right to welcome and guide them all into the Roccacio Juice and Latte Bar on the ground floor for a round of wheatgrass and white cacao and vanilla-foamed africanos, or whatever. There is no reason, thinks Clive, that today will not be a perfect day.

In 1974 Nelson Derrick lived, or slept anyway, at the mercy of St. Bart's in a tiny annex of the church once used for storing gym mats. It had its own door to the outside that opened onto an alleyway that's just outside the frame of the photograph Clive looked at this morning while stirring, stirring, stirring his Metamucil into a cold glass of apple cider. The alleyway ran behind backyards from Ray Street through to Locke where the Salvation Army sat in a small brown building on the corner. Nelson Derrick wore flowered bell-bottomed blue jeans that he would have been too old to wear even during the summer of love. A denim jacket and sole-thwacking sneakers completed the year-round wardrobe. In the winter, he had a giant swaying brown bag of a coat given to him by someone at the church. He had gorgeous long hair, like a woman's, and he kept it clean and silky and he never drank or smoked but only lugged his faithful duffle bag through the alley up to the Salvation Army where he spent his days largely in silence, reading every last word of yesterday's newspapers by the side doors to the soup kitchen.

He had a halting half-lidded shyness about him and said things along the lines of "Uhuh. Oh, uhuh. Now, well. My," if you asked him something specific, like: "Hey Nelson, what's in the bag, man?" None of that "wisdom of the downtrodden" for Nelson. There were Derricks at Clive and Carl's school but they disavowed any connection. Clive's grandfather seemed to remember something about pop bottles for a bus ticket to Halifax, but as far as Clive and Carl were concerned Nelson had been living in the gym-pad cupboard forever. They don't make bums like Nelson Derrick anymore. He was of those days when young children walked themselves to school through back alleys and large parks, and after supper were asked only to be home before the streetlights came on. His shambling hobo-hippy self, blond and blown, burdened and slow, was at one with the neighbourhood and nobody gave him a second thought.

The thing that Carl has written about in the letter – the thing that had Clive digging through the photo albums this morning – happened in a storm sewer that could be accessed by prying open a manhole cover at the halfway mark between Ray and Locke in the alley behind the church. That they could open this secret door at all was a trick they'd discovered the summer before when Carl had taken a piece of fence pipe and wedged it diagonally into one of the holes in the iron. The two of them bouncing on the lever until it magically came lip up with a satisfying scrape onto the crumbling asphalt.

There was a dainty metal ladder that disappeared into the blackness and a smell that steamed up as though every rotten head cheese and kielbasa in the city had been dumped at this one spot. Dropped down fifteen feet, the inside was dark like a cave and dripped and echoed – a low tunnel with a slimy pebbled, plastic-garbaged trench in the middle, concrete, brick, and mud seeping through the cracks.

They found the body of a dead raccoon twenty feet from the manhole entrance in near complete and stinking darkness. The animal's skin was in such a state of desiccation that a stick could be pushed through it with little effort. Creeping further and further into the blackness with the ebb and flow of droning Locke Street traffic like sucking giant's breath never failed to titillate. The still and foul tunnel seemed to somehow represent a truer, or at least more possess-able, world for little boys. It was as though they'd discovered the location for the private thoughts of the city where secrets were stored that, while hidden, were nonetheless imminent, dark, and poisoning.

When the snow began to fall it was early on a Thursday morning, and there was no wind at first so that giant flakes fell in lacy columns from the sky and patted hugely on faces and hands at recess and continued to accumulate on top of the grass yard at Borden Elementary. It was almost knee high after school with no sign of letting up. The talk was of a coming snow day and the feeling of melt soaking through Clive's and Carl's pants on the trudge home was the feeling of wild freedom. Clive celebrated by slam-dunking Carl into a mound of snow by the tire swings. "I yam what I yam!" he yelled. "And I'll be swimmin with bare naked women!" Carl yelled back.

The alley was already drifted steeply on its northern side and only just traversable on the opposite edge, even then there being some necessity to hand-over-hand it along the top boards of the occasional fence. There was a smooth bowl at the halfway point where the rising heat seeping upward through the manhole had resisted the storm somewhat and Carl had the idea to jimmy it open now before continuing home so that they would be able to find and enter it the next day.

Carl slept over on the floor of Clive's room that night. They ate their macaroni in the back section of Clive's room in which a huge blanket with a spaceman motif had been hung to create a fort for Clive's monster models. It was a childish thing but it was okay for Carl to see it since Carl had helped him build it. They consulted Clive's book of *Ancient Egyptian Mysteries* and talked themselves into a frenzy of fear, imagining the "dead eyes of the boy king held open in his golden sarcophagus" and the beating hearts of bald and beaded slaves sacrificed up for devouring by a god with a head like a collie. They felt the mysterious kingdom, its secret knowledge and power, stretch its sinewy arm across forever and scoop them up into its confidence.

The photograph was taken the next morning when the snow had stopped and the radio had confirmed the school closing. Everybody in the city just waited it out, relieved and happy. They were Egyptians all morning, that morning. Egyptian 1 and his sidekick, Egyptian 2. And in the afternoon they adventured up the alley in search of passage to the mummy underworld. The yawning opening, its shucked lid just a slender new moon of metal peeking out from under the white, was surrounded on all sides by deep snow that had to be bodily ploughed through in their parkas.

And what it was, the thing that Carl raised in his letter after such a long time removed, was that Nelson Derrick had obviously come home the previous afternoon. And he'd obviously not seen or hadn't had the wherewithal in the first place to simply watch his footing in the deep snow. Hadn't thought, couldn't think. And Nelson Derrick lying there, broken, blond hair clumped and twisted, at the bottom of the ladder and his duffle bag snagged and torn on one tip of it and thousands and thousands of old lottery tickets spilled out around the rim of the manhole and plastered with wet to everything.

And it was like nothing to push it all safely into the sewer, where it belonged and dig free and slide the cover closed and simply leave and wait until the snow had melted away in the sun and washed down through the intakes along the streets. That long and still like nothing. And wait even for the spring to disappear the winter, and the small mystery of Nelson Derrick, all together with new greenness before Carl took a flashlight and shone it down through one piercing in the manhole while Clive put his eye to another. A hint of grey and echo and then the first taste of a whole and unexpected universe of experience, the flip side to everything exposed, its horror spun face up, its pleasure spun face down. And the possibility of ruin.

Dear Carl, I haven't given a thought to Nelson Derrick in many, many years. Not to say that I didn't feel regret, etc., during the odd moment in the shower all through high school and even leading into my early years at university. But I've got so many things on my plate now – as you likely know, since I can see from your letter that you've done your homework for Clive 101. The past is behind us, Carl. For a long time now it's been my philosophy to blinker out the noise, focus on what's in front of me, and let what's moved beyond take care of itself. It doesn't concern us anymore. There's a new world being forged and we have to chew through the old one to get it. We don't dwell on the old. We process its parts into something new. See things my way, I guarantee you'll feel better.

Clive's watch says 1:34. Minutes, minutes. He works a seed from this morning's muesli loose from between two molars and crushes it between his teeth. A slight bitterness. Brandon has climbed onto the very top of the kayak stands and Fiona has given up or is just beguiled by the play of light on the moving water. His watch says 1:34. The moment was soon or the moment could be now. No one has yet bothered to remove the paint can. It's as if life is a constant rehearsal for some people, and never the real thing. He himself is ready where he should be. A large silhouette against the sparkles.

"Go get them, will you?" Clive motions his daughter down the dock with a sweep of his arms. She looks at him like he's an infomercial for denture cream. There are people watching. The cameras are trained on the ribbon stretched and waiting. Bob Nausmann's hypocritical Smart car is turning the corner and about to come right into the complex. They'll be five minutes gathering and making their way to the rise and down to the water. He remembers to take off his gloves.

With considerable management of the pounding pumps and pistons inside of him, he clops down the grated aluminium toward the pontoons and the water to settle things himself. A photograph seems so real. It begs to be taken seriously. But it's just a trick of emulsion, of chemicals and human perception. There is no such repository for the moment.

"Brandon – Brandon – do you remember what you're going to say to . . . look at me . . . Please. Do you remember . . . ! Fiona? Can you do something to help? Can you turn the fuck around and please drag him to the ribbon where everybody is now on their way?"

Fiona sucks in a whisper and comes to from some minor reverie. "Brandon, listen to your daddy."

"I thought you were going to be on my side today," says Clive. "I am starting to feel so disappointed."

"Do you think it matters to anyone but you who gives Bob the scissors?" says Fiona.

"Come down here, Brandon." Clive stomps the dock and the reverberation travels through the wood and plastic and ripples out into the waterway.

The members of the board are coming. The event co-ordinator is talking to the woman with the green scarf. Bob Naussman is smoking a cigarette by a brushed-steel bin. There's nothing wrong. They can all meet at the lampposts. They can rise up to meet everyone, like a family that's just been having fun, that's just been looking for the shadows of playful fish around the slime-free moorings that anchor the dock to the sea bed.

Clive steps back from rack and the opens his arms. "Come on, Brandon, jump down. I'll catch you. It's fun." He smiles up at his son, imagining the way the two of them might look from above against the water's sparkle and flash. A strong father and his gleeful son, relaxed enough to forget themselves and play on such an important day.

"Who's your Baghdaddy!" says Brandon and leaps with a mid-air back-kick flourish of total trust.

The two of them fall after the paint can into the water. The paint rises to the surface in swirling Tremclad Cotton globs as Clive loses Brandon in a blast of cold against his chest and his heavy overcoat turns him round and up and round and up in a current whose strength he'd never imagined staring down into the water from the promenade. The surface is mirrored above and there's a vague sense of his own self, a flash of shape, some colour, reflected on the dull tin of it. The undersides of the white pontoons, a set of almost two-dimensional ovals, are all that remains of the ceiling world. All around him there's a soft sound like muffled pan pipes.

Brandon is a writhing tangle above him and his panicked boot catches Clive in the face, spinning him downward and deeper. His clothes offset the natural buoyancy of his body and he sinks then floats underwater like a sleeping humpback whale. The bottom of the waterway is shot through with veins of astonishing blue that disappear into the gloom of the deeper coursing. Hundreds, thousands of worn Jenn Cola bottles are crusted to the seaweed with tiny armoured life. The bottles are broken, scrubbed soft and porous but also lucent and unsullied. Clive floats. And before he breaks the surface directly in view of his first, most precious unit buyers, before he lugs his wailing child up the finger of the dock toward the crowded landing full of everything groomed and polished and loaded, before he himself sullies the viewing platform at the head of the promenade with diluted drips of white paint draining in a circle around him from his eight-hundred-pound coat, Clive feels the current tug at his boot heels and struggle to release him deeper, set him drifting toward the shapes of things further away – fish, garbage, fallen leaves – that flicker and glint in and out of perception as they race through the dim water, ceaselessly surrendered to the persistence of that flow out into Victoria's inner harbour, out beyond the breakwater which stills the waves for the cruise ships in dock, before finally disappearing into the appetite of the pounding ocean.

DORETTA LAU

HOW DOES A SINGLE BLADE OF GRASS THANK THE SUN?

My dragoons and I were gathered to discuss our plans for neighbourhood domination. Yellow Peril, the Chairman, Suzie Wrong, Riceboy, and I, the Sick Man of Asia, converged every Friday night to chop suey like a group of triad bosses. Chingers, all of us. Slanty-eyed teenage disappointments with no better place to haunt but the schoolyard near the abode of my *ma ma* and *ba ba*.

Tags covered the walls of our institution of mediocre learning. Every overzealous territory marker in the area had hit the walls like vicious dogs, making it difficult to discern that the school had once been grey. The poor spelling that appeared in most of the graffiti was evidence of the region's subpar education system; the choice was not a self-aware homage to hip hop influences. To one-up all the noddies and ain't-gonna-everbees, last winter the Chairman had stencilled OBEY MAO on the basketball court blacktop. He even included an image based on the portrait of Mao at Tiananmen Square, but the only thing that looked right in the Chairman's version was

Mao's giant mole, located on his chin. Some of the neighbour-hood children thought the tag said OBEY YAO; they had a rather limited knowledge of history, no respect for our people's illustrious past.

The Chairman and I had a re-education program for the neighbourhood youths, which consisted primarily of lectures and rigorous beatings. We enjoyed thrashing sense into the ignorant youngsters. The Chairman elected to go the Bruce Lee way of the empty hand, while I preferred the traditional tools of corporal punishment. Nothing pleased me more than placing a dunce cap on an eight-year-old simpleton's head while making jokes about dimwits and slow learners and applying the strap to tender hands. Riceboy took offence to this, which was why he refused to partake in the re-education scheme – he had been subjected to ESL classes during elementary school despite his fluency in the language of the colonizer.

Anyhow, the stupider the children were, the harder we would hit them. The Chairman and I made the little noddies stand in urine-stained corners, holding their ears, while we unleashed our fury upon them. No mercy for the retards, either. The Chairman didn't stand for any PC bullshit. "We're equal opportunity," he once said, while smacking a child whose IQ was reported to be in the low seventies. "Retards are kids too. Why should we make them feel lesser than their fellow nose-picking classmates? They should be included in all the reindeer games. As you know, I'm anti-exclusionary policy."

My own mantra while administering lashings with the feather duster was, "I'm doing this for you, not for me." This was my *ma ma*'s favourite phrase, and she was a wise woman. Anything good enough for me was good enough for that lot of simpletons and punks. From time to time I considered asking my *ma ma* to etch those very words on my back so I could have my own version of the story of *Yueh Fei*, one of my favourite heroes of Chinese history. I imagined that, like him, I was on a mission to save my country.

On this particular Friday night, we were gathered without an agenda. The previous week we had screened *Hero* and *The Emperor and the Assassin*, much to the delight of the Chairman, who believed in the first emperor's concept of *tian xia*. On this point he and Yellow Peril differed. Peril's family was Taiwanese and she believed with occidental-eyed earnestness that someday Taiwan would "liberate China from Communism."

At the end of that evening, Riceboy and I had to physically restrain Peril – she was ready to get all assassin on the Chairman. I have to say, touching her arm got my heart beating all allegro-like, but I wasn't ready to act on those feelings.

This week, a showdown between me and Riceboy was playing out. Riceboy was getting ready to chop friend because I had said that Johnnie To had surpassed John Woo as an action director.

"You have to admit that John Woo has the most *ging* shoot-outs," Riceboy said, adjusting the giant gold chain around his neck.

"I'm not dismissing Woo," I said. "I often dream of the day he remakes *Le Cercle Rouge* with Tony Leung Chiu-wai as the Alain Delon character and Fatty Chow as the alcoholic marksman. It's just that –"

"Are you *still* trying to get the whole Fatty Chow thing to catch on?" Suzie asked. "Chow Yun-Fat is famous in the West now. People know who he is. He's been in a zillion Hollywood films."

"The *A Better Tomorrow* years are still upon me," I said in my defence, even though I could sense that the Chairman was growing bored of our conversation. He considered the Cantonese cinema a bourgeois diversion and refused to acknowledge its existence.

"*The Bulletproof Monk* years, more like it," Riceboy scoffed.

Suzie Wrong started girl-talking with Yellow Peril separate from the group. I thought I heard my name, so I leaned in a fraction, but they were speaking at such a low decibel that I could not eavesdrop. I wanted to agitate Suzie Wrong, all ninety pounds of her. I wanted to cause something of a scene so that Yellow Peril would engage with me, even if only to defend Suzie. So, for lack of Einstein conversation, I started water-torturing Riceboy on his *nom de guerre*.

"Why'd you choose such a dickless name?" I said, spitting on the ground with gusto, just like I'd seen those coolie-types and fresh-off-the-boats do in Middle Kingdom Town. I was practising to be the best possible Chinaman I could be, embracing the vices as well as the virtues with equal dedication.

"The Sick Man of Asia? How's that any better?" Riceboy hiked up his giant pants, which were riding so low they would have revealed his boxer shorts, except he was wearing a T-shirt that nearly reached his knees. He was taller than me and had a twenty-five-pound advantage, but his style choices were a definite handicap in a fight.

"It's a reclamation," I said. "I've taken the slang of the West and altered the meaning for my own usage, thereby exercising a certain mastery over the language of the colonizer. So I ask again, why'd you choose such a dickless name?"

"Chigga, what?" Riceboy raised his fists at me.

"Why do you have to emasculate him?" demanded Suzie Wrong. Apparently she had been listening to us the whole time, despite her side conversation with Peril. 'You say dickless as if it were an insult."

It took the kind of willpower it takes to wake up every morning before dawn to tend a rice field to keep from smiling. I had her attention, which meant I had Yellow Peril's as well. My heart beat faster, as if I'd won a giant stuffed animal doing something manly at the carnival.

"Yeah, Sick. I don't feel the lack," Yellow Peril chimed in, thrusting her pelvis forward. I noticed that she was wearing a very fetching pair of knee-high boots. I wanted to get up in her lack, so I feigned interest in her words. I nodded.

The Chairman looked at me slantways. Even in his pyjama-like costume he stank of authority. I tolerated his propaganda mongering because he meant well. Our views on the Motherland differed, but we lived in Lotus Land, so that was the tit we had to suck on. No use in raging over petty details and ideologies, especially since the Chairman believed that Riceboy and I were colonized dogs who were resistant to the Chinese voice of reason. The Chairman always had the advantage – his family was from the Mainland, while my family, as well as Riceboy's, hailed from Hong Kong.

"The name fits with the nomenclature, comrade," the Chairman said.

Finally, Riceboy spoke. He opted to unleash his flawless Cantonese. *"I hope your sons are born without asses."* The ultimate curse.

I spat on the ground and held back a sigh. Yes, I had insulted his manhood, even though I knew from experience how difficult it was to be a yellow man in the new world. I should have known better. Yet, I resented his words – I had insulted him as an individual while he had insulted my family to be. But instead of confronting him, I opted to redirect the evening.

"*Silencio*," I said. "Order, order, and all that. What is our business this fine spring night?"

"Chaos and destruction," said Yellow Peril. The way she said it made me worship her all the more. I started imagining what she looked like naked. I wondered if she had freckles on her tits, or if she had funny tan lines from her bikini.

"Excellent," I said, snapping out of my daydream. "What to destroy, now that is the question."

"No pillaging," insisted Riceboy, tugging on the waistband of his jeans.

"That's something I can't guarantee, Liceboy," I said, cooliefying my English, still a little sore that he'd cursed my unborn children.

Last week, to divert attention away from the feud between Peril and the Chairman, I had suggested we trespass upon the Riceboy family laundry. I thought we could smash a couple of stereotypes in the process. Riceboy did not find this funny in the least. He told me that my ideas were stupid. *Ideas*. As in, all of them, not just this particular one. Yeah, he was sore about the whole thing, so sore that he had become a festering week-old wound.

The laundry business had existed for three generations. It had history, the kind that inspires Lotus Land novelists to fill reams of paper with stories featuring multigenerational conflict and politically correct resolution. Riceboy's parents thought that he would take over once he completed an MBA.

One thing about him that I envied: his clothes always looked clean and neatly pressed, even if they were a bit roomy.

The Chairman sensed tension between us and decreed, "Let's make like SARS and spread."

So we got in Riceboy's rice rocket – a vehicle recognizable at a hundred paces because of its magnificent spoiler and dozens of anime figurines populating the ledge next to the rear window – and he rickshawed us through the wet Lotus Land streets.

"Let's go to Middle Kingdom Town," Suzie suggested.

Riceboy floored it. He was excellent behind the wheel, a regular Tokyo-drifting god, which was why I had appointed him our official driver months earlier. Also, he was the only one of us who didn't have to ask his parents permission to borrow the family car.

Ten minutes later, we arrived at our destination. Middle Kingdom Town was crowded, a real picture of humanity. There were the coolies, the FOBs, the Lotus Land-born, and the tourists. Oh, how I detested the tourists. They looked for authenticity in a place that could not provide it. Middle Kingdom Town could not stand in for the Motherland. My dragoons and I knew this well. But there were fools who thought that thousands of years of culture could be compressed into the poorest neighbourhood in the city.

As we walked down Pender, I noticed Scott Wilson, who is sick with yellow fever, standing next to hundreds of little toys. He was flirting with the girl selling them. I imagined he was complimenting her camel toe, saying, "Baby, I love how tight your jeans are. Let me give you herpes."

"Hey, three-inch egg roll boy!" he shouted when he saw me.

He grabbed his crotch and made a big production of insulting me. The beads in his Buddhist bracelet clattered. For a moment I thought he was going to whip out his penis and a measuring tape to prove his worth in inches. Lucky for all in the vicinity of Middle Kingdom Town, he kept his little boy in his pants.

Scott's hostility was deep-rooted. The situation was this: last month he asked Suzie Wrong out on a date. Well, he asked her for a lot more than that, but I'm a gentleman and not some gossip-mongering auntie hunched over a mah-jong table, so I'll stick to the date euphemism. Suzie had no interest ("Not even if I had AIDS and no one else wanted to touch my sick ass," she confided to me later) and told him as politely as she could, no. Then he said, "It's in your Asian genes to be a whore or mail-order bride or work at a massage parlour." "You forgot about nail-salon technician," she deadpanned, not losing her cool for a moment. Scott nodded, thinking that he had scored points with Suzie. He was the biggest simpleton that we knew, dimmer than poor Edward Yip, who had suffered some raging fever as an infant and processed thoughts at the pace of a dial-up internet connection.

When I heard about this incident, I threatened to de-man Scotty boy and make a Rice Queen out of him. I told him that he was cruising for a Bobbitting. This took him a day to decipher because he didn't have any older sisters who remembered with filtered-water clarity the current events of the nineties. When he finally figured out what I'd meant, after some sleuthing on the internets, he chose to put a brick through the windshield of Riceboy's rice rocket with a note attached that said YOUR CHINK ASS IS SO DEAD. "Sorry, Riceboy," I said when I saw the damage. "I guess we all look same."

"Hey, villain," I said to Scott, ignoring the insult to my manhood. "Confucius say *diu lei lo mo*."

Scott looked confused. No amount of studying Suzie Wrong's ass could prepare him for non-English insults. None of the other Chingers liked him, so he didn't know the choice swears of any dialect.

"Whatever, egg roll boy," he muttered, unable to produce a fresh insult. "*Ching chong ching chong*, motherfucker." The expression on his face was comical. He seemed confused and afraid and violent and entitled all at once. His mouth was agape. The girl at the toy stand shot me an amused glance. She knew the mother tongue. My dragoons whooped. Victory! We sauntered past, and stepped into the Noodle Shop.

Once inside, we got our own table. No sharing for us since we were five. The waitress came up to us and said, "What do you want?" No "hello." No "how are you tonight?" This was how things were done in Middle Kingdom Town. The masochist in me enjoyed this treatment very much. Plus, we could get away with tipping far less than fifteen per cent.

I ordered a red bean ice and fried egg sandwich, Suzie had a half-and-half and dumplings, Peril wanted fish balls and noodles, the Chairman refused to eat in public, and Riceboy, well, he had fried rice and a Diet Coke.

"What's wrong with sugar?" I asked.

"Chigga, what?" Riceboy glowered at me.

"You heard me. What's wrong with sugar?" I hit his can of Diet Coke with a pair of chopsticks.

"Why you have to be that way, son?"

"Your chigga accent does us no favours," I said. "Why do you have to appropriate another culture when you speak? We have our own trials and tribulations to draw from. We don't have to pilfer the pain of others in order to achieve some kind of authenticity."

The food arrived, ending the conversation.

I was hard on Riceboy because I loved him like the brother I didn't have – I had two older sisters. My parents tried very hard to have me, precious son, keeper of the family name. Or so they said, but they seemed rather disinterested in me. It was as if they had exhausted their all-star parenting skills on my sisters. One was a doctor and the other a lawyer. Suffice to say, they were prime specimens, a credit, as it were, to the race. That's what our neighbour said last year. She's ninety, so instead of leaving a bag of burning dogshit on her front porch, I forgave her for being an ignoramus.

I looked around the table. Yellow Peril was slurping up her noodles with gusto. Riceboy was shovelling rice into his mouth like a champion competitive eater, while Suzie Wrong took big gulps of her drink. The Chairman looked on as if he was posing for a painting. I was poking at the red beans in my glass. We had so much potential, but sometimes it seemed as if we would amount to nothing. It was clear – my dragoons and I needed a little structure in our lives. We needed to achieve a goal.

"We must do something tonight," I said. "We need an activity."

"Cat burglary!' Yellow Peril suggested.

"Revolution," the Chairman said.

"What we need, dear friends, is a heist," I said.

"What about the mural?" asked Yellow Peril. There was a mural down by one of the beaches that we wanted to paint over. We talked about doing this at least once a month. The mural depicted the joys of colonial life, roughing it in the wilderness, and the triumph of the settlers over the natives. We wanted to remove the near-naked depictions of First Nations people (the region was far too cold for the skimpy traditional costumes pictured, of this I was almost sure) and paint moustaches on all the settlers.

"We don't have any paint," I said.

"There's a ton of leftover paint at my house," Suzie said. "My parents just painted the kitchen. There should be enough left for our purposes."

"Excellent," I said.

We paid the bill, leaving a ten per cent tip, and walked out onto the sidewalk. The air was cool and smelled clean, like rain. It was a perfect Lotus Land night.

We got in the rice rocket and sped toward Suzie's house. The thing about Suzie is that her surname is Wong, but her first name isn't really Suzie. Her parents are not so lacking in English skills or understanding of Western popular culture to give her the same name as a fictional hooker.

When we reached the Wong residence, I gave out a series of commands. "Suzie, show Riceboy and the Chairman where the paint is. They'll carry it back."

The three left the car. My plan had worked. I was alone with Yellow Peril.

"So, Peril, did you just get your hair cut?" I asked, brushing a lock of hair away from her face. I knew the answer, because I had overheard Peril telling Suzie all about her genius Japanese stylist.

"Yesterday," she said, touching her hair. I noticed that she had on a bright red lip gloss that made her mouth look like a delicious hard candy.

"You look fetching," I said. I was all ready to move in for the kill, to lean in and kiss her shellacked shiny lips, when Riceboy threw the door open.

"Am I interrupting something?" He smirked knowingly, and slid into the driver's seat. He let a big fart rip and it had the unfortunate characteristics of being both loud and stinky.

I sighed. Peril opened the door to get some air. I really had to mend my relationship with Riceboy, or he would go around festering and foiling all my plans. If I didn't do anything, he would continue on like this, acting as if he was just goofing things up by mistake, all the while pulling up his pants. There would always be an edge of malice in all his dealings with me if I didn't apologize in some way.

After the Chairman loaded the cans of paint and the rollers, pans, and brushes into the trunk, we headed to the beach.

Riceboy shredded the scenic route, motoring down narrow streets that had a view of the ocean and the mountains. I peered at my friends again, examined their faces and slouched postures. These were my dragoons. In the moonlight they looked like the kind of people to whom the poets of yesteryear would dedicate verse.

Riceboy halted the car. We had arrived. We were ready to launch.

I got out, popped the trunk, and put a drop cloth over the back licence plate. I'd eyeballed enough movies to be an expert on side-stepping issues with the law. Riceboy draped his oversized coat over the front plate. The Chairman marched the cans of paint over to the mural, and Peril and Suzie gathered the remaining supplies.

We approached the mural with the fanfare of a winning army, whooping and menacing our way down the path. The mural had a sinister vibe. Under the streetlight, the settlers appeared to have leers upon their faces. They looked like zombies or cannibals or vampires or some type of unknown monster that fed on the flesh of humans.

"It's really in need of a touch up," Suzie said.

Everyone nodded in agreement.

The Chairman filled a pan with paint, then another. Peril handed me a roller. Riceboy and Suzie grabbed the brushes. We were not jibber-jabbering, but somehow we had all sidled up to the same conclusion: we were going to paint over the entire mural.

We laboured like the Chingers that we were, and, in less than an hour, the task was finito.

"That summer you spent slaving for that painting company was worth it," I said to Riceboy. "This is an example of fine craftsmanship." Despite all that had transpired that night, the corners of my mouth pulled up – a smile. Riceboy's face held the same expression. I imagined that this was forgiveness, or something like it.

Peril was next to me, an opportunity. I got up in her personal space and seized her hand. Her hair smelled like a field of wild flowers, and I was a bee wanting to gather her pollen. She didn't treat me like a leper. Instead, she held my hand like it was a giant wad of cash she was afraid to drop.

The wall was now beige, slick like the Wongs' kitchen. There was no evidence that there had once been a mural. My dragoons and I gazed at the blank slate before us. Light drizzle began to fall, but we continued to stand at attention. Though it's said that the Great Wall of China is the only man-made thing visible from space, at that moment it felt as if anyone looking down upon the Earth would have seen that expanse of beige wall, and us, sleeping giants shaking off a long slumber, presiding over it.

ZOEY LEIGH PETERSON

SLEEP WORLD

Forty-seven minutes is a long time to wait in a mattress store when you don't need a mattress. For the first couple of laps, the salespeople kindly ignore Kathryn. She has explained that she is waiting for someone. It's early on a Tuesday morning, and the salespeople are still handing each other cups of coffee and debriefing on last night's television.

Kathryn wanders the store, trying to look purposeful. She studies each mattress in turn. She contemplates their regal names. She peers into a small cutaway section of mattress with its isolated springs pressed up against the Plexiglas. They look battered and desperate, like the animals in the brochures that still come to the house.

Eventually, one of the young salesmen is sent over to check on her. Kathryn affirms, again, that she is waiting for a friend, that it is the friend who needs a mattress, and that she herself is entirely content with her current mattress, though this is not strictly true. Her own bed is sagging and problematic, but Chris likes it.

The young salesman returns to the pack with this information. They keep talking amongst themselves about this show and that show, but Kathryn can feel them watching her with suspicion. She tries to imagine what they might suspect. That she is going to sneak out of the store with a queen-size box-spring in her bag? That she is going to slit the long, soft belly of a mattress and hide evidence inside? That she is going to move into their showroom with several temperamental cats and set up camp? What is their worst-case scenario?

Now that Sharon owns a car, she is late to everything. The car was part of a story that began with Sharon not having a baby and ended with her and Kyle moving to a condo with cream carpets.

On paper, their new place is not even that far away. A forty-minute ride from Chris and Kathryn's – thirty if you really pedal. Kathryn and Sharon had routinely cycled twice that distance when they were in grad school together, but the miles feel somehow longer in this new direction. Bike paths end unceremoniously in the middle of the block, spitting you out onto noisy highways. The cars move faster and seem angrier, and you arrive unhappier than you were when you left.

Back when Sharon and Kyle lived across the alley, the four of them would see each other almost every day. Sometimes to borrow a lemon or envelope or screwdriver, other times because the news was too terrible to watch alone.

Now though, they don't show up at each other's back door with a bottle of wine or half a birthday cake. They don't phone each other and say, We made too much pasta, do you guys want to come eat with us? Instead they say, What does week after next look like? They say, Can we do it at our place? They say, Hey I'm coming into town to look at mattresses, why don't you come along and we can catch up?

When Sharon arrives, much is forgiven. The salespeople are not suspicious of Sharon. They are charmed and intrigued by her princess-vs-pea dilemma – a series of fine beds that all felt perfect for the first hour, but then this nagging ache that would creep up her leg and into her spine. It's fun to watch Sharon do her thing. She is getting everyone on board, like they are her students. Kathryn feels lucky to be here with Sharon on a Tuesday morning while her work sits at home on the desk.

Here is what I propose, says Sharon to the gathered sales force. You guys pretend I'm not here and let me lie around in your beds all day like a weirdo. Then at the end of the day, I hand you my credit card and show you the bed you just sold me.

This amuses the salespeople and they bring out special paper booties and special pillows for different kinds of sleepers – side sleepers, stomach sleepers – and a secret notebook with all the pricing information and talking points. And so equipped, Sharon and Kathryn are set adrift in the sea of mattresses.

Okay, says Sharon once they are alone, let's get in bed and then I want to hear all about this Emily thing.

Kathryn had told Sharon about the Emily thing in an inadvertent phone call inspired by Neanderthals. She'd been on the couch watching a BBC program on Neanderthals, the last of a people, and she had suddenly felt so much love for Sharon, and so much longing, that she picked up the phone and dialled the number without thinking.

Sharon was half-watching the same show and paying some bills, and they talked about work for a while and how it must feel for an actor to be cast as a Neanderthal.

Then Sharon had asked what was up, and asked in such a way that Kathryn felt that something should be up. And so, to have something to say, Kathryn told her that Chris had a crush on some Emily from work – which is fine, people get crushes – but that he had invited this person to stay in their apartment while they were away for the long weekend, to house-sit, to sleep in their bed, and that that felt weird. This got Sharon's interest. They talked about it hotly for several minutes – Sharon being emphatic and scandalized in gratifying ways – until Sharon was so sorry, but she had to go to a strata meeting.

Now Sharon is going to want the whole story. Everything is a story now with Sharon. But Kathryn isn't sure what else to say. Chris hasn't mentioned Emily since that weekend. After bringing her up constantly in the weeks leading up to her stay, now he can't even be drawn into conversation about her. When Kathryn asks what Emily looks like or what colour her hair is, Chris can't say. All that Kathryn knows about Emily is what she left behind in their apartment: in the bathroom, a tin of lip balm with a sliding lid that is satisfying to open and close; in the recycling, a half-rinsed jar of some paste that makes the whole house smell velvety; in the bedroom, nothing, although both their clock radios were unplugged; and on the refrigerator, a three-page letter of thanks, politely addressed to both of them, but clearly written for Chris and filled with such candour and fellowship that it felt too intimate to read. Kathryn had read it twice. All this she has already told Sharon on the phone while the Neanderthals failed to adapt.

Kathryn considers now telling Sharon about the misspellings in the letter, not just Kathryn's name, but in almost every line. But she cannot think of a way to say this without feeling dirty. Finally, she resolves to say this: There is no story. There are just these feelings that come and go. Feelings without a beginning, middle, and end.

But by the time they are settled into a bed, they are already talking about sex.

Since buying the condo, Sharon and Kyle have been out of sync, sexually. Morning has always been their time. Truthfully, morning and night. But especially morning. These days, though, Kyle's brain wakes up making lists and doesn't remember it has a body until it's time to leave for work. Now Sharon has found a solution: oats before bed. Apparently, half a cup of Scottish uncut oats right before bed has Kyle waking up like his former self.

That's why I was late getting here, Sharon says. She doesn't actually wink.

Kathryn rolls onto her side and stares out over the empty mattresses. They're like ice floes. Can you steer an ice floe? Or do you just go where it takes you?

How did you figure that out, Kathryn asks. The oat thing.

Ann-Marie, from our building, she told me about it, says Sharon.

Kathryn has met this Ann-Marie, once, at Sharon and Kyle's housewarming. Ann-Marie was in the kitchen blending margaritas and warming tortillas in a cast-iron pan she'd brought from her place across the hall. Let me take that, said Ann-Marie, plucking a dirty plate from Kathryn's hand. This kitchen is exactly like mine, so I already know my way around, said Ann-Marie, though Kathryn could see the sink right there.

You should try it, says Sharon of the oats. This, Kathryn understands, is a reference to Chris, and Kathryn feels a vague urge to defend him.

Chris has what Kathryn calls a high cuddle drive. He kisses her awake every morning, he reaches out to touch her arm while they read the paper, he hugs her for whole minutes, which she loves. But sex, when it comes, comes in slippers. Still, over the years they have found a sort of equilibrium. And it's nice, the sex, when they have it.

This isn't working for me, says Sharon, rising from the bed. Too mooshy, she says.

They drift through the beds, Sharon pressing her palm firmly down into each mattress and holding it there, eyes closed, as if communing with the bed's essential nature. Kathryn looks at price tags. Some of the beds are so unaccountably expensive, that Kathryn – if it were up to her – wouldn't even pause in front of them, wouldn't give them the satisfaction.

Sharon is lingering over a four-thousand-dollar bed. She has slid her hand under the foam pad and is palpating the springs, dispassionately, like a doctor. She is in fact a middle school teacher.

Didn't they just buy a bed, Sharon and Kyle? (Kathryn remembers precisely: it was an engagement present to themselves.) Did they sell that bed? Where does four thousand dollars come from? How do you buy a condo, and then a bed, and then another bed?

There was a time when she might have asked Sharon these questions. Actually, there was a time she wouldn't have *had* to ask – the answers would have bubbled to the surface while they helped each other put away groceries or stood in line together to cash their student loans. When they were part of the slow unspooling of each other's lives.

Sharon has sunk herself into the four-thousand-dollar mattress. Kathryn is converting the price in her head. Four thousand dollars is her food for an entire year. It is the dental work Chris needs. It is x hours of copy-editing plus y hours of indexing, over the ten-year life of the bed, for a total of z hours per year. Kathryn climbs into the exquisite bed.

Sharon holds Kathryn's hand as they lie staring up at the acoustic panels.

This is the one, Sharon says. Her hand feels softer than it used to, and bigger, in a four-thousand-dollar bed.

Sharon used to be cheap. When they were students, when money was a thing, Sharon was flamboyantly frugal, a loud champion of all things scrounged or redeemed.

One time, Sharon and Kyle had shown up at their door late one evening, exultant, because the video store was throwing out old VHS tapes. Sharon had rescued *The Great Muppet Caper* from a cardboard box on the sidewalk, just as the rain was starting to fall.

Chris pulled the futon off the frame and onto the living-room floor, and the four of them sardined themselves under two overlapping blankets and watched and cheered and made amazing jokes, until Kathryn thought she might hyperventilate.

Later, exhausted by their own hilarity, they watched in silence, a blissful stupor washing over their bodies. And Kathryn loved these people, loved living on this futon island with them, and it was at this moment – as the movie rounded into the third act – that Kathryn began to think about the four of them falling asleep here in front of the TV, and the four of them waking up in the morning and making breakfast together and deciding what to do with their Sunday, the four of them. Kyle was already drifting off, soughing faintly between songs. And then Chris was asleep, furrowing and scrunching his sincere face. And then it was just Sharon and Kathryn holding hands and fading in and out as the tireless puppets saved the day. Then the credits were rolling and Sharon was squeezing her hand, then letting it go. She was reaching for Kyle's shoulder, rubbing him slowly awake.

You guys can stay, Kathryn had said. You should stay.

Sharon smiled, and kept rousing Kyle, who made a low, assenting rumble.

You should stay, Kathryn said again. It felt urgent.

But now Kyle was standing up, his eyes still closed, and Sharon was leading him to the door.

Thank you for a perfect night, Sharon said.

Kathryn locked the door behind them and stood there trying to reabsorb her feelings. She could hear Chris stirring in the other room. He was calling out to her – making an endearing joke that had threaded through the evening – and she was suddenly irritated and hot and a kind of angry that she could not name. She did not answer. She washed the dishes loudly and wrestled the futon back onto the frame and did not go to bed until Chris was surely asleep. And by the next day, Sharon and Kyle were engaged.

—

This, ladies, is as good as it gets. So says the salesman. The reigning king of beds, he says. He begins to enumerate the many features of this noble mattress. Kathryn can see the contents of his nostrils.

They have only been in this bed for half an hour, and Kathryn waits for Sharon to drive the salesman away, remind him of their deal. But Sharon does not drive him away. She encourages him. She calls him Gary, which is his name. She asks Gary how long the warranty is, she asks about coil count. They talk admiringly to each other about the bed while Kathryn stares into a halogen light. She is thinking again about that letter, magneted to her fridge.

And what do you think, the salesman asks Kathryn. Kathryn doesn't understand the question.

She's just keeping me company, Sharon says, letting go of Kathryn's hand. Sharon explains to the salesman that her boyfriend – fiancé actually – can sleep on anything and so bed-shopping with him is impossible because he dozes off on every bed they try.

The salesman makes a half-neutered observation about men and women and Sharon laughs. Sharon and the salesman begin to rehearse the differences between men and women.

But Chris would be here. If Kathryn had a pain in her leg, if Kathryn was unable to sleep at night, Chris would be here beside her, even if he was bored. But he wouldn't be bored. He would be engaged. He would make it into a game. He would make up life-stories for each mattress. He would tell her about their childhoods as beanbags, imbuing each bed with hopes and ambitions and tragic flaws that he and Kathryn might recognize and grow to love. And Kathryn would mostly listen, but would occasionally blurt out some bit of business that he would seamlessly integrate into the story.

And when the time came to decide, Chris would listen to her messy, rambling anxieties about where the bed was made, what the factory conditions were for the workers, and did she really need a new bed at all, and didn't most of the world sleep on mats not half as comfortable as the bed they already had. And when she got overwhelmed by the morality of it and all the choices and the expense and the materialism and she started to panic, he would put his arm around her and guide her out of the store and across the street to the Chinese place and he would order dumplings and put them in front of her. And he would sit there and take all the terror and despair and just surround it with his goodness and absorb it like charcoal until she could stand herself again and could go back across the street and buy a bed. And when some salesman told them that men are like this and women are like that, she would know that she and Chris were on the same side and that Gary was on the other. Because she and Chris are a team.

Sharon is sitting up now, digging through her bag. She is buying the four-thousand-dollar bed. Kathryn wonders at the quiet snap of this decision. How one minute Sharon did not know, and then the next minute she did. It is only 11:30 in the morning.

Kathryn has not said any of the things she meant to say. She meant to say that, yes, the thought of Emily eats at her. That she feels colonized by that letter, planted like a flag in her kitchen. That sometimes when she comes home and the letter has been moved slightly, she wishes that Emily would disappear and have never existed, but that sometimes she wishes it was Chris who would disappear, or she herself, or that nobody had ever existed and the planet was still choked with algae and God was pleased. Other times, she hears some dumb song on the radio that makes her feel connected to everything – mattress salesmen and deer ticks and crying babies – and she wants Chris to do whatever he needs to be happy. If he needs to kiss Emily, then kiss her. Or worse. She just wants him to be happy. She wants him to be happy so he can make *her* happy.

Sometime this week would be ideal, says Sharon.

Sharon has her day-planner out, making arrangements for the mattress to be delivered. Kathryn gazes blankly at the appointments and the half-familiar names. It's mostly wedding stuff. Then she sees her own name:

Sleep World
(w/Kathryn!)

Next to her name is drawn a small heart. The whole day is blocked off. Kathryn wonders if they will now have lunch and sit on some heated patio drinking bellinis and talking about big and small things, or if the unexpected efficiency of her purchase will inspire Sharon to see how many other tasks she can accomplish today.

Kathryn doesn't mind either way. She is ready to go home. She has something to say to Chris. It is starting to take up space in her mouth. She wants him to be happy. What is her worst-case scenario?

ELIZA ROBERTSON

MY SISTER SANG

S eated and stowed.
   Thank you, all set.
   [Sound like cockpit door closing.]
Oh, that fucking door again.
What's wrong?
This.
Oh.
You have to slam it pretty hard.
[Sound like cockpit door closing.]

———

This one is: Plane Ditched in Columbia River after Multiple Bird Strikes. Three serious injuries. One fatality. Forty-three passengers treated for hypothermia. On my desk Monday morning: the stats, the snaps, the autopsy, the tapes. (The .FLAC files.) (We still say tapes.) Linguists identify speech – loss of thrust, loss of trust, one five zero knots, one five zero, not. I take the acoustics. Engine noise, aircraft chimes, whether the captain has reclined his seat.

———

Flaps one, please.
Flaps one.
What a view of the Columbia today.
Yeah.
After takeoff checklist.
After takeoff checklist complete.
[Sound of chime.]
Birds.
Whoa.
[Sound of thump.]
Oh shit.
Oh yeah.
Uh oh.

———

Sometimes you hear the pilots snap photos. Would you look at those Rockies. Or: photo of the FO clicking a photo of that fighter. Also, they swap jokes.

Welcome to the George Herbert Walker Bush Intergalactical Airport.

[Sound of laugh.]

I can't fly anymore. Free flights, if I wanted, but I can't coax myself past security. I take trains.

———

Mayday mayday mayday mayday.

Caution, terrain terrain terrain.

Too low. Terrain.

Pull up. Terrain.

We're goin' in the river.

Say again, Jetblue?

Pull up. Pull up. Pull up. Pull up. Pull up.

———

The Oregonian featured the accident on the front page. I bought a copy at lunch. The girl's on A3: Backup Singer Dies in Plane Crash. In the photo, she's surrounded by honeycomb. Her hair's the same colour. Yellow in the waxlight, how sun warms through a sheet of gold tack.

———

Name: VERNON, Joy. Case #1734512, age: 19, race: white, sex: female.

Cause of death: cerebral hypoxia

   due to: asphyxiation

   due to: aspiration of water into the air passages

Manner of death: drowning

———

In the autopsy photo, her eyes are open. Brown irises. Eyes like wood like warm like walnut. Report says sclerae clear. Report says ears pierced once each lobe and nose unremarkable.

———

She sang back-up for Fiona Apple, says the newspaper. And LuAnne de Lesseps. She also released a single of her own, which you can purchase on iTunes for $1.29.

———

My sister sang before she married. Christian pop, which her manager sold as gospel. We weren't religious – our car wore a Darwin fish. But her manager said there was a market. He said, Praise radio will eat her up with double catsup and a side of fries.

I never liked him. He wore T-shirts with milk stained down the front. Cheerios, he'd say. Sometimes it's so hard to get them in the mouth.

———

The new linguist started today. She'll analyze the resonant frequencies of vocal tracts. F-values, she calls them. How we form words from the lips and the teeth and the tongue and the lungs. She combs her hair very smooth. I think she must use a bun-setter.

I brought a coffee to her computer station to introduce myself. I said, "Well if it doesn't work out here, I think the CIA is hiring."

She typed the rest of her sentence, then pointed to the small ceramic pig on her desk. It wore a Post-it. The Post-it said, *Cunning linguist jokes: $1.*

She's bright. But she knows she's bright, which makes it less attractive. Still.

We work in the basement where you don't see the sun. You see: two computer monitors with equalizer waves; desks made from highly recyclable aluminum; ergonomic chairs, whirly. Our lab is fragrance-free and climate-controlled, volume-controlled, light-controlled. Plants cannot grow here. We keep a synthetic lemon tree by the vending machine.

———

To isolate the voices on a CVR tape, you have to clear the extraneous noise in layers. The engine roar, the static. Like filing sand off a fossil, stratum by stratum. Blowing off the dust. Audio archaeology, let's say. Let's say Indiana Jones.

I like to listen to routine take-offs and landings. The pilots sound like performance poets. I picture them crinkled over the control board in black berets, anemic fingers snapping, clasping espressos, eyes cast to the far corner, too cool for contact, for the stewardess with the pretzels and the can of V8.

Flaps five.

Flaps five.

Flaps one.

Flaps one.

Flaps up.

Say what?

Flaps up.

Flaps up.

———

My sister toured once, ten years ago, after her junior year of high school. She hit the major towns on the Praise radio circuit. Lubbock, Texas, to Lynchburg, Virginia. Lynchburg, I had said when she showed me her itinerary. Lynchburg? She shrugged. They have the world's largest evangelical university.

The tour was eight weeks, to private Christian schools and rodeos. Her merch team sold chastity rings. She brought me home a mug that said *TEAM JESUS* and filled it with prayer jellybeans. Red for the blood you shed. Black for my sinful heart. Yellow for the Heaven above, and so on. I still have them. I think she meant it as a joke.

She died in childbirth. A C-section that led to a blood clot that led to a stroke. We talked on the phone the night before. She told me they had painted the nursery yellow, which the decorator described as "String." She said that yellow can be shrill; it's hard to get yellow right. She said she got it right. She said, you know the colour of a wheel of lemon when you hold it to the sun? I said, perfect. Have you settled on a name? She said yes. Jaime. Because on paper it reads like *j'aime*.

———

Jaime turned four last month. I talked to her on Skype. When she grins she thrusts her chin out like a goat. I can picture her in a garden this way, neck craned to the sun, as daylilies do, and sunflowers. Heliotropism, I think it's called.

———

After lunch, I found Joy Vernon's single on YouTube. The song is called *Delilah*, the video shot at her father's bee farm. She sings against a barn wall in a breezy shirtdress, and she picks her banjo. A low, pinging banjo, against that wall, and her voice is blue and dusky.

Halfway through the video, I felt a brush at my elbow, and I turned to find April, the new linguist, behind me in her chair. She had wheeled it from her desk across the aisle. I shifted, and she rolled nearer.

"She's lovely, isn't she?" she said when the video ended.

"Yes," I said.

"Could you play the song again?"

I dragged back the play bar. We watched the video from the start. Bees in the wisteria. Joy's hair in her eyes as she bows to see the strings.

"Carrot slice?" said April. She had packed her lunch in a Japanese bento box. Everything compartmentalized. A slot for the chopsticks.

"Thank you." She passed a carrot into my palm. It looked carefully cut. On a diagonal, the edge serrated.

"I used to work in Homicide," she said. "Voice ID from emergency phone calls, and so on." We still faced the computer screen – Joy at the barn again, strumming the banjo between verses. "This one case, the vic was an opera singer." She paused to snap her lunchbox. "I never liked opera. But after a week on the case, I ordered her recording of *Evita* online. I listened to the tracks over and over."

I nodded. The YouTube video had ended. April turned to me. Her cheeks looked worn somehow, smooth and unsunned, but as if the skin were pulled too tightly to her ears.

She continued, "When you replay a voice in evidence for eight hours a day, you can almost know them. And when you catch a glimpse of their life before, you get immersed. I get immersed. In the knowing of them."

I stared at her.

She looked down. "Unprofessional, I know."

When she raised her eyes, I was still staring. She held the eye contact. In that moment, I understood that she understood that I understood everything she said.

———

I often see her at the vending machine. She never buys anything, but she slides her eyes over each item through the glass. I stopped once. When she noticed me, she turned toward the elevator. I said, "Too many choices?" and she smiled and waggled her lunch kit.

———

You get into the habit of transcription: sound of Smarties dispensed from the machine, sound of Coke can, sound of leather soles on a vinyl floor. Sometimes you try to adjust the levels. At the crosswalk, when I race a yellow light. Sound of honk. At home, when the neighbours yell, and one of them unhooks the fire extinguisher. Sometimes my fingers stretch for the mouse.

———

After work today, I returned to the newspaper stand and bought the last fifteen copies of *The Oregonian*. I don't know why. But they were only one dollar each.

———

For Jaime's fourth birthday, I mailed an Easy-Bake Oven. She loved it. The cookie dough turns pink. She said to me on Skype, "This present is my number two favourite." But I want to send a gift I didn't find on page one of the Toys"R"Us flyer. Origami, maybe. Her mother loved origami. I have this Polaroid of her folding paper cranes – thirty of them, for her classmates on Valentine's Day instead of cards or cinnamon hearts. Are four-year-olds into paper?

———

My sister and I bought ants on television once. *An entire colony, queen included.* We converted our fish tank into a two-storey formicarium – poured plaster over a plastic wall, over the clay tunnels we had shaped with our palms. Plus leaves and sand. The leaves you call "forage," plant material for grazing live-stock, a term we adopted. Livestock. Can't play soccer after school – have to check the herd.

She sang for them. I played rhythm: chopsticks on an empty plastic jug. The ants go marching one by one, hurrah, hurrah. Work songs. You could watch them for hours, and sometimes we did. The entire colony shimmering through the chambers, a still black line, though every ant moved. Frames of celluloid projected on a screen, like a river, like blood cells. How motion can be static – it gets you thinking.

When we spotted an ant too close to the cheesecloth, she would fetch petroleum jelly from the bathroom, and we fin-gered streaks of it around the lip of the aquarium. I told her they harvested vaseline from jellyfish. She said, Do not. I said, Do too, and smeared a daub of it into her bangs.

We later experimented with radio and production speed. Which is to say, crawling. Which is to say, with speakers situated on either side of the formicarium. Do ants file faster to "The Imperial March" or ABBA? The study proved inconclusive.

After a couple of months, the plaster moulded and ants found their way into the kitchen, into the paper sack of flour and the dried figs. My mother made me dump the tank in the park "at least two blocks from our house." My sister started piano. She signed up for voice lessons twice a week with an Italian woman who sang off-Broadway. I took up coin collection. There was money in coins. Ha, ha.

———

And they all go marching down.
   To the ground.
      To get out of the rain.

———

A quick hello from your cockpit crew, this is Flight 166 with service to New York. We'll be flying at 38,000 feet, mostly smooth, for four hours and fifteen minutes, takeoff to landing.

———

I've heard the cabin safety announcement so often, I could probably be a flight attendant. In preparation for departure, please be certain your seat back is straightened and your tray table stowed. There are a total of eight exits on this aircraft: two door exits at the front of the aircraft, four window exits over the wings, and two door exits at the rear of the aircraft. To start the flow of oxygen, reach up and pull the mask toward you. Place the mask over your nose and mouth. Place the elastic band over your head. The plastic bag may not inflate.

———

I have this shirt with a soundboard printed on the front. The caption says, *I know what all these buttons do*. I think a pilot could wear this shirt also.

———

Today, April wears a wool sweater the colour of eggshells, the colour of string. She's hennaed her hair very red. Poppy, I'd say. I'd say: hellzapoppin. I think she must attract hummingbirds.

At break, I stopped behind her at the vending machine and watched her scan the items. I don't even think she brought her wallet. I stood there for a full minute before I caught her staring at me through the glass. Then it was me who jumped.

She turned. She said, "Go ahead, I'm not in line."

I said, "Me neither."

She shifted her eyes to the potted plant.

"You know they're scented?" I said.

"I'm sorry?"

"The lemons."

She drew her eyes up the tree to the yellow baubles of plastic fruit.

"Real wood, too," I continued. "We voted for it last year. They emailed options from a catalogue."

The elevator dinged open and one of the techs from Fifth Floor strolled out behind us. April stepped for the door. I stepped with her.

"What were the other options?" she said.

"Orange." I walked inside the elevator and leaned against the far wall. "Banana. Bamboo."

"I would have voted bamboo."

The elevator opened at the main floor. I followed her through the lobby into the courtyard, an urban "greenspace" designed with white-slab cement, birch mulch, a stand of honey locusts, and a fountain.

I said, "They described the lemon trees as *evergreen.*"

She said, "Well. I don't suppose they lose leaves."

We bought coffees from an espresso bar across the street and carried them back to the fountain – a rectangular pond like a wading pool, with a hunk of granite in the centre for the spout. In fact, I'd seen the fountain used as a wading pool a few times. And as a birdbath. And as a urinal. But such is public art.

I offered her a piece of my croissant – one stuffed with chocolate, so what I said was, *"Pain au chocolat?"*

She said, "No, thank you."

I sipped my coffee.

She said, "I'm not supposed to have this, but you want to hear?" She outstretched her iPhone, the white wires of earbuds looped around her thumb.

I nodded.

"One of the survivors posted it on YouTube. I downloaded the video file before they took it down."

She offered me an earbud and plugged the second into her own ear. We bowed over the phone. I could feel the friction of the space between our foreheads. There's a point where technology mimics the past. iPads like slates, like the Flintstones, like chisels. The iPhone felt divinatory – as though we should be bent over a bowl of water.

She tapped the screen and opened the file. She pressed PLAY.

Rain blew into the camera, diagonal sheets of it into the aluminum, into brown water. The camera jolted up and you could see people, their orange life vests, crowded onto the wing. The rear slides had extended. They floated uselessly, like boneless arms, or slapstick rubber chickens. What you could hear was shouting – passengers shouting to passengers in the water – *Grab here* – *Grab my hand* – passengers shouting to passengers to swim away – *Dive* – *Before* – *it goes* – crew shouting to passengers to stop shouting. What you could hear was rain. Drumming into metal, into hard water, pinging off the life vests. And a continuous chime from the interior of the aircraft, ding ding ding, like your door's open, like a friendly reminder before you leave the parking lot. And there, in the corner of the frame, you could see her treading water. She had floated the farthest from the wreck, her hair starfished out around her shoulders. She drifted farther from the plane with every paddle. Her mouth opened and closed, but not in communication, her eyes unfocused, or focused on a distance. She was singing. You could see she was singing.

———

To fold a paper crane, your paper must be square. With sixteen newspapers and scissors from Reception, you can cut a lot of squares. I began with a lifestyles story on the 2002 Miss America. I pressed her face right in half. Then I folded the same line onto the reverse side, whitespace for an AT&T ad. I followed the dotted diagram from www.papercrane.org. I ignored the video how-tos and the photographs. For my sister, there was no such thing as Google.

April found me at 8:30, after she cycled back to work for her phone. I had moved to the floor at this point, to the strips of paper I snipped from the squares. I stored the completed cranes in an emptied recycling box – fired them from where I sat, like paper planes. Paper cranes. Nose first into the box, or onto the surrounding carpet.

When she saw me, she backed up, then stepped forward, then stood very still. "We used newspaper for my guinea pig," she said. "You look like my guinea pig."

"You have a guinea pig?"

"I left my phone."

"Okay."

"When I was twelve." She folded her arms over her ribs. "Her name was Rosa."

She helped me fold cranes. We plugged in her iPhone. We listened to the soundtrack from *Evita* on repeat. *Don't cry for me, Argentina*. By midnight, we needed to borrow another recycling box from the lab across the hall. I noticed we both folded A3 so that Joy Vernon's face pointed outward, from the tail of the crane, or the wings.

I think I can fit the cranes into three oversized boxes from UPS. I'll mail the Polaroid of my sister with the first parcel. In the photo, she hovers a blue gingham crane above her head. She balances the wings between her fingers like she will demonstrate flight. Like she knows the crane will stay suspended when she drops her hands.

Steven Benstead is the author of two novels. His short fiction has appeared in *Grain*, *Prairie Fire*, *Pierian Spring*, *Secrets from the Orange Couch*, and *Manitoba Myriad*. He wrote the text for *Winnipeg: City at the Forks*, and has recently completed a new novel, tentatively titled *Soldier, Soldier*. He has worked in Winnipeg as a bookseller since 1983.

Jay Brown is a writer and librarian living and working in Toronto. His short fiction has appeared in *The Vancouver Review*, *Grain*, *Prairie Fire*, and the anthology *Darwin's Bastards*. "The Egyptians" is his second work to appear in *The Journey Prize Stories*. He is currently at work on a novel.

Andrew Forbes has published music and film criticism both online and in print, and his fiction has appeared in *The Feathertale Review*, *Found Press Quarterly*, *Scrivener Creative Review*, *The New Quarterly*, and *PRISM international*. He is a co-founder and senior editor of the sportswriting website *The Barnstormer* (thebarnstormer.com), and he has recently completed his first collection of short fiction. He lives in Peterborough, Ontario, with his wife and three children.

Philip Huynh's stories have appeared in *The Malahat Review*, *Prairie Fire*, and *The New Quarterly*. "Gulliver's Wife" was the runner-up for *The New Quarterly*'s 2012 Peter Hinchcliffe

Fiction Award. He is working on a novel, along with more short fiction. He lives in Richmond, British Columbia, with his wife and twin toddler daughters.

Originally from Halifax, **Amy Jones** is a graduate of the MFA Program in Creative Writing at UBC. Her short fiction has appeared in several Canadian publications, and she was the winner of the 2006 CBC Literary Award for Short Story in English. Her first short fiction collection, *What Boys Like* (Biblioasis, 2009) was the winner of the 2009 Metcalf-Rooke Award, and was short-listed for the 2010 ReLit Award. Amy currently lives in Thunder Bay, where she is working on a novel.

Marnie Lamb earned a Master of Arts in Creative Writing from the University of Windsor before living abroad for two years. Her short stories have appeared in several literary journals, including *filling Station*, *The Nashwaak Review*, *blueprint*, *Room*, and *The New Quarterly*. Currently, she is working on a collection of Japan-themed short stories, which includes "Mrs. Fujimoto's Wednesday Afternoons," and a young adult novel. Now a Toronto resident, she runs Ewe Editorial Services, which provides copy editing, indexing, and permissions research services.

Doretta Lau is a journalist who covers arts and culture for *Artforum*, *South China Morning Post*, *The Wall Street Journal Asia*, and *Bazaar Art Hong Kong*. She completed an MFA in Writing at Columbia University. Her fiction and poetry have appeared in *EVENT*, *Grain*, *Prairie Fire*, *PRISM international*,

Ricepaper, *subTerrain*, and *Zen Monster*. She divides her time between Vancouver and Hong Kong, where she is at work on a novel and a screenplay. In 2014, her short story collection will be published by Nightwood Editions.

Laura Legge is equal parts the Socratic paradox "I know that I know nothing" and the Shaquille O'Neal rap song "(I Know I Got) Skillz." She's honoured you read her story, and hopes to meet you sometime so you can tell her some of yours.

Natalie Morrill is a multi-genre writer from Ontario, and is finishing an MFA in Creative Writing at UBC. Her poetry and short fiction have appeared in *Ultraviolet Magazine*, *filling Station*, and the anthology *Lake Effect 4* (Artful Codger Press, 2009); she also has new poetry forthcoming in *CAROUSEL*. Her work has been recognized by the Alberta Magazine Publishers Association (Silver, 2013 Showcase Award for Fiction). She's at work on a novel set in post-war Austria: so far, this involves at least one magic fish.

Zoey Leigh Peterson's fiction has appeared in various publications, including *The Malahat Review*, *Grain*, *PRISM international*, and *The Walrus*. "Sleep World" originally appeared in *The New Quarterly*, where it was the winner of the Peter Hinchcliffe Fiction Award. Zoey lives in Vancouver, where she is at work on a novel about the whole Emily situation.

Eliza Robertson grew up on Vancouver Island. She studied writing and political science at the University of Victoria, and pursued her MA in Prose Fiction at the University of East

Anglia, where she received the UEA Booker Scholarship and the Curtis Brown Prize. She has been twice long-listed for the Journey Prize and was a finalist for the 2013 CBC Short Story Prize. She is the regional and overall winner for the 2013 Commonwealth Short Story Prize. She now lives in England, where she has started a PhD.

Naben Ruthnum lives and writes in Toronto, and has previously published in *Riddle Fence*, *Joyland*, *Qwerty*, and *Ellery Queen's Mystery Magazine*. His pseudonym, Nathan Ripley, recently completed a thriller called *Scrapbook*. He's currently working on a novel based on the characters in "Cinema Rex."

For more information about the journals that submitted to this year's competition, The Journey Prize, and *The Journey Prize Stories*, please visit www.facebook.com/TheJourneyPrize.

The Dalhousie Review has been in operation since 1921 and aspires to be a forum in which seriousness of purpose and playfulness of mind can coexist in meaningful dialogue. The journal publishes new fiction and poetry in every issue and welcomes submissions from authors around the world. Editor: Carrie Dawson. Submissions and correspondence: *The Dalhousie Review*, Dalhousie University, Halifax, Nova Scotia, B3H 4R2. Email: dalhousie.review@dal.ca Website: www.dalhousiereview.dal.ca

EVENT features the very best in contemporary writing from Canada and abroad, from literary heavyweights to up-and-comers. For over four decades, *EVENT* has consistently published award-winning fiction, poetry, non-fiction, notes on writing, and critical reviews – all topped off by stunning Canadian cover art. Recent stories first published in *EVENT* have gone on to win both the Gold and Silver National Magazine Awards in Fiction in 2012 and 2011, and the Western Magazine Awards in Fiction in 2012 and 2010. *EVENT* is also home to Canada's longest-running annual non-fiction contest, and a Reading Service for Writers. Editor: Elizabeth Bachinsky.

Managing Editor: Ian Cockfield. Fiction Editor: Christine Dewar. Submissions and correspondence: *EVENT*, P.O. Box 2503, New Westminster, British Columbia, V3L 5B2. Email (queries only): event@douglascollege.ca Website: www.eventmags.com

filling Station is Canada's experimental literary magazine. *fS* exists to promote innovative and original poetry, fiction, and literary journalism while encouraging dialogue among local and national writers, assisting the creative advancement of Canadian literature, and bringing this important work to the reading public. By consistently providing an exciting contrast to more traditional literary and arts journals, *filling Station* remains unique among literary magazines both in Canada and abroad. Managing Editor: Caitlynn Cummings. Fiction Editor: Jon R. Flieger. Submissions and correspondence: *filling Station* Publications Society, P.O. Box 22135, Bankers Hall RPO, Calgary AB T2P 4J5. Email: mgmt@fillingstation.ca Website: www.fillingstation.ca

Grain, *the journal of eclectic writing*, is a literary quarterly that publishes engaging, diverse, and challenging writing and art by some of the best Canadian and international writers and artists. Every issue features superb new writing from both developing and established writers. Each issue also highlights the unique artwork of a different visual artist. Editor: Rilla Friesen. Associate Fiction & Nonfiction Editor: Kim Aubrey. Associate Poetry Editor: Adam Pottle. Art Editor & Designer: Betsy Rosenwald. Submissions and correspondence: *Grain*, P.O. Box 67, Saskatoon, Saskatchewan, S7K 3K1. Email: grainmag@sasktel.net Website: www.grainmagazine.ca

The Malahat Review is a quarterly journal of contemporary poetry, fiction, and creative nonfiction by both new and celebrated writers. Summer issues feature the winners of *Malahat*'s Novella and Long Poem prizes, held in alternate years; the fall issues feature the winners of the Far Horizons Award for emerging writers, alternating between poetry and fiction each year; the winter issues feature the winners of the Constance Rook Creative Nonfiction Prize; and the spring issues feature winners of the Open Season Awards in all three genres (poetry, fiction, and creative nonfiction). All issues feature covers by noted Canadian visual artists and include reviews of Canadian books. Editor: John Barton. Assistant Editor: Rhonda Batchelor. Submissions and correspondence: *The Malahat Review*, University of Victoria, P.O. Box 1700, Station CSC, Victoria, British Columbia, V8W 2Y2. E-mail: malahat@uvic.ca Website: www.malahatreview.ca Twitter: @malahatreview

The New Quarterly is an award-winning literary magazine publishing fiction, poetry, personal essays, interviews, and essays on writing. Now in its thirty-first year, the magazine prides itself on its independent take on the Canadian literary scene. Recent issues include The QuArc issue (a 290-page flip book on the interstices of science and literature undertaken with *Arc Poetry Magazine*) and The TNQ Extra (writers on their collections and obsessions). Editor: Pamela Mulloy. Submissions and correspondence: *The New Quarterly*, c/o St. Jerome's University, 290 Westmount Road North, Waterloo, Ontario, N2L 3G3. E-mail: editor@tnq.ca, orders@tnq.ca Website: www.tnq.ca 2012

Prairie Fire is a quarterly magazine of contemporary Canadian writing that publishes stories, poems, and literary non-fiction by both emerging and established writers. *Prairie Fire*'s editorial mix also occasionally features critical or personal essays and interviews with authors. Stories published in *Prairie Fire* have won awards at the National Magazine Awards and the Western Magazine Awards. *Prairie Fire* publishes writing from, and has readers in, all parts of Canada. Editor: Andris Taskans. Fiction Editors: Warren Cariou and Heidi Harms. Submissions and correspondence: *Prairie Fire*, Room 423, 100 Arthur Street, Winnipeg, Manitoba, R3B 1H3. Email: prfire@mts.net Website: www.prairiefire.ca

PRISM international, the oldest literary magazine in Western Canada, was established in 1959 by Earle Birney at the University of British Columbia. Published four times a year, *PRISM* features short fiction, poetry, creative non-fiction and translations. *PRISM* editors select work based on originality and quality, and the magazine showcases work from both new and established writers from Canada and around the world. *PRISM* holds three exemplary annual competitions for short fiction, literary non-fiction and poetry and awards the Earle Birney Prize for Poetry to an outstanding poet whose work was featured in *PRISM* in the preceding year. Executive Editors: Sierra Skye Gemma and Jennifer Neale. Fiction Editor: Anna Ling Kaye. Poetry Editor: Leah Horlick. Submissions and correspondence: *PRISM international*, Creative Writing Program, The University of British Columbia, Buchanan E-462, 1866 Main Mall, Vancouver, British Columbia, V6T 1Z1. Website: www.prismmagazine.ca

Submissions were also received from the following publications:

The Antigonish Review
(Antigonish, NS)
www.antigonishreview.com

Brick, A Literary Journal
(Toronto, ON)
www.brickmag.com

Broken Pencil Magazine
(Toronto, ON)
www.brokenpencil.com

carte blanche
(Montreal, QC)
www.carte-blanche.org

The Claremont Review
(Victoria, BC)
www.theclaremontreview.ca

Descant
(Toronto, ON)
www.descant.ca

*ELQ/Exile Literary
Quarterly Magazine*
(Holstein, ON)
www.exilequarterly.com

The Fiddlehead
(Fredericton, NB)
www.thefiddlehead.ca

Found Press Quarterly
www.foundpress.com

FreeFall
(Calgary, AB)
www.freefallmagazine.ca

Geist
(Vancouver, BC)
www.geist.com

Joyland Magazine
www.joylandmagazine.com

Little Brother Magazine
(Toronto, ON)
www.littlebrother
magazine.com

Little Fiction
(Toronto, ON)
www.littlefiction.com

Matrix Magazine
(Montreal, QC)
www.matrixmagazine.org

The New Orphic Review
(Nelson, BC)
http://www3.telus.net/
neworphicpublishers-
hekkanen

On Spec
(Edmonton, AB)
www.onspec.ca

Plenitude Magazine
www.plenitudemagazine.ca
*Prairie Journal of Canadian
Literature*
(Calgary, AB)
www.prairiejournal.org

The Puritan
(Toronto, ON)
www.puritan-magazine.com

Queen's Quarterly
(Kingston, ON)
www.queensu.ca/quarterly

Room
(Vancouver, BC)
www.roommagazine.com

The Rusty Toque
(London, ON)
www.therustytoque.com/
index.html

subTerrain Magazine
(Vancouver, BC)
www.subTerrain.ca

Taddle Creek
(Toronto, ON)
www.taddlecreekmag.com

The Windsor Review
(Windsor, ON)
www.windsorreview.
wordpress.com

* Winners of the $10,000 Journey Prize
** Co-winners of the $10,000 Journey Prize

1

1989
SELECTED WITH ALISTAIR MACLEOD

Ven Begamudré, "Word Games"

David Bergen, "Where You're From"

Lois Braun, "The Pumpkin-Eaters"

Constance Buchanan, "Man with Flying Genitals"

Ann Copeland, "Obedience"

Marion Douglas, "Flags"

Frances Itani, "An Evening in the Café"

Diane Keating, "The Crying Out"

Thomas King, "One Good Story, That One"

Holley Rubinsky, "Rapid Transits"*

Jean Rysstad, "Winter Baby"

Kevin Van Tighem, "Whoopers"

M.G. Vassanji, "In the Quiet of a Sunday Afternoon"

Bronwen Wallace, "Chicken 'N' Ribs"

Armin Wiebe, "Mouse Lake"

Budge Wilson, "Waiting"

2

1990
SELECTED WITH LEON ROOKE; GUY VANDERHAEGHE

André Alexis, "Despair: Five Stories of Ottawa"

Glen Allen, "The Hua Guofeng Memorial Warehouse"

Marusia Bociurkiw, "Mama, Donya"

Virgil Burnett, "Billfrith the Dreamer"

Margaret Dyment, "Sacred Trust"

Cynthia Flood, "My Father Took a Cake to France"*

Douglas Glover, "Story Carved in Stone"

Terry Griggs, "Man with the Axe"

Rick Hillis, "Limbo River"

Thomas King, "The Dog I Wish I Had, I Would Call It Helen"

K.D. Miller, "Sunrise Till Dark"

Jennifer Mitton, "Let Them Say"

Lawrence O'Toole, "Goin' to Town with Katie Ann"

Kenneth Radu, "A Change of Heart"

Jenifer Sutherland, "Table Talk"

Wayne Tefs, "Red Rock and After"

3
1991
SELECTED WITH JANE URQUHART

Donald Aker, "The Invitation"

Anton Baer, "Yukon"

Allan Barr, "A Visit from Lloyd"

David Bergen, "The Fall"

Rai Berzins, "Common Sense"

Diana Hartog, "Theories of Grief"

Diane Keating, "The Salem Letters"

Yann Martel, "The Facts Behind the Helsinki Roccamatios"*

Jennifer Mitton, "Polaroid"

Sheldon Oberman, "This Business with Elijah"

Lynn Podgurny, "Till Tomorrow, Maple Leaf Mills"

James Riseborough, "She Is Not His Mother"

Patricia Stone, "Living on the Lake"

4
1992
SELECTED WITH SANDRA BIRDSELL

David Bergen, "The Bottom of the Glass"

Maria A. Billion, "No Miracles Sweet Jesus"

Judith Cowan, "By the Big River"

Steven Heighton, "A Man Away from Home Has No Neighbours"

Steven Heighton, "How Beautiful upon the Mountains"

L. Rex Kay, "Travelling"

Rozena Maart, "No Rosa, No District Six"*

Guy Malet De Carteret, "Rainy Day"

Carmelita McGrath, "Silence"

Michael Mirolla, "A Theory of Discontinuous Existence"

Diane Juttner Perreault, "Bella's Story"

Eden Robinson, "Traplines"

5
1993
SELECTED WITH GUY VANDERHAEGHE

Caroline Adderson, "Oil and Dread"

David Bergen, "La Rue Prevette"

Marina Endicott, "With the Band"

Dayv James-French, "Cervine"

Michael Kenyon, "Durable Tumblers"

K.D. Miller, "A Litany in Time of Plague"

Robert Mullen, "Flotsam"

Gayla Reid, "Sister Doyle's Men"*

Oakland Ross, "Bang-bang"

Robert Sherrin, "Technical Battle for Trial Machine"

Carol Windley, "The Etruscans"

6
1994
SELECTED WITH DOUGLAS GLOVER;
JUDITH CHANT (CHAPTERS)

Anne Carson, "Water Margins: An Essay on Swimming by My Brother"

Richard Cumyn, "The Sound He Made"

Genni Gunn, "Versions"

Melissa Hardy, "Long Man the River"*

Robert Mullen, "Anomie"

Vivian Payne, "Free Falls"

Jim Reil, "Dry"

Robyn Sarah, "Accept My Story"

Joan Skogan, "Landfall"

Dorothy Speak, "Relatives in Florida"

Alison Wearing, "Notes from Under Water"

7

1995

SELECTED WITH M.G. VASSANJI;

RICHARD BACHMANN (A DIFFERENT DRUMMER BOOKS)

Michelle Alfano, "Opera"

Mary Borsky, "Maps of the Known World"

Gabriella Goliger, "Song of Ascent"

Elizabeth Hay, "Hand Games"

Shaena Lambert, "The Falling Woman"

Elise Levine, "Boy"

Roger Burford Mason, "The Rat-Catcher's Kiss"

Antanas Sileika, "Going Native"

Kathryn Woodward, "Of Marranos and Gilded Angels"*

8

1996

SELECTED WITH OLIVE SENIOR;

BEN McNALLY (NICHOLAS HOARE LTD.)

Rick Bowers, "Dental Bytes"

David Elias, "How I Crossed Over"

Elyse Gasco, "Can You Wave Bye Bye, Baby?"*

Danuta Gleed, "Bones"

Elizabeth Hay, "The Friend"

Linda Holeman, "Turning the Worm"

Elaine Littman, "The Winner's Circle"

Murray Logan, "Steam"

Rick Maddocks, "Lessons from the Sputnik Diner"

K.D. Miller, "Egypt Land"

Gregor Robinson, "Monster Gaps"
Alma Subasic, "Dust"

9
1997
SELECTED WITH NINO RICCI; NICHOLAS PASHLEY
(UNIVERSITY OF TORONTO BOOKSTORE)
Brian Bartlett, "Thomas, Naked"
Dennis Bock, "Olympia"
Kristen den Hartog, "Wave"
Gabriella Goliger, "Maladies of the Inner Ear"**
Terry Griggs, "Momma Had a Baby"
Mark Anthony Jarman, "Righteous Speedboat"
Judith Kalman, "Not for Me a Crown of Thorns"
Andrew Mullins, "The World of Science"
Sasenarine Persaud, "Canada Geese and Apple Chatney"
Anne Simpson, "Dreaming Snow"**
Sarah Withrow, "Ollie"
Terence Young, "The Berlin Wall"

10
1998
SELECTED BY PETER BUITENHUIS; HOLLEY RUBINSKY;
CELIA DUTHIE (DUTHIE BOOKS LTD.)
John Brooke, "The Finer Points of Apples"*
Ian Colford, "The Reason for the Dream"
Libby Creelman, "Cruelty"
Michael Crummey, "Serendipity"
Stephen Guppy, "Downwind"
Jane Eaton Hamilton, "Graduation"
Elise Levine, "You Are You Because Your Little Dog Loves You"
Jean McNeil, "Bethlehem"
Liz Moore, "Eight-Day Clock"
Edward O'Connor, "The Beatrice of Victoria College"
Tim Rogers, "Scars and Other Presents"

Denise Ryan, "Marginals, Vivisections, and Dreams"

Madeleine Thien, "Simple Recipes"

Cheryl Tibbetts, "Flowers of Africville"

11

1999

SELECTED BY LESLEY CHOYCE; SHELDON CURRIE;
MARY-JO ANDERSON (FROG HOLLOW BOOKS)

Mike Barnes, "In Florida"

Libby Creelman, "Sunken Island"

Mike Finigan, "Passion Sunday"

Jane Eaton Hamilton, "Territory"

Mark Anthony Jarman, "Travels into Several Remote Nations of the
World"

Barbara Lambert, "Where the Bodies Are Kept"

Linda Little, "The Still"

Larry Lynch, "The Sitter"

Sandra Sabatini, "The One With the News"

Sharon Steams, "Brothers"

Mary Walters, "Show Jumping"

Alissa York, "The Back of the Bear's Mouth"*

12

2000

SELECTED BY CATHERINE BUSH; HAL NIEDZVIECKI;
MARC GLASSMAN (PAGES BOOKS AND MAGAZINES)

Andrew Gray, "The Heart of the Land"

Lee Henderson, "Sheep Dub"

Jessica Johnson, "We Move Slowly"

John Lavery, "The Premier's New Pyjamas"

J.A. McCormack, "Hearsay"

Nancy Richler, "Your Mouth Is Lovely"

Andrew Smith, "Sightseeing"

Karen Solie, "Onion Calendar"

Timothy Taylor, "Doves of Townsend"*

Robert Mullen, "Alex the God"

Karen Munro, "The Pool"

Leah Postman, "Being Famous"

Neil Smith, "Green Fluorescent Protein"

15
2003
SELECTED BY MICHELLE BERRY;
TIMOTHY TAYLOR; MICHAEL WINTER

Rosaria Campbell, "Reaching"

Hilary Dean, "The Lemon Stories"

Dawn Rae Downton, "Hansel and Gretel"

Anne Fleming, "Gay Dwarves of America"

Elyse Friedman, "Truth"

Charlotte Gill, "Hush"

Jessica Grant, "My Husband's Jump"*

Jacqueline Honnet, "Conversion Classes"

S.K. Johannesen, "Resurrection"

Avner Mandelman, "Cuckoo"

Tim Mitchell, "Night Finds Us"

Heather O'Neill, "The Difference Between Me and Goldstein"

16
2004
SELECTED BY ELIZABETH HAY; LISA MOORE; MICHAEL REDHILL

Anar Ali, "Baby Khaki's Wings"

Kenneth Bonert, "Packers and Movers"

Jennifer Clouter, "Benny and the Jets"

Daniel Griffin, "Mercedes Buyer's Guide"

Michael Kissinger, "Invest in the North"

Devin Krukoff, "The Last Spark"*

Elaine McCluskey, "The Watermelon Social"

William Metcalfe, "Nice Big Car, Rap Music Coming Out the Window"

Lesley Millard, "The Uses of the Neckerchief"

Adam Lewis Schroeder, "Burning the Cattle at Both Ends"

Michael V. Smith, "What We Wanted"
Neil Smith, "Isolettes"
Patricia Rose Young, "Up the Clyde on a Bike"

17
2005
SELECTED BY JAMES GRAINGER AND NANCY LEE

Randy Boyagoda, "Rice and Curry Yacht Club"
Krista Bridge, "A Matter of Firsts"
Josh Byer, "Rats, Homosex, Saunas, and Simon"
Craig Davidson, "Failure to Thrive"
McKinley M. Hellenes, "Brighter Thread"
Catherine Kidd, "Green-Eyed Beans"
Pasha Malla, "The Past Composed"
Edward O'Connor, "Heard Melodies Are Sweet"
Barbara Romanik, "Seven Ways into Chandigarh"
Sandra Sabatini, "The Dolphins at Sainte Marie"
Matt Shaw, "Matchbook for a Mother's Hair"*
Richard Simas, "Anthropologies"
Neil Smith, "Scrapbook"
Emily White, "Various Metals"

18
2006
SELECTED BY STEVEN GALLOWAY;
ZSUZSI GARTNER; ANNABEL LYON

Heather Birrell, "BriannaSusannaAlana"*
Craig Boyko, "The Baby"
Craig Boyko, "The Beloved Departed"
Nadia Bozak, "Heavy Metal Housekeeping"
Lee Henderson, "Conjugation"
Melanie Little, "Wrestling"
Matthew Rader, "The Lonesome Death of Joseph Fey"
Scott Randall, "Law School"
Sarah Selecky, "Throwing Cotton"

Damian Tarnopolsky, "Sleepy"
Martin West, "Cretacea"
David Whitton, "The Eclipse"
Clea Young, "Split"

19
2007
SELECTED BY CAROLINE ADDERSON;
DAVID BEZMOZGIS; DIONNE BRAND

Andrew J. Borkowski, "Twelve Versions of Lech"
Craig Boyko, "OZY"*
Grant Buday, "The Curve of the Earth"
Nicole Dixon, "High-water Mark"
Krista Foss, "Swimming in Zanzibar"
Pasha Malla, "Respite"
Alice Petersen, "After Summer"
Patricia Robertson, "My Hungarian Sister"
Rebecca Rosenblum, "Chilly Girl"
Nicholas Ruddock, "How Eunice Got Her Baby"
Jean Van Loon, "Stardust"

20
2008
SELECTED BY LYNN COADY; HEATHER O'NEILL; NEIL SMITH

Théodora Armstrong, "Whale Stories"
Mike Christie, "Goodbye Porkpie Hat"
Anna Leventhal, "The Polar Bear at the Museum"
Naomi K. Lewis, "The Guiding Light"
Oscar Martens, "Breaking on the Wheel"
Dana Mills, "Steaming for Godthab"
Saleema Nawaz, "My Three Girls"*
Scott Randall, "The Gifted Class"
S. Kennedy Sobol, "Some Light Down"
Sarah Steinberg, "At Last at Sea"
Clea Young, "Chaperone"

21

2009

SELECTED BY CAMILLA GIBB;
LEE HENDERSON; REBECCA ROSENBLUM

Daniel Griffin, "The Last Great Works of Alvin Cale"

Jesus Hardwell, "Easy Living"

Paul Headrick, "Highlife"

Sarah Keevil, "Pyro"

Adrian Michael Kelly, "Lure"

Fran Kimmel, "Picturing God's Ocean"

Lynne Kutsukake, "Away"

Alexander MacLeod, "Miracle Mile"

Dave Margoshes, "The Wisdom of Solomon"

Shawn Syms, "On the Line"

Sarah L. Taggart, "Deaf"

Yasuko Thanh, "Floating Like the Dead"*

22

2010

SELECTED BY PASHA MALLA; JOAN THOMAS; ALISSA YORK

Carolyn Black, "Serial Love"

Andrew Boden, "Confluence of Spoors"

Laura Boudreau, "The Dead Dad Game"

Devon Code, "Uncle Oscar"*

Danielle Egan, "Publicity"

Krista Foss, "The Longitude of Okay"

Lynne Kutsukake, "Mating"

Ben Lof, "When in the Field with Her at His Back"

Andrew MacDonald, "Eat Fist!"

Eliza Robertson, "Ship's Log"

Mike Spry, "Five Pounds Short and Apologies to Nelson Algren"

Damian Tarnopolsky, "Laud We the Gods"

23

2011

SELECTED BY ALEXANDER MACLEOD;
ALISON PICK; SARAH SELECKY

Jay Brown, "The Girl from the War"

Michael Christie, "The Extra"

Seyward Goodhand, "The Fur Trader's Daughter"

Miranda Hill, "Petitions to Saint Chronic"*

Fran Kimmel, "Laundry Day"

Ross Klatte, "First-Calf Heifer"

Michelle Serwatuk, "My Eyes are Dim"

Jessica Westhead, "What I Would Say"

Michelle Winters, "Toupée"

D.W. Wilson, "The Dead Roads"

24

2012

SELECTED BY MICHAEL CHRISTIE;
KATHRYN KUITENBROUWER; KATHLEEN WINTER

Kris Bertin, "Is Alive and Can Move"

Shashi Bhat, "Why I Read *Beowulf*"

Astrid Blodgett, "Ice Break"

Trevor Corkum, "You Were Loved"

Nancy Jo Cullen, "Ashes"

Kevin Hardcastle, "To Have to Wait"

Andrew Hood, "I'm Sorry and Thank You"

Andrew Hood, "Manning"

Grace O'Connell, "The Many Faces of Montgomery Clift"

Jasmina Odor, "Barcelona"

Alex Pugsley, "Crisis on Earth-X"*

Eliza Robertson, "Sea Drift"

Martin West, "My Daughter of the Dead Reeds"